PRAISE

Ramón a

"*Ramón and Julieta* is a passionate and joyful romance about honoring family legacies, celebrating your heritage, the importance of community, and the power of love. A beautiful novel!"
—*New York Times* bestselling author Chanel Cleeton

"This novel's got a little Shakespeare and a lot of tacos, with a very steamy haters-to-lovers relationship at its core."
—NPR

"Albertson gives *Romeo and Juliet* the rom-com treatment in the delightful *Ramón and Julieta*."
—PopSugar

"As this love story shaped by the complexities of Latinx communities unfolds, Albertson insightfully dramatizes the contrasts between Julieta and Ramón as he becomes increasingly conflicted about his identity as a Mexican American and his business plans for the neighborhood and its impact on the culture."
—*Booklist*

ALSO BY ALANA QUINTANA ALBERTSON

Ramón and Julieta

Kiss Me, Mi Amor

Love & Tacos

ALANA QUINTANA ALBERTSON

BERKLEY ROMANCE
New York

BERKLEY ROMANCE
Published by Berkley
An imprint of Penguin Random House LLC
penguinrandomhouse.com

Copyright © 2023 by Alana Albertson
Readers Guide copyright © 2023 by Alana Albertson
Penguin Random House supports copyright. Copyright fuels creativity,
encourages diverse voices, promotes free speech, and creates a vibrant culture.
Thank you for buying an authorized edition of this book and for complying
with copyright laws by not reproducing, scanning, or distributing any part of it
in any form without permission. You are supporting writers and allowing
Penguin Random House to continue to publish books for every reader.

BERKLEY and the BERKLEY & B colophon are registered
trademarks of Penguin Random House LLC.

Library of Congress Cataloging-in-Publication Data

Names: Quintana Albertson, Alana, author.
Title: Kiss me, mi amor / Alana Quintana Albertson.
Description: First edition. | New York: Berkley Romance, 2023. | Series: Love & Tacos; 2
Identifiers: LCCN 2022054537 (print) | LCCN 2022054538 (ebook) |
ISBN 9780593336243 (trade paperback) | ISBN 9780593336250 (ebook)
Classification: LCC PS3617.U589655 K57 2023 (print) |
LCC PS3617.U589655 (ebook) | DDC 813/.6—dc23
LC record available at https://lccn.loc.gov/2022054537
LC ebook record available at https://lccn.loc.gov/2022054538

First Edition: July 2023

Printed in the United States of America
1st Printing

Book design by Kristin del Rosario
Title page art: Sugar skulls pattern © xenia_ok / Shutterstock

This book is dedicated to my nana,
Susana Quintana Viramontes,
who raised ten children.

KISS ME, MI AMOR

CHAPTER ONE

E nrique Montez bit into his carne guisada taco. The spices from the braised beef were cooled from the neutralizing dollop of fresh crema.

"Thank God," Enrique said to his older brother, Ramón, gesturing across the table with the taco still in hand, "that this badass woman agreed to marry you."

His future sister-in-law, Julieta Campos, had cooked a meal for her family and his brothers at their now weekly Sunday dinner in her restaurant, Las Pescas. Julieta and her mother, Linda, adored taking care of their loved ones, which now luckily included Enrique.

Julieta's lips twisted in a wry smile. Ramón simply looked at her with eyes of love. "I thank God every day." He pressed a kiss to her hand, then looked back at Enrique. "But after putting up with you for the past twenty-eight years, I deserved a miracle."

Enrique glared across the table at Ramón and his future bride. His brother whispered something into Julieta's ear, which caused her to giggle.

Enrique rolled his eyes. He should simply be happy for his brother and his fiancée. Still, a brief stab of envy tore through him . . . "Man, you're so whipped. I'll never be like that."

His younger brother, Jaime, rolled his eyes. "Yeah, because no one would deal with your weird bullshit. Do you have to do yoga on our deck every morning?"

"Better than you flipping tires in our yard," Enrique retorted.

Julieta's cousins Tiburón and Rosa laughed while Julieta's mother scooped out a huge portion of rice onto everyone's plates. What a trip to see the Montezes and the Camposes, formerly mortal enemies, breaking bread—well, more accurately, tearing tortillas—around the table. Notably absent, and most certainly not invited, was Enrique's father, Arturo. He'd begun the family feud decades ago when Arturo stole a fish taco recipe from Linda, his spring break fling. But Enrique was a peacemaker, and he hoped that even though his father's actions were unforgivable, one day, his father would repent and make amends with Linda, Julieta, and Ramón, though deep down he knew that with his father's deeply ingrained machismo, that fantasy happy ending was probably a pipe dream.

Enrique's immediate concern was spending quality time in a warm family environment that he and his brothers had never known. This connection had already changed Ramón significantly. His elder brother had benefited in amazing ways, even though Enrique teased him. Ever since Ramón and Julieta had become engaged, his workaholic sibling was now all about the family life. Ramón spent his free time playing Lotería with Julieta's overbearing tías, and he'd started volunteering at the Barrio Logan College Institute in his newly adopted community. He even hosted the weekly La Vuelta Lowrider Cruise with Tiburón.

Enrique studied Ramón, who had a big grin on his face. Enrique couldn't imagine being in such a committed relationship. Not until he struck out on his own and became something more than just the middle Montez brother. Ramón was the smartest, Jaime was the cutest, and Enrique was always the peacemaker.

"¡Salud!" Linda held up her sangria, and everybody clinked glasses before continuing to eat. This was the life—family. All together.

Exhaling a healing breath, Enrique reflected on how much he had changed in the past year. After the social media attention from their company's quest for gentefication turned ugly, Enrique spiraled into depression. He had spent the last several months working on himself . . . therapy, meditation, yoga.

In the meantime, he would continue to work for the family business, though Enrique didn't have an extreme desire for wealth, like his father had, or like Ramón had once had, for that matter. Ramón used to be focused on the bottom line—growing their corporation's assets and increasing the profit margin. His plan was to buy the land where Julieta's restaurant was located and turn the beloved neighborhood into a gentrified street full of chain stores. But Julieta had exposed Ramón to the true cost of these acquisitions—hurting lively communities and real people. Ramón did the right thing and returned the land to Julieta's mom. And now, Ramón was a changed man—aware of the societal effects of their business deals. And all of the brothers finally knew what it was like to belong to their community.

Enrique had never cared too much about money—he had seen the perils of that lifestyle early on, especially in his parents' relationship. They would spend lavishly on exotic vacations but couldn't stand to be in the same room together without fighting. And though they had enough wealth to comfortably provide for many generations to come, his father was always trying to expand the company. But all the money and success could never heal the deep wounds in their family.

At least Enrique understood his father's drive. In fact, Enrique could feel that he himself had grown too comfortable. His job was beyond secure, but it no longer challenged him.

In fact, nothing challenged him.

Time to change that.

Enrique clinked his glass with a fork, which caused Ramón to immediately kiss Julieta.

Enrique smirked. "I thought the kiss after the glass clink was only for weddings."

Ramón shrugged. "We're just practicing."

"Get a room, you two." Tiburón threw a tortilla chip at Ramón and Julieta, which Ramón caught and then crushed in his hand.

The warmth from their new family radiated throughout the restaurant—though maybe that was just the heat coming from the terra-cotta fireplace. Las Pescas was so magical, especially during the holiday season. Mariachi music played over the stereo, paintings from local vendors hung on the walls, the Talavera accents colorfully contrasted against the Saltillo tiles, and there was a Christmas tree in the corner, decorated with hand-painted ornaments created by local children.

Enrique took a sip of his michelada. The spicy Tajín-coated rim drew fire to his lips, but the Clamato juice cooled off the heat. "I have an announcement."

"What is it?" Ramón cocked his brow.

Enrique's stomach knotted. He should've run his plan by his brother, who had become the CEO of the Montez Group after he'd ousted their father. But for once, Enrique didn't want to ask permission from anyone to do anything. He wanted to be his own man—

out of the shadow of his father and brother—and his idea was sound. If the Montez Group contracted their produce through farms that had track records of treating their employees fairly, they could truly make a difference in their community—not to mention, do the right thing.

Enrique was no prodigal son—that title definitely went to Jaime—but even so, Enrique could never top Ramón's two Ivy League degrees, and now his engagement to the beautiful and talented Julieta. Not that Enrique was any slouch—no, quite the contrary. Enrique didn't want to compete with his brother; he had never even applied to Stanford and was more than happy to spend his college years surfing at Cal Poly San Luis Obispo. The eco-conscious atmosphere that he had immersed himself in when he was there called to him now, which was why he knew it was time to go and spend some time on the Central California Coast.

"I'm heading up to Santa Barbara for the holidays. I arranged a meeting with a farmer up in nearby Santa Maria." He glanced around at his brothers. Ramón squinted his eyes, which now had lines around them, and Jaime's baby face contorted.

Ramón didn't waste any time. "A farmer? But why? We're already contracted with enough farms."

"I know, but we need to reassess all of our agricultural relationships. I want us to contract with ethical operations only. The owner of this farm is amazing. She used to work on the farm herself with her parents and recently acquired it when it went up for sale. She raised the money through speaking engagements around the country and educating others about farmworkers' rights. She was just named one of *Time* magazine's most influential Hispanics."

Julieta opened her mouth. "Can we please use the word *Latines*? It's more inclusive."

Jesus. "Not the point. I'm not going to get into the Latino/Latine/Latinx/Hispanic semantics game."

"She?" Rosa asked, curiosity lacing her voice. Rosa was pretty and strong, like her cousin.

"Yes, she. Carolina Flores is one of the top female farmers in the state. She owns Flores Family Farm in Santa Maria. Make that one of the top farmers, period."

Jaime looked up from scrolling through his phone. "Carolina Flores? Isn't she the girl who had those viral graduation photos in the strawberry patch?"

Enrique nodded. "That's the one."

Tiburón interjected. "Flores? Any relation to Señora Flores at the café next door?"

Julieta rubbed her fiancé's arm. "Yeah. Luísa Flores is her aunt, but from what she told me, she isn't close to them."

Enrique scratched his chin. "Really? I didn't know that." He had met Señora Flores many times—he was a sucker for her freshly baked conchas—but he had no idea she was related to Carolina.

Ramón pursed his lips and glared intently at his brother. "Okay, I thought we talked about this. You know Apá reached out to her father a couple of years ago with disastrous consequences when the Flores family bought the farm. Victor Flores does not want to distribute to us."

Enrique smirked. "Right, you told me that, but it's his daughter's farm, not his."

Tiburón chuckled.

Enrique glared at him. "Something funny?"

"Nope. Just that you clearly don't understand the dynamic of a traditional first-generation Mexican family. It doesn't matter if she owns it, not him. He's her papá."

Enrique gulped. Nothing was more accurate. He was a third-generation Mexican-American. He didn't have a clue what it was like to be raised in his culture. "True, I don't. But she seems to be a savvy businesswoman. And Señor Flores said no when he only knew Papá. He doesn't know *us*, and I arranged a meeting with her, not him. She's in charge now, though you're right—he could still be involved in the decision-making. And you only talked to him on the phone. Ramón, I've done my research. Señor Flores is a family man—he's old-school. He's nothing like Apá, and neither are we. I'm going to go there in person, spend some time with her, get them to trust us. And Carolina wrote me a nice email back. She invited us to her farm. Maybe she will accept our proposal with her father's approval. The options are endless."

"Options?" Julieta rolled her eyes. "What's your plan? Start contracting with them and then buy out their farm like you bought our block?"

Enrique gritted his teeth, but at least her tone was teasing, not serious.

Ramón pinched Julieta. "Come on, babe. I made it right, didn't I?"

"Yes, you did." She scrunched her face, and she and Ramón rubbed noses.

Another wave of uneasiness hit Enrique. He couldn't imagine being so in love that he would be so affectionate in public.

Jaime tossed a bacon-wrapped, chorizo-stuffed jalapeño popper drenched in chipotle crema into his mouth. "I'll come with you. I love Santa Barbara. We can stay at Apá's house in Montecito for Christmas."

Enrique shook his head. Nope. Montecito was the celebrity enclave of Santa Barbara, and definitely not his scene. Enrique had already rented a hotel room on West Beach near downtown because he had no desire to stay at their father's vacation home, though he loved the view and the beach access. Why did his father need another home in the middle of the state? Apá had bought it when Enrique had been accepted to Cal Poly. He had claimed it was an investment, but keeping a multimillion-dollar estate empty seemed ridiculous. If Enrique had the opportunity to get to know Carolina, he did not want her to realize his father just wasted money, especially because she came from such humble beginnings.

But the house wasn't even half the problem. Enrique didn't want his baby brother tagging along. This was a serious trip for Enrique to make a name for himself in the company without his brothers, without his father. The last thing he needed was Jaime nagging him to go party every night and hitting on one of Señor Flores's ten daughters—especially Carolina.

What an impressive woman she was. She had worked on the farm her entire life while maintaining a top grade point average and dancing with the local Ballet Folklórico group. Her parents had taken her with them every day to pick berries in the fields—rain or shine, no matter if they were scorched by the rays of the sun or frozen by the chill of the night. She would work in the evenings until the wee hours, sleep for a brief time, wake up, and go back to school. She was accepted to Cal Poly San Luis Obispo, which was no easy task. For college graduation, she had hired a photographer to take pictures of herself in her cap and gown, picking produce with her parents to honor their hard work and sacrifices. When her sister Blanca had posted them online, those photos went viral. The media attention had catapulted her career and made her an in-demand speaker at Hispanic events around the United States. And when her farm was for sale a couple of years ago, she'd raised enough money to buy it.

Enrique was in complete awe of her.

But she had a complex reputation around the farm-owning community. She definitely treated her employees right, but there had been rumblings that she was ruthless. A shrew . . . d businesswoman. That she didn't hesitate to tell off distributors or fire long-term staff members who weren't pulling their weight.

Enrique didn't believe any of that nonsense. When Ramón was cutthroat in his business, people hailed him, not demonized him. How misogynistic and frankly racist for these rich non-Hispanic farm owners to give a hard time to one of the only Mexican-American female proprietors in the state, or in the country, for that matter.

Enrique had seen a picture of the entire family on the Flores Family Farm website. All the daughters were beautiful, especially Carolina. Her long, dark curly hair, huge brown eyes, and those curves. *Man.*

But no matter how smart, successful, and sexy Carolina was, Enrique was not interested in her romantically. At all.

Enrique had learned his lesson from Ramón about mixing business with pleasure. Sure, his brother's story had a happy ending, but Enrique was certain that was due to luck more than anything.

"I know a great club in Santa Barbara," Rosa said, tugging on her cousin Tiburón's arm. "Perhaps we could come for a short visit and show you."

Tiburón gave a fist bump to his prima.

Enrique shook his head. "No thanks, guys. I'll do this one on my own."

Ramón shook his head. "Jaime's right. Someone should go with you."

"Okay, *Dad.* I can handle business on my own."

"I know you can." Ramón pointed at his brother. "But I don't want you to spend the holiday alone."

Enrique shrugged, ran a hand through his long, dark hair, and surrendered. "Fine." He hated the way Ramón always overrode his business decisions. But Enrique didn't want to ditch Jaime for the holidays. Since Ramón wasn't speaking to their father, it would fall on Jaime to go over there alone this Christmas if Enrique was gone.

If they were both out of town, their father would simply make other plans. And their mother was on a cruise in Italy.

Enrique turned to his younger brother. "Jaime, you can come, but I'm serious. He has ten daughters. You cannot hit on them—not even one."

Jaime was a regular Don Juan—love them and leave them. Which was fine. He was young. Maybe he'd grow up one day and change his mind.

Maybe not.

Jaime laughed and leveled Ramón and Enrique with his eyes. "Why do you both think I'm some kind of Neanderthal? I can talk to women and not hit on them. It is possible." He exhaled, causing his long bangs to flap up before taking their resting place, skimming his eyebrows. "Look at Rosa and me. We're just friends."

Rosa smacked him playfully on the head. "We are family, you foo. Plus, I would never put up with your shit. I pity the girl who falls for you. You're cute but you're a fuckboy."

Jaime grinned. "That's not what you said last night."

Rosa lunged at him, but Jaime stopped her.

Enrique shook his head—what was going on with those two? He didn't want to ask. It didn't matter—Jaime would never settle down. Ever. Rosa was right—what kind of woman would ever put up with his antics? Jaime was a model. When he wasn't doing social media for the Montez Group, Jaime was showing off designer sweats in La Jolla as a side gig, and he definitely had the surfer/beach vibe look down.

Enrique turned his attention back to his food. He took a big bite of his next taco and contemplated the scenario. Ramón was right— having Jaime come would be better after all. It would be nice to have some company on the trip. Bringing another member of his family along would show Señor Flores how serious they were. From what he could tell, Señor Flores was a traditional Mexican man and would not be receptive to either of Enrique's proposals, even if Carolina was, and Enrique wasn't sure how much sway Señor Flores had over Carolina, though after what Tiburón said, Enrique feared it would be a lot. Either way, Enrique would fight for this. He actually cared about farming, the environment, and the health of the workers who picked the food for their restaurants—this was more than just business and the family name.

This was their future, too.

It would work out. This would be a great partnership for the Montez Group, which they really needed.

They had received positive publicity after Ramón had given the block of Barrio Logan to Linda—not that he'd done it for publicity. Enrique was thrilled that they had done right by Barrio Logan. The Montezes, minus Papá, had been welcomed into the community, which was worth all of the hate they had initially received.

But it wasn't enough; it was a Band-Aid, and Ramón and Enrique knew it. Years of their father's business decisions displacing local taco shops and serving whitewashed versions of Mexican favorites had made the Montez Group persona non grata in San Diego. In fact, recently there had even been an online campaign for the Taco King chain to be shut down. A Twitter boycott slowed sales for a bit, but Julieta's presence quickly quelled the social media mob's anger, so they moved on to a new target. Even so, the constant threats that were DM'd to Enrique had taken a toll on him. He felt so helpless and so guilty and was unable to cope back then. But he was in a much better place.

Because now their father was out of the company; Ramón was in charge. And Enrique was committed to growing the business and creating lasting changes for their legacy.

Ramón took a swig of his beer. "When are you leaving?"

"Tomorrow morning." The sooner, the better. He'd lock down the deal first, and then hang with Jaime. Maybe wake up early, go surfing, and spend the rest of the day chilling on the beach. One thing Enrique loved about California was that he could be in the ocean year-round, as long as he had a good wet suit.

Julieta put her hand up in a stop sign. "Enrique, we'll go with you, too. It is important that we spend Christmas together as a family."

Ramón's jaw dropped, and he gave her a pointed look but remained silent. Smart man.

Enrique paused. Christmas hadn't meant anything to him since he'd been an adult. The holidays held numb memories of car rides back and forth between his dad's cold mansion and his mom's equally chilly beachfront casa in La Jolla Shores, or long stays with nannies while both parents went on separate tropical vacations with their significant others of the week. No. He didn't need extra family with him for a holiday that was essentially just another day of the year.

"No. It's okay. I don't really get into the full Christmas thing. Besides, don't you have a restaurant to run?" Enrique asked.

"Of course I do, but one of the best things I've learned from your brother is achieving work-life balance. Las Pescas is operating smoothly, and I feel comfortable taking a hard-earned vacation."

"Wouldn't you rather go somewhere else? Hawai'i, perhaps?"

Julieta didn't give up. "Nope. I love the Central Coast. It'll be fun. And you've never celebrated Christmas as part of my family. I'm going to make you love it! Have you ever participated in Las Posadas? There is one in Old Town."

"No." Enrique had never been to Las Posadas and didn't even know much about the tradition, even though he was technically a Catholic. "What happens?"

Julieta clasped her hands together as her eyes danced. "Oh, they are so much fun. Basically, the community gathers to recreate the journey of Joseph and the Virgin Mary to seek shelter. They walk to different homes where they are repeatedly refused shelter, and at the final house on the block, they are welcomed in with tamales and punch and piñatas for the kids."

Hmm. That sounded incredibly awkward. Enrique wasn't religious, unless you counted him chanting kirtan at yoga. Plus, he barely spoke Spanish. He was interested in learning about his culture but wanted to keep the separation between church and his heritage. Traditional Catholic values didn't align with his beliefs; he was a fan of birth control, gay marriage, and a woman's right to control her body. "Cool, when is it? Maybe I can come after the trip."

Julieta checked her phone, and then looked back at Enrique. "It's this week—we could participate in the holiday and then go with you after it."

"That sounds great, but I really need to be up in Santa Maria as soon as possible—and you couldn't up and leave with twelve hours' notice. I'd love to finalize a contract with the Flores Family Farm right away so their produce can be used as soon as the season changes."

Julieta stared at him, then shook her head.

"What, Julieta?"

"It's just that it's Christmastime. From what Señora Flores told me about her family, her brother is very old-school—it doesn't sound like he would want to do much business during the holidays. In super traditional Mexican families, the patriarch has a lot of control. Her father is probably head of the household until she gets married, whether she wants to wed or not."

Ugh, she was right. "Good point. But Carolina agreed to meet with me, so I'm going to go."

"Well, I don't mind missing Las Posadas this year to spend the

holidays together as a family. Maybe we can find one up there."
Julieta stood up, went into the kitchen, and returned to the dining
room and handed Tiburón a beer with a lime nestled in its neck.

Linda pointed her finger at her daughter. "I'm in, as long as Arturo doesn't show up."

Jaime typed something on his phone. After a few minutes, he
smiled. "Just texted Dad. He said no problem about using his place."

"I'm down," Tiburón said as he scrolled through his phone. Enrique peered at Tiburón's phone from his seat next to his future
primo-in-law and watched as Tiburón changed the location on his
dating apps to Santa Barbara. Tiburón's eyes lit up, and he began
swiping on every dark-eyed, big-bootied beauty that graced his
screen. Surprisingly, though, Jaime did not follow suit. Enrique grimaced at Tiburón, realizing Jaime might not be the only one to keep
an eye on around the Flores daughters.

"It'll be a nice break for us." Ramón and Julieta kissed.

Enrique threw up his hands. Fabulous. "Fine. You all win. I'm
going to go home and pack."

Downing his michelada, Enrique walked out of the restaurant.
His solo quest had now turned into the Campos-Montez Central
Coastal California Christmas Vacation.

Feliz fucking Navidad to me.

Chapter Two

⟪❀⟫

Carolina Flores took a sip of her sandía agua fresca on her porch and looked out across the scenic landscape of her lush farm, mesmerized by the clear blue sky overhead, the rows of colorful Swiss chard lined up like little soldiers, and the fields of red onions, ripe for picking. It wasn't strawberry season yet, her favorite, but she loved the calm of the winter months. A cool coastal breeze wafted the fragrant scent of garlic through the air, and Carolina marveled at the contrast between the snowcapped Santa Ynez Mountains in the distance and the food growing on the land.

Mi tierra.

She owned the farm, and her entire family worked on it. When Carolina finally raised enough money to make the purchase, Papá had vowed that everyone in the family would learn to do all jobs, and that no one was too good to perform the hard labor. Luckily, Carolina was passionate about farming, but her siblings had dreams of their own that didn't involve cultivating the earth for the rest of their lives.

Papá had pointed to their staff. "We are no better than them just because we own the place now. They are just like us. Exactly like us."

And Carolina took his words to heart. Technically, she owned the farm, not him, but she happily shared all her assets, including the farm and the accompanying owner's house, with her family, grateful for their hard work and sacrifice to get her a better life. Her parents had worked on this farm since immigrating to America in their teens from Mexico. They had met on these fields and fallen in love. Even throughout droughts and a pandemic, the Flores family never gave up. Though, with Papá's health failing, it would soon be completely her responsibility. Papá definitely had wanted a son, hence her mother's ten children. Well, that and the fact that they were devoutly Catholic. But they'd only had girls. As the eldest of ten daughters, Carolina had finally convinced her father that she was the future of the farm, and that it would be best kept in her hands. He still held out hope that one day she would marry, and her husband would take over the business, but that would never happen.

Ever.

She was sick to death of Papá's archaic rules about women. The thought of dealing with more of the same in a marriage to another traditional man made her throat close like she was having an allergy attack.

Sure, there were more progressive men out there, but Carolina's father would never approve of a nontraditional guy. And even if she did rebel and find a guy with modern sensibilities, she seriously doubted he would want anything at all to do with her family. Any normal man today would never agree to have her over-involved family all up in his business. It was hopeless, which was fine by Carolina. She loved her independence. She'd never felt that flutter in her heart that her younger sister Blanca always talked about experiencing every time she flirted with any man who caught her eye. Carolina had a few crushes growing up, and definitely could appreciate a handsome, well-dressed man, but just the thought of dating gave her anxiety.

Papá supported Carolina when she'd decided to go to Cal Poly San Luis Obispo and get a combined bachelor's and master's degree in agricultural science with the pipe dream of buying a farm one day, though honestly, he had probably been more excited about the prospect of her obtaining her Mrs. title while she was there, rather than her master's. Much to her father's dismay, Carolina had never been engaged. Or had a serious boyfriend—or any boyfriend, for that matter. She was nothing like Blanca, who had a full battalion of suitors but, because of their father's traditional rules, was not allowed to date until the eldest Carolina did. Poor Blanca was out of luck.

Carolina had no desire to be a traditional Mexican housewife like her mother. Not that she looked down on Mamá—Carolina admired and respected her for raising ten children and keeping their home full of love, but Carolina wanted to work outside the home.

And Carolina had worked hard to make her dream come true. As the new CEO of the Flores Family Farm, she had a great vision for the future. She would update the technology, streamline the production process, and most importantly, focus on farmworkers' rights.

The Flores Family Farm prided themselves on providing their employees, who were almost exclusively people of color, with a living wage and healthy working conditions. And to that end, they only partnered with ethical farm-to-table restaurants for their produce. Those high-end places were willing to pay exorbitant prices to ensure not only was the produce picked at its peak freshness, but also that the farmworkers were given the best possible care and were treated with the respect and dignity they deserved.

Sure, the margins were low, and during the drought and the pandemic, her commitment to their workers had almost caused them to go bankrupt. But there was never too steep a price on doing the right thing.

She had turned their business around recently with a weekly subscription box service for families who wanted fresh food without going to the grocery store. And it had been wildly successful, just like Carolina prayed it would be.

But Carolina couldn't think too far into the future right now—it was time for her to prepare for the holidays. Tomorrow was Las Posadas—her favorite part of Christmas. Ever since the day as a little girl when she'd been chosen to be the angel who led the procession through the streets of her town, Las Posadas had held a special place in her heart.

The celebration took on a new meaning now that she was an adult; this year, she had been lucky enough to be chosen to play the Virgin Mary. Though the holiday was technically religious, members from the entire town, no matter what religion or nationality, took part in the tradition. Many immigrants related to the experience of Mary and Joseph seeking shelter and being refused. It was cultural, even if you weren't a Catholic.

And Carolina loved every aspect of this tradition. From the spiced, warm ponche that soothed her throat after walking through the streets to the sweet basket of treats containing cookies, it was all divine.

And don't even get Carolina started on the scrumptious tamales. As long as she didn't have to cook them herself.

But there was only one problem—she didn't have a Joseph.

Well, she *had* a Joseph, her cousin Roberto, who had unfortunately caught the flu, so now he was out. But even if he had been healthy that would've been a disaster—it was embarrassing enough that she had to use a relative and did not have a boyfriend or a husband to play Joseph, not that she wanted to get married or anything.

Why were men always required in order for her to do the things she loved?

Carolina's other passion, besides sustainable farming, was dancing with the local Ballet Folklórico. The dances were stories in themselves—representing different regions in Mexico, but many were influenced by cultures from around the world. Some were about animals, some depicted moments in history, all were amazing. She loved the vibrant costumes, the ribbons she wore braided through her long black hair, and the sound of her feet tapping on the floors. But again, she needed a male partner to perform the dances she loved most. Her friends danced with their boyfriends or husbands, which simply wasn't an option for Carolina. She finally quit last year. Without a partner, it was pointless. And she had a farm to run.

She sighed. She didn't need a man to be happy, but she used to need a man to dance and currently needed one to be her Joseph. She had posted on Facebook again, asking for a volunteer. Someone would answer her call. She had faith. She had even prayed for a Joseph to appear in her life, but so far, God had not given her an answer.

Carolina pushed her thoughts aside, turning away from the beautiful fields, and walked into her home.

The scents of cumin and citrus filled the air, mixed with the fresh pine from the Christmas tree. Papá had nodded off and was slumped on his old vinyl recliner with an unfinished crossword puzzle by his side. She tiptoed by him and peered into the kitchen. Her mother was stirring something in a pot. Carolina wasn't sure what, but it smelled delicious. Carolina always had a good nose, despite being a complete disaster in the kitchen. She'd never had any patience to learn.

Warmth filled Carolina's chest anticipating another festive holiday; Carolina couldn't feel more blessed.

Well, perhaps she could.

She checked her phone. No one had replied to the post she'd placed on Facebook asking for a volunteer to be her Joseph.

If her sister Blanca had put up the post, she'd have been inundated with offers. But perhaps Carolina had said no to men too many times as she concentrated on her studies, and now no one wanted to help her in her time of need.

Ah well. She had her family.

But where exactly were they? The house was silent. Prior to purchasing the farm, they were all crammed into a small two-bedroom, one-bath home on the farm. Ten girls slept together in one room with bunk beds crammed in a small space. Nothing said good morning like waking up with your sister's foot in your face, as they had to sleep each head on either end of the bed. At least Blanca always had pretty painted toenails. But the farm came with a five-bedroom home. Carolina gave her parents the master, out of respect. She now finally had her own bed but did still share her room with Blanca. Even in the new space, with a family of twelve, the house was always bustling. But it was surprisingly quiet right now. Even Chuy, the family's yappy Chihuahua, didn't bark when she walked in.

Carolina decided to embrace the rare silence. She didn't want to wake Papá, or even worse, be forced to help Mamá in the kitchen, so she sat on the old tan corduroy sofa and grabbed a book. It wasn't her first choice to read—one of her dad's crime thrillers in Spanish—but she focused on the words on the page and enjoyed the quiet.

When she was a few chapters in, the door flew open.

Blanca stood in the doorway. Her waist-length black hair hung down her back, with a few wisps landing right on her perfectly flat midriff, which was currently bare since she was wearing a tube top and low-slung jeans.

Blanca was a knockout. No wonder every man in Santa Maria wanted her.

Carolina lowered her voice to a strong whisper, careful not to wake Papá. "What are you wearing, Blanca? Hurry and change before Papá sees you!"

Blanca glanced at their father, who had turned in his chair but was somehow still asleep.

"Good call, Cari." She bit her pouty lip and grabbed a sweatshirt that hung on an antique coatrack near the door but didn't put it on. At least it was in reach if Papá woke up. Blanca was no dummy. It may have been the twenty-first century, but make no mistake—Papá still treated his daughters like it was the 1950s.

Blanca motioned Carolina to come outside. Carolina quickly followed her onto the porch.

"¿Qué tal?"

"Oh my God! I just heard from Lupe, who heard it from Viola, who heard it from Gina that the Montez brothers are in town!"

"¿Quién?"

"Ay! They run the Taco King empire! You know who they are. Like the three hottest men ever. Ramón was *People en Español*'s most eligible bachelor."

Carolina was not impressed. "Why do I care?"

Blanca rolled her eyes. "Because, silly. They are all *so* hot. And rich."

Carolina shook her head. She adored her younger sister, but she couldn't fathom how her only goal in life was to marry some rich guy and become his trophy wife.

Sure, all the girls in the Flores family had grown up working on the farm alongside the strawberry pickers. Carolina's earliest memories were of plucking berries next to her parents. So she could understand that Blanca wanted to have an easier life than they'd had growing up. But there was so much more to her than her looks. Blanca was stylish and sweet and compassionate. And she spent her free time designing the cutest clothes. Carolina thought she should go to college and then maybe get into fashion design.

But there was no use in lecturing her now.

"I have my eye on Jaime. He's so fine. You should go for Enrique. I read that Ramón is taken. The rumor is he was asked to be the first Mexican-American guy on *The Bachelor*, but he turned it down because he's in love with this girl who runs a restaurant. Can you believe that? What type of guy turns down that kind of celebrity for true love?"

An honorable one. "One who is not a narcissist."

"Well, he doesn't need to be on *The Bachelor*. Every Chicana knows about Ramón—and his brothers."

"Not every one—I didn't know."

Blanca took out her phone and showed her a picture of them. "¡Mira!"

Carolina studied the picture from an article. Tall, dark, and handsome. Similar features but each was distinct. Ramón was the most clean-cut, Enrique had a SoCal surfer vibe, and Jaime looked like a pretty boy.

They were all good-looking, for sure, but Carolina knew men like them.

And she wanted nothing to do with them. She hated the way they seemed to abandon their culture and community when they made it big. Some of the wealthiest farm owners in Santa Maria were Mexican, and many of them treated their workers horribly.

And even if she found a decent guy who happened to be rich, she wouldn't feel comfortable in their world. She liked her life. One earned by hard work and sacrifice. Sure, the couch she had been sitting on was faded, and their house had avocado-colored appliances from the eighties, but they had a good roof over their heads and delicious food on the table, and most importantly, one another.

Blanca clutched the glass of agua fresca that Carolina had left out earlier and drank it.

"This spa water is the best."

Carolina rolled her eyes. "Don't start with me." Restaurants were now serving traditional Mexican aguas and rebranding them as spa waters. It was so ridiculous.

Blanca laughed and took another sip. "Well, I want Jaime." She touched her sister's hand and gave her a pleading look. "¿Ayúdame?"

"That's a hard no." Carolina refused to help her. Blanca was well aware of Papá's archaic rules—especially the one that stated that Blanca, who was twenty-one years old, wasn't allowed to seriously date until twenty-three-year-old Carolina did, which was ridiculous because Blanca was legally allowed to drink but not date. And Carolina didn't want to date. So that was the end of that story, though it really was Carolina's duty to help break her father's iron fist.

Blanca dramatically clasped her hands. "Please! Daddy never lets me do anything. I'm an adult, Cari. You at least got to go to college."

"Don't start with me, Blanca. You could go to school."

Blanca flipped her hair. "Yeah, I could, but not really. I would have to live at home and commute like you did. And then how would I go to parties?"

Carolina never went to parties in college.

Though sometimes, when she left campus late, she'd watched all the other girls heading to the events. They were all so carefree and happy. Carolina had envied their freedom.

But as a first-generation college student, she'd had responsibilities, pressures, and expectations not only to succeed but to return and help her family. And don't even get her started on all the rules her parents imposed. She still had a curfew, even though she was a grown-ass adult at twenty-three. Her non-Hispanic friends couldn't fathom that she still had to be home by eleven during the week and by midnight on the weekends. But rules were rules. She owned a farm, and she could technically afford to live on her own—but Papá would never allow it unless she was married. Sometimes, she laughed when she would go online and watch videos made by influencers who talked about toxic families and their advice to just say adiós to them and live your truth. Carolina was Mexican with a traditional family—those freedoms didn't apply to her life. It was what it was, and Carolina had just accepted it.

"College is for studying, not for meeting men."

She pouted. "You're no fun. I don't ask for anything. Just meet with the Montez brothers!"

Carolina was almost willing to do that to end the conversation. "And how do you expect me to do that? I don't have their phone numbers."

Blanca's sable eyes lit up. "Oh, but you do." She pulled up the Flores Family Farm email account on her phone and pointed to a message. It was from Enrique Montez.

Dear Miss Carolina Flores,

My name is Enrique Montez. I greatly admire your advances in sustainable farming and your business acumen. I'm equally impressed with your campaign for farmworkers' rights. You are an inspiration.

I would like to meet with you to discuss a possible collaboration between our businesses. I can be in Santa Maria in the month of December. Please let me know when a good time would be to set up a meeting.

Sincerely,
Enrique Montez

Carolina's heart constricted. Collaboration? What did that mean?

No, gracias.

Papá had worked on the farm for over twenty years, and the Flores family had now owned it for two. Papá had worked his way up from an employee, and theirs was now one of the few Hispanic-owned farms. She didn't want to supply food to just anyone, and definitely not the Montez fast-food empire.

"That message was from a month ago. I don't care if he's coming to town. What did you reply?" Blanca handled all the emails for the company. She was diligent and actually liked sitting behind a computer. Carolina preferred working her hands through the earth to tapping on a keyboard.

Blanca pulled on Carolina's black pants. "Just meet with him. What's the harm?"

"Plenty. The Taco King owners have a reputation for buying out small businesses—not that we are for sale. They are like Richard Gere in *Pretty Woman*."

"But I love that movie! And you're not a hooker. Besides, I doubt he wants to buy out the business. He probably just wants to talk to us. Or you," she teased. "He said you were an inspiration."

"He was trying to butter me up. Anyway, I have no desire to provide them produce for their awful food. They can buy cheap, wilted lettuce elsewhere."

Gravel crunched. An engine roared up the road, interrupting their conversation. That was weird—they weren't expecting any company...

An outrageously expensive SUV with gold rims drove up the long and windy drive and approached the home. Who would drive such an ostentatious car? Especially one with a license plate like ... did that say T8C0 K1NG?

A horrifying thought crossed her mind. One look at Blanca's wide eyes and Carolina's fears were confirmed.

She pulled her sister's hair. "Blanca María Flores, tell me you didn't agree to a meeting."

"I can't lie."

Ay, Dios mío! Blanca had written them behind her back and invited them over? The Montez brothers were here, now? Carolina looked down at her clothes—a grass-stained formerly white T-shirt and black Dickies. Her work boots were caked with mud, and her dark hair was in a messy braid.

"You just did. You told me you heard a rumor they were in town— not that you set up a meeting with them!"

"Both those things are true!" Blanca's head turned toward the driveway. "Wait here. And don't be mad at me, Cari. One day, you will thank me." Blanca ran toward the garage. A blacked-out Tesla SUV was now parked in the driveway.

I'm going to murder Blanca! Just wait until Papá hears about this!

A minute later, Blanca returned, trailed by four men. Three of them, Carolina recognized as the Montez brothers. The fourth one had a tattoo of a shark on his neck. If Papá saw him, he'd kick him off the property!

One of the Montez brothers held a bouquet of bright yellow and orange sunflowers—which happened to be her favorites, but that was beside the point. Why would he bring flowers to a business meeting? What were his intentions?

He flashed a wide smile with perfectly white teeth. His dark brown skin glowed in the sun, highlighting his muscular arms. He had great arms. If she was into that type of thing. Which Carolina was most certainly not.

His hands were manicured; her nails were filled with dirt.

But even though she tried to look away, their eyes met, as if the magnetic pull of the earth drew them together.

A pulse of electricity shot through her. She lowered her head and stared at the ground. The silence was awkward. She raised her chin and met his eyes.

And he was grinning at her.

"Mucho gusto, Señorita Flores. I'm Enrique Montez, and these are my brothers, Ramón and Jaime. And that is my soon-to-be cousin-in-law, Tiburón. Thanks for agreeing to meet with me."

Chapter Three

Enrique stood at the bottom of the porch, clutching the huge bouquet of sunflowers he had picked up for Carolina at the local stand.

Her headshot on the website didn't do her justice. Her hair was in a loose braid, and she didn't wear a hint of makeup. She had beautiful copper-brown eyes and full lips, even if they were pursed in an angry scowl. Her tight white T-shirt and close-fitting black pants showed off her curves. It made him want to grab her hips and pull her close.

But the last thing Enrique should be thinking about was hitting on this accomplished woman. No. He needed to learn more about her farm, not sow his oats.

Carolina didn't say anything. She sneered at her sister and then gritted her teeth.

Why did Carolina look so shocked?

Uh-oh, had she not been expecting him? Was he early? No, he was sure he'd had the time right.

She grabbed a sweatshirt from her sister and quickly covered herself.

Strange. She looked fine now—as she had before—though he had been a bit shocked that she was wearing work clothes for their business meeting. But maybe since she was a hands-on farm owner, she wanted to show him the day-to-day operations.

"Speak, bro." Tiburón nudged his shoulder.

Enrique took a cautious step toward Carolina and reached out his arm to hand her the flowers. "Miss Flores. I'm sorry if I caught you by surprise. Did I get the time wrong?"

Her little sister grinned and took a step closer to Jaime. She examined him head to toe but surprised Enrique by turning her attentions to Tiburón. "Nope! Right on time. I'm Blanca, by the way. Her super charming and very single sister."

Carolina slapped Blanca's arm. Blanca laughed and twirled her hair.

Enrique's gaze returned to Carolina. "Like I said in the email, I was hoping I could talk to you about a possible collaboration with our restaurant group. Should we reschedule?"

Carolina cleared her throat and waved her index finger at the flowers as if she was offended by them.

Hmm. Maybe Enrique shouldn't have brought the flowers. That was sexist—he wouldn't have brought a man flowers. He should've brought a bottle of wine.

Blanca reached over and grabbed them. "I'll just take these. I love flowers. And so does Carolina, but you can call her Cari. Sunflowers are her favorite. Personally, I prefer poppies." She smiled and turned to Tiburón. "Why don't you all sit on the porch? I'll get some drinks for us, and we can get to know one another."

Tiburón didn't waste any time. His eyes not so subtly grazed over her body as he walked toward a porch swing. "Don't mind if I do."

At least Jaime was behaving himself for once. He didn't so much as check out either Carolina or Blanca.

Carolina pulled her sister's arm. "That won't be necessary, and despite what my sister said, you can call me Ms. Flores." She turned to face Enrique. "I'm sorry for any miscommunication, Mr. Montez. I had no idea you were coming—my sister replied to your email impersonating me. She doesn't have the authority to set up meetings for me, and I will deal with her after you leave."

What? Carolina hadn't written the email?

"That is unfortunate, and we don't mean to intrude. But since we drove all the way from San Diego, I would appreciate if you would give me a few minutes of your time."

Carolina shook her head, and her braid flung around her shoulders like a whip. "We're not interested. We're doing quite well at the farm and are not looking for any new restaurants to distribute to—especially yours."

Enrique balked. Not *theirs*? "Why on earth not?"

"We don't work with chains. We mostly work with local farm-to-table restaurants and provide them with high-quality produce. We are a small farm and not able to serve the needs of a fast-food conglomerate." Carolina folded her arms, her body language clear. "If you would like further information on our farm, or would like to visit, we have tours on Mondays and Thursdays. You can sign up online."

Enrique took a step back. His mouth dropped open. Tours? Like he was some sort of common tourist? Enrique wasn't used to being shut down so thoroughly. His name normally opened doors to opportunity, not slammed them shut in his face. He had to try another approach. "I'm sorry for the confusion, Ms. Flores, I had no idea you didn't agree to this meeting. I really think we can offer something fantastic for both your farm and our restaurant group. Please hear me out."

Carolina zipped up her large sweatshirt and put her hand up like a stop sign. "I'm sorry as well. But we're not interested. To be clear, I am not interested. Please leave."

Ramón placed his hand on Enrique's shoulder. "See? I told you so. Let's just go. We've wasted enough time up here."

Enrique shook his head. He would not just go. He had driven more than five hours to see her. Not to mention, now his entire family was up here, too, thanks to Julieta's desire to have one big happy family Christmas. What a complete nightmare.

But Enrique wasn't the type of man to quit. Not when he wanted something. And he wanted to learn everything about the Flores Family Farm. What new hydroponic techniques they were using, how they crossbred and pollinated their plants, and how they became financially viable without taking advantage of their workers.

And most importantly, he wanted to get to know this woman who wouldn't even give him the time of day. How could she hate him so much when she didn't even know him? Was the Montez name so tarnished that he wouldn't even get the opportunity to prove himself?

Not to mention that he was wildly attracted to her. The sweat glistened off her forehead, and wisps of her hair blew in the wind. He imagined her body slick and wild as he kissed her everywhere.

Dammit—instead of warning Jaime off lusting after Carolina, he should've heeded his own advice.

But he couldn't help it—Carolina, or Ms. Flores, was gorgeous.

"I'm happy to leave and come back another day later this week if that's better for you. But we drove up from San Diego and are spending the holidays in Santa Barbara, well, Montecito, actually, so I could make this meeting upon receipt of Blanca's email. I promise I just want to learn about your farm, tell you more about our company, and discuss how we could possibly be mutually beneficial to each other's missions. Please, find some time for us." He stared into her kind eyes. "For me?" He threw in a wink for good measure.

Carolina's head tilted, and for a second, Enrique thought he might have made headway. "I'm sorry for the inconvenience. I hope you have a wonderful time in Santa Barbara."

Enrique shook his head, his patience turning to anger. "Are you serious right now? I came here for a confirmed meeting with you. I'm not some tourist."

"Not sure what to tell you. But sometimes it's fun to play tourist. You could pay a visit to the Queen of the Missions or feed an African spurred tortoise at the zoo."

"The zoo? We have the best zoo in San Diego. No. I want to spend time in Santa Maria."

Blanca interjected, a sly look on her face. "Well, if you want to hang out here, tomorrow we're celebrating Las Posadas in town. Carolina is playing Mary." She paused and lowered her voice. "Well, maybe. She doesn't have a Joseph yet."

"¡Ay! Blanca!" Carolina threw up her hands and glowered at her sister, who smiled like a cat who just caught a mouse.

Las Posadas? There they were again. This was the second time in two days that Enrique had heard about the holiday that he'd never celebrated and knew nothing about. First from Julieta, and now from Blanca.

It had to be a sign.

Enrique always believed in signs and deeper meanings; in fact, he started reading people through their astrological signs. He had never been into it until an ex-girlfriend did his chart. First, he thought it was bullshit, but the more he studied the planets and their interpretations, the deeper into it he got. He read that some CEOs even made business decisions with the guidance of an astrologer. Enrique hadn't crossed that line yet, but he was still fascinated by the topic. He was a Pisces, and according to his research, Carolina was an Aries. She was headstrong and feisty; he was fair and calm. And he would win her over.

He smirked. "I'll be your Joseph."

Tiburón burst out laughing, and Jaime joined him, cackling. Ramón just shook his head and let out a mirthless laugh.

Jerks.

Carolina grimaced. "Las Posadas are important to this community. I don't appreciate you mocking me, my religion, or my customs. Please go."

Enrique stepped forward. "I'm not mocking you, Ms. Flores. I mean it. I'll do it."

"Does he get a donkey?" Tiburón roared, and Jaime high-fived him.

Enrique gave them a death glare.

"Yes, actually. He would." Carolina's eyes widened, and her tone was cautiously hopeful. She uncrossed her arms.

Enrique smiled. Progress.

Carolina narrowed her gaze at Enrique. "Really? You don't even know me, and you aren't from here. You're willing to play Joseph in Las Posadas? Are you even Catholic?"

He smiled cockily. "Technically, yes. I'm confirmed, but I don't go to church regularly. I'm not into organized religion, actually. I'm more of a spiritual man. I prefer to meditate and practice yoga."

Tiburón put his head in his hands, and Carolina's face wrinkled.

Okay, maybe Enrique shouldn't have mentioned his love of Downward Dog, but he was always open and honest about who he was.

Jaime grabbed Enrique's arm. "Okay, José. We need to be going."

He turned to Carolina. "Sorry about him; sustainable farming really gets him going. You should see him at Whole Foods. He freaks out over Romanesco broccoli and microgreens."

"*Basta*, Jaime." Enrique shook his brother off, and Jaime walked toward the edge of the porch. Enrique would leave, too—he wouldn't stay where he wasn't wanted. But he needed Carolina to know this about him.

Enrique tried again. "He's right. Sustainable farming is so important to me—it's why I came here. And even if you don't partner with me, I want to learn how to improve the lives of the farmers on the farms we contract with."

"You can do that without me. It's not my responsibility to educate you about basic human rights."

He took a step closer to her. "You're right; it's not. But you're the best at what you do, and I want to learn from the best."

She tilted her head. "True. I am the best."

He grinned, enjoying her confidence. "And I can help you, too. The kind of money and resources we have will benefit so many people." Her face softened. "Are Las Posadas important to you?"

She nodded. "Yeah, they're my favorite part of the holiday."

"If you really do need someone to be your Joseph, I'm your man."

Carolina bit her lower lip. "Are you serious? You would play Joseph? I've been looking for someone for weeks. Everyone has refused or is busy."

"I'd love to. I've never celebrated Las Posadas. I never really knew anything about the holiday until yesterday, actually. Julieta, Ramón's fiancée, told me about it. She's in town also. I'm sure she'd love to attend."

Carolina stepped closer to him. There was something wildly erotic about this woman who was fresh off a hard day of work and not dressed to impress him.

"Hmm. Well, I'm glad someone in your family is familiar with the event. You have to dress like Joseph and walk with me. But it's really easy besides that."

"I can walk, run even." Enrique could think of so many more physical activities he'd like to do with this woman but kept those thoughts to himself. "That's all we have to do?"

"Pretty much. It celebrates Mary and Joseph's search for a place to stay on the night of Jesus's birth."

His face crinkled. "Why couldn't they find a place to stay? Didn't they have a house?"

Carolina gave a warm smile. "Are you sure you were confirmed?"

"Yes, but I wasn't paying any attention in CCD." Those catechism classes were never-ending.

"They were traveling from Nazareth to Bethlehem. Traditionally, it's for nine days—which represents the nine months of Mary's pregnancy or the nine-day journey they traveled. In Mexico and some other places, it's celebrated over nine days, but here we celebrate it in one night. It's simple. We just walk together and knock on the doors of houses in the neighborhood and ask for shelter. The residents deny us and then the last house lets us in. Then there's a huge party, we dance to great music, and the kids strike a piñata. It's delightful."

He wasn't religious, but he was down for anything. Regardless, spending more time with her was priceless. Even if he had to ride an ass.

"I'm in, no strings attached." He considered making her promise that in exchange for playing Joseph, she would take him on a personal tour around the farm, but he decided against it. If he couldn't get her to trust him after spending time together and offer to take him herself, then he didn't deserve a tour or a collaboration. She didn't owe him anything.

Her eyes lit up and she clasped her hands together.

Enrique grinned. Finally, a smile on her face. A tingle radiated through his chest.

"Well, thank you. You are really helping me out. I'm sorry for my rudeness, earlier. But it will be a fun time. I promise. Ballet Folklórico performs as well. I used to dance with them . . . but not this year." Her voice lowered and she cast a downward glance. Her smile had now vanished as quickly as it had come. "They are having a huge perfor-mance this week and I am working with local restaurants to get the food donated." She cast an inviting look at his brothers and Tiburón. "You're all welcome to attend."

Tiburón gazed at Blanca. "If you're there, I'm there."

Blanca laughed and tossed her hair. Man, Tiburón's effect on women was mesmerizing to watch. Bad boy for the win.

Ramón spoke up. "We can help with the food if you like. My fian-cée is the best chef."

Carolina shook her head no. "I appreciate the offer, but we should be hearing back from the restaurants soon."

Enrique brushed her hand. "No, really, it's okay. I'm sure you don't want our Taco King food, but Julieta is amazing and can take over the local kitchen and we can cater this for you."

Blanca grinned, then batted her eyes toward Tiburón, then turned her attention back to her sister. "Wow, Cari. You really lucked out."

Carolina pointed at her. "Wow, what? *You* are the one who is lucky, hermanita. I was about to march inside and tell Papá about the stunt you pulled, but since Señor Montez here has agreed to help us celebrate my favorite holiday, you are forgiven. But don't ever put me in a situation like this again."

Uh-oh. Enrique tried to break the tension. "Please call me En-rique. When you say Señor Montez, I think of my dad."

"I'll call you Joseph tomorrow."

Enrique raised his eyebrow at her. "Oh yeah? What will you call me on Wednesday?"

She licked her lower lip. "Nothing. Because after Las Posadas ends, I'll never lay eyes on you again."

Enrique laughed. He reached out his hand to her, and she offered it up in a shake, but he flipped the script and kissed it. "We'll see about that. Good night, mi amor."

She glared at him. "Mi amor?"

His hand grazed hers. "Yeah. You're my wife, right?"

"For one night only. And then I'll never be anyone's wife again. Meet me at the St. Mary of the Assumption Catholic Church tomorrow at five. Adiós, José."

Enrique waved goodbye and walked back to his SUV. This meeting hadn't gone exactly as planned, but it didn't matter. He had another chance with her mañana.

And he wasn't going to blow it.

Chapter Four

Carolina shut the front door. Nerves and anger swirled in her body. What on earth had just happened? Carolina could murder Blanca. How dare her little sister put her in that situation. She knew better.

Carolina never, ever wanted to let competitors or industry big shots on her farm. Tourists were one thing—they took tractor rides around the farm, picked some fruit while posing for Instagram photos, then shopped for treats in their gift shop. The sweet strawberry syrup and spicy salsas were their bestsellers.

But Enrique Montez wanted something else. Carolina wasn't quite sure what, but she was more than certain that she wouldn't like it.

At all.

He couldn't possibly have good intentions toward her farm. After she'd bought it, it had taken a while to turn a profit. They were fine now; comfortable, not rich.

She didn't need a new restaurant to provide produce for—

especially when the restaurant was a chain. Something like that could ruin her reputation with the high-end farm-to-table places she serviced. She didn't want her long-term clients to desert her, which was a realistic possibility. Especially if the Montez brothers tried to squeeze her for more produce, lower prices, faster turnarounds—which they would. People like that always did—she'd have all her eggs in one basket. No thank you.

But Enrique had given her the one thing she wanted most for Christmas—a partner for Las Posadas. If it wasn't for him, she would be the laughingstock of the town, the only woman in the history of Santa Maria's Las Posadas who couldn't find a man to play Joseph to her Mary.

Her father roused from his sleep, squinting, the deep lines on his eyes making him look even older than his age of fifty-five. Years of backbreaking labor in the bright, hot sun of the fields and a lack of medical care had taken a toll on him. "What time is it, mija?"

She knelt by his side. "Time for dinner, Papá." She inhaled the scent from the kitchen. "I'll go help Mamá."

He kissed Carolina on her cheek. A rough, wheezy cough escaped. Papá had suffered respiratory issues for years, but this cough sounded different. She hoped it wasn't bronchitis. She made a mental note to schedule an appointment tomorrow for him to see the doctor. Then she stood up and went to the kitchen.

"Hola, Mamá." She leaned on the kitchen counter. "What's for dinner?"

Mamá was chopping up cilantro, her hair in a tight bun and her body wrapped in a loose apron.

"Carnitas. Call your sisters to set the table. They just got back from Tío Alberto's. He needed help painting his house. I was going to tell you to go, but Blanca told me that you had a very important meeting."

Ah, so that was where they all were. And of course, everyone knew about the meeting but Carolina.

Carolina went to the backyard. "Dinner!" Sofía, the youngest at five, who they all affectionately called Baby, ran up to Carolina. "Did you meet him?"

"Who?"

"Your future husband!" She made a kissy-face. "Blanca told me that tonight you both were meeting the men you were going to marry."

Ay! Carolina would never forgive Blanca for this. "I'm not getting married, Baby." Not now. Not ever. Her body shuddered in horror at the thought. "Go inside before Mamá yells."

The rest of her sisters, Adela, age nineteen, Eva, age seventeen, Juanita, age fifteen, Valentina, age thirteen, Pia, age eleven, Daniela, age nine, and Victoria, age seven, trickled inside in pecking order, and the house was bustling with laughter and chaos.

Valentina pulled Pia's hair, causing Pia to let out a scream. Pia raced after Valentina, almost knocking to the ground Carolina, who tripped on Victoria.

Damn, Carolina really wanted to move out.

Carolina returned to the kitchen and caught a glimpse of the fresh handmade tortillas in the corner of the bench, right next to the salsas. Made from scratch, of course.

"One day, you need to learn how to cook, mija," her mamá said, following her gaze.

"Nah, I'll just eat." A chef, Carolina would never be. There was a reason DoorDash was so popular. Takeout and Mamá's leftovers suited her just fine.

Mamá shook her head. "Then you will never find a husband."

"Fine by me," Carolina said, aware her words would provoke a reaction. The crinkled brow on Mamá's face turned into a scowl.

Carolina threw in a sprinkle of hope with a grin. "Maybe I'll find a man who cooks for me."

"Do you want to send your father to an early grave?" Her mother made the sign of the cross and clasped her hands in prayer.

That was another reason Carolina never wanted to get married. What if her husband wanted her to be like her mother? Or, most likely, if he was raised in a similar Mexican household, like *his* mother? She would be expected to give up her career and cook and clean all day and raise babies, which at the moment, she wasn't even sure she wanted. She was practically a mother already, after helping to raise her sisters.

No, Carolina certainly didn't want that life and didn't want that type of man.

But Enrique didn't seem to be like that at all. Though it was probably just a front because he wanted *something* from her, he had seemed kind and respectful.

Where had that thought come from? It didn't matter how sweet he was, or how sexy he looked in that short-sleeved ocean-blue button-up shirt and his navy slacks. Or that his hair was dark and shiny, and his eyes were soulful. This man was just visiting Santa Barbara for the holidays—Montecito, in fact! He probably had a multimillion-dollar home there.

Ugh, why was she even stressing about him? All that mattered was, thanks to a handsome stranger, she would have a partner for Las Posadas. She couldn't be more blessed.

Blanca barreled through the kitchen and dramatically fanned herself with a napkin.

Carolina pinched Blanca's arm. "Ay, Blanca. I'm livid with you. You blindsided me."

"Qué?" their mother asked.

Carolina hopped up on a stool. "Why don't you tell her what you did."

Blanca poured herself a glass of water and downed it. "It's nothing—Carolina is overreacting. The Montez Group emailed asking to set up a business meeting with Carolina. I replied that of course they could meet with us, but I totally blanked about telling her. They showed up today, and Carolina was completely rude to them. She tried to kick them off the farm!"

"Carolina Yvonne!" Mamá yelled. "You have no manners. You need to be nice to all visitors. I taught you better than that."

"Whatever, Mamá. I don't owe them anything. And Blanca, you know that isn't what happened! This is my house and my farm, and I didn't invite them."

"It's *our* farm." Blanca rolled her eyes before continuing. "One of the men really wanted to see the entire operation, so when Carolina mentioned Las Posadas and not having a Joseph, he volunteered to be Joseph! He's super handsome, too. I think he likes her."

Carolina's cheeks burned. She couldn't believe her sister just said that, especially to their mother, who was so desperate to marry off her eldest daughter that she had once created a fake Tinder account for her. It had been a complete disaster—men had shown up at their home expecting to go on dates with her, but she'd refused to even accept one invitation. A few had even asked her father's permission, which of course he had given, but Carolina still wouldn't date them.

Mamá clasped her hands to her chest. "He did? What a great man! He must be a good, devout Catholic boy if he would agree to portray Joseph."

Carolina threw up her hands. "Nope. He even said he wasn't really Catholic anymore, though he was confirmed. He never goes to church and prefers yoga instead. He's probably one of those Cafeteria Catholics who just shows up for Easter and Christmas. You know who he is, Mamá—Enrique Montez. His family owns the Taco King chain."

"He's rich, Mamá! Like super crazy rich! I saw a magazine with pictures of his house. He drives a Tesla SUV." Blanca whipped out her phone and found a picture of the Montez men. Ramón, Enrique, and Jaime. They all shared strong jawlines and devastatingly dashing dimples. Even Carolina had to admit that Enrique was good-looking. Devilishly handsome. Even more so in person.

Mamá rubbed her hands together like she was plotting something. "Smart and rich? And considerate enough to participate in a cultural and religious tradition for you? When is the wedding?"

"Right?" Blanca high-fived Mamá. "And then *I* can finally marry."

Carolina exhaled. She would never hear the end of this. "Stop, Mamá." She tapped Blanca's head with a rolled-up newspaper. Hey, it was better than being hit with Mamá's chanclas. Those slippers hurt! "I'm already angry with you. Why are you making it worse?"

"Because of Tiburón! He's so dreamy. I think he likes me."

Now it was Carolina's turn to laugh. "I thought you wanted Jaime because he's a Montez."

Blanca twirled her hair. "Jaime is cute and all, but more of a pretty boy. Tiburón is all man."

Carolina quickly plotted her revenge against Blanca. "Well, you're right. He couldn't *stop* staring at you." She turned to Mamá. "And he had a neck tattoo! Of a shark!"

That should get Blanca back for filling Mamá's head with crazy ideas that a millionaire had any romantic interest whatsoever in Carolina. Enrique most certainly did not. Not that she cared one way or another if he did. She wasn't interested. Not even a little bit.

Carolina had always imagined that if she ever fell in love, it would happen naturally. Like maybe with a family friend, or someone from high school. But the well of potential suitors had run dry years ago in her super traditional town where almost everyone coupled off young. All of her high school classmates were either married or in serious relationships, or seriously unstable. And her parents' friends had no prospective sons to date. She had met practically everyone in this town by now, since so many families in the community celebrated events together.

Besides, she was married to her business. If she'd messed around dating, it was unlikely she'd have been successful enough to buy her own farm.

Mamá shook a wooden spoon at Blanca. Bits of carnitas flew through the air. "A neck tattoo! Blanca, your papá would never let you date a man with any tattoos, let alone one on his neck. Is he in a gang? Aren't the Sharks a gang?"

Blanca giggled. "Yeah, in *West Side Story*, Mamá. And you're so judgmental—he is not in a gang."

"Well, you don't know that. Si camina como un pato."

Carolina adored Mamá's idioms. "He doesn't walk like a duck, but maybe he swims like a shark."

Blanca shook her head. "I can't believe you two!"

Mamá pointed her nail at Blanca. "You don't want to embarrass your papá. You know his blood pressure is high."

A twang of guilt settled over Carolina. She had encouraged her mom to shame a guy just because he had a tattoo. Fine, many tattoos. He could still be a good man. Carolina didn't judge people by their skin color or their skin art, though she would never get a tattoo herself.

Blanca hugged Mamá. "Give Tiburón a chance. He seems like a great guy."

Mamá scowled. "You aren't allowed to date, Blanca!"

Ha. Blanca knew the rules. She couldn't date until Carolina had a boyfriend. And that was never happening. So basically, Blanca would be single for the rest of her life, too.

Carolina thought that rule of their father's was ridiculous. Blanca was an adult, and Carolina was certain if their father didn't change his mind, Blanca would rebel.

"You can't stop me. I'm going to date Tiburón if he asks me out!"

Mamá yanked Blanca's hair. "You will do nothing of the sort. You are not dating anyone, especially someone who doesn't live near us. I need your help with your sisters. Carolina runs the farm now that your Papá is sick. You have responsibilities, Blanca. Speaking of which, go call everyone for dinner. But take that bright red lipstick off your face before your papá sees it, and change your top first. You look like a streetwalker."

Blanca pouted but didn't say a word. Smart girl. She stuck her tongue out at Carolina, who sneered back.

Once alone, Mamá handed Carolina a spoon. Carolina stirred the carnitas, which was the extent of her cooking skills.

"So, that was really nice of this young man to offer to be Joseph. His parents must've raised him right."

Nope. Carolina didn't like where this was going. "It's doubtful. I read a profile on them. His parents are divorced. And they are very wealthy. That is never a good combination." She had met kids like him at college—filthy rich, without a care in the world, and no stable influence to ground them. They seemed to have everything, but honestly, Carolina felt sorry for them. She wouldn't trade all the wealth in the world for her intact home life.

Her parents had immigrated from Mexico with nothing. Her dad had worked on the farms for years, arduous labor to provide for his family. But he'd always made time for his kids, no matter what. He'd attended every Ballet Folklórico dance performance that Carolina was in, and every night listened to her talk about her day. Though he could never help her with her homework, he'd supported her educational dreams.

Admittedly, she had recently started to question her father's rules. Her independence and education had afforded her the ability to think for herself and question old principles. And lately, she couldn't help being more combative with her papá. She wanted to challenge his ideologies and stop him from treating his wife and daughters as his property.

But she hadn't made much progress.

"Well, mija, maybe not. But you have to wonder if him showing up before Christmas is a sign from the Lord. I have prayed for a man like him to come into your life."

Carolina swallowed. She didn't want to admit it . . . but she had prayed for him, too.

Chapter Five

Enrique sat on the redwood deck overlooking the ocean on Butterfly Beach in Montecito. He loved it up here. It was so different from San Diego. The coast was rockier, and the hills had wildflowers. Sea anemones and starfish dotted the sand and shiny rocks, and a glorious whale danced in the distance. The waves were rougher, the water cooler.

Then again, he thought everywhere along the California coast was magical.

Linda had left the house an hour ago to run errands. Enrique had offered to go with her, but she'd insisted on going alone. Though Linda seemed content in her life since she'd retired, Enrique still wondered what really had happened with her and his dad. Linda and Arturo had met in Baja California in the late seventies during spring break. Linda had served him a fish taco that gave him the idea to open Taco King. They had fallen madly in love and had vowed to reunite. Ramón had told Enrique that their father said he returned to propose to her but found her with another man, who turned out to be Julieta's father. Clearly, that was the best outcome for all parties—especially Julieta, and Enrique and his brothers, who wouldn't have existed if Linda had married their father.

But there was one lingering question.

Why? Why hadn't Linda waited for him?

Sure, she might've doubted that he would return, but Enrique didn't buy it. If Papá loved Linda the way Ramón loved Julieta, Enrique couldn't fathom why she wouldn't have waited just a bit longer for him.

Maybe Enrique was more of a romantic than he thought.

Tiburón opened the French doors and joined Enrique on the deck. Ever since Ramón and Julieta got engaged, Enrique and Tiburón had vibed. The dude didn't surf and couldn't care less whether his salad was organic, but they'd found some common ground over their love of cars and horror flicks.

Tiburón relaxed in a lounger. "Where is everyone?"

"Well, while you were having your siesta, Ramón and Julieta decided to go on a date and Jaime and Rosa went to the movies."

"Which movie?" Tiburón crooked an eyebrow.

"*Die Hard*. It's Jaime's favorite Christmas movie."

"That movie is dope. Wish they woke me."

They sat in silence for a few more moments until Tiburón spoke again. "This is the life. How long has your dad owned this place? If I were you, I'd be here all the time. Hell, I'd move in."

Tiburón had a point. Why didn't Enrique come here more often? "Dad always loved it up here. We used to vacation at the San Ysidro Ranch as kids. He bought this property when I was accepted at Cal Poly, but I haven't spent much time here since college. I used to come up here on the weekends and surf."

"Cool. I love it out here, though I'm usually farther up north. My Tío Tomás lives in Salinas."

Enrique's interest was piqued. "Oh, cool. My uncle is a farmer up in Salinas. Is yours a farmer, by any chance?"

Tiburón nodded. "Yeah, he is. Maybe they know each other. He's a solid dude. I don't visit him and my cousins a lot, but I spent some summers up here." He looked over the water. "I'll tell you what, though—that is some crazy-ass hard work. My uncle is fucked-up from all the years working in the dusty fields. He has some respiratory illness that makes his voice sound like sandpaper, and he coughs up blood and shit. We're like three and a half hours away—maybe I'll go up there and see him."

Enrique's stomach coiled. "I'll go with you. We could visit my uncle, too." Though that was unlikely. Tío Jorge had a huge falling-out with his sister, Enrique's mom. Back in the day, Tío Jorge's farm was one of the first to provide produce to the Montez Group. But Arturo started demanding cheaper prices and Tío Jorge eventually told his brother-in-law to go to hell. Enrique hadn't seen his uncle since.

Was Tío Jorge healthy? Enrique needed to visit him and renew that relationship. So many farmers endured countless health problems, but Enrique had never seen the effects of the labor firsthand. His skin wasn't calloused from picking produce, and his back wasn't sore from bending to the earth.

How arrogant was Enrique to show up and ask Carolina to teach him about farming when he'd never spent a day of his life working like a typical bracero? Yes, Enrique and his brothers had their own small farm, but it only provided produce for the test kitchen, so who was he kidding?

Theirs was artisanal and featured high-end equipment. They hired workers, families like Carolina's, to harvest the crops. He'd visit weekly, tend to some of his rare hybrid herbs, stroll through the plot he had given Julieta, and call it a day.

Carolina was right to kick him off her farm. She probably saw him as some entitled and privileged Mexican. What an idiot he was. His skin burned.

He needed to figure out how he could win her trust the following night and let him meet with her about the farm later in the week.

Maybe he could drop some facts and figures into their conversation as they went from house to house. Or he could bring some Taco King food from the test kitchen to the closing party—convince her they weren't the worst Fast Mex chain in the United States.

Ugh, no. He was being ridiculous.

The front door opened.

"Enrique! Ven!" Linda Campos shouted from inside the house.

Enrique glanced inquisitively at Tiburón. He shook his head. "Don't look at me. I don't have a clue what she wants. But one word of advice, bro. *Go*."

Enrique stood and walked back inside into the kitchen, which was vastly different from his sleek and modern one in San Diego. This place was cozy. The wood was rustic, there was shiplap on the walls, and white linen curtains waved in the ocean breeze.

Julieta's mother was clutching a modern but basic sewing machine underneath her arm and a skein of brown wool and an array of both earth-toned and bright fabrics.

"Where did you get a sewing machine?" he asked.

"At the store, silly. Now sit." She pulled him onto a chair in the dining room. "We don't have much time to prepare." She took out a pattern for a robe. What was she making a robe for? Surely, she couldn't—

Oh.

Oh *no*.

Lord, what had Enrique gotten himself into? "Señora Campos. You don't need to make me a costume. I'm sure Carolina has an outfit ready."

Linda ignored him, put the machine down on the table, plugged it in, and whipped out a measuring tape. She tugged on Enrique's sleeve, calculated the length of his arm, scratched out some numbers on a yellow notepad, and then sat in front of the machine to wind up the bobbin.

"I'm serious. It's your holiday. You shouldn't waste your time sewing."

"It isn't a waste; it's an honor to remember the journey of Mary and Joseph. And yes, you're right. The church probably does have an outfit, but it could be big and old and smelly. You are a Montez! You can't look shabby. Especially since you are playing José." She made a quick sign of the cross. "I will create something suitable for you. No, it will be exquisite."

Enrique shook his head. He'd gone a bit overboard by volunteering to play Joseph, but what was the harm? He welcomed learning about the Mexican traditions that his family had never participated in . . . though he had to admit, he felt uncomfortable playing Joseph when he himself didn't practice the religion. He definitely should've paid more attention in catechism. But the nun was mean to him. Plus, he didn't see the point of going to church after his parents stopped attending. They didn't take their vows seriously, so why should he be expected to be pious?

Tiburón walked inside and pointed at Linda's fabric. "What are you doing?"

"I am making Enrique an outfit fit for a king," she said as the machine whirred to life.

"Ah. For your debut as Joseph." Tiburón grinned. "So how do you feel about your wife being pregnant with another man's child? You don't buy into this Immaculate Conception bullshit, do you?"

Linda's hands dramatically dropped to the fabric. She stood up and smacked Tiburón on the head. "You will not talk about the Virgin like that!"

"Ay, Tía, it was a joke."

Linda scowled at him, made another sign of the cross, and sat back down. The buzz from the machine drowned out the words she was murmuring.

Enrique smirked. "I'll never hear the end of this, will I? I just really want to convince Carolina to partner with us."

Tiburón high-fived him. "I get it, bro. I'd make an ass out of myself, too, for a woman that fine. Hell, I'd do anything for that sister of hers. I'd even be one of the Three Kings. Blanca. Did you see that booty? She's fire."

Enrique nodded. "Yeah, she's pretty. They both are. But we aren't here to hit on them."

Tiburón grabbed a beer from the refrigerator. "Speak for yourself. That's exactly why I'm here. It's Christmas vacation, and I'm not a Montez. I can hit on who I want—I don't have to listen to you, foo." He lightly shoulder-checked Enrique as he passed.

Of course, Tiburón was right—he could do whatever he wanted. The Montez men had always been taught to focus on duty over desire.

But Tiburón better not ruin Enrique's chance to get to know Carolina.

"Good luck with that. Señor Flores is super traditional."

Tiburón rubbed his hands together. "Traditional is my thing. Don't worry about me. I never have a problem with the ladies." He leaned over his aunt's shoulder. "Tía Linda, you got that seam all wrong. Get up. I'll do it."

She stood and patted him on the back. "Gracias, Tiburón."

Tiburón sat down, pulled the fabric taut, and fed it through the foot. The hum from the machine blended with the sound of the waves crashing against the rocks outside.

Tiburón sewed? Enrique took a step closer to the machine and eyed his even work. "You stitch, Tib?"

Tiburón cocked his eyebrow, and Enrique focused on the vertical slit separating it into two parts. He'd noticed it before but had never mentioned it. Was that a scar?

"Yup. You got a problem with that?"

"No. I think it's cool. When did you learn?"

He glared at Enrique. "In prison."

Alrighty then. It wasn't a secret that Tiburón had a record. But he hadn't opened up about his past, and, though they were cool, Enrique didn't feel like it was his place to ask about what happened. Tiburón would tell him when he was ready.

Linda walked into the kitchen. "You boys hungry?"

"Starved," Tiburón answered without a beat.

Enrique didn't want Linda to cook for him. "I could eat, but we can get takeout. This is supposed to be your vacation."

She flapped her hand. "Cooking in *this* kitchen is a vacation."

Enrique paused to reflect on how food for Linda and Julieta represented family, while food for the Montezes was a means of making money.

He glanced back at the fabric, which had begun to take shape. He barely knew about this holiday, but Carolina had been so happy to have a Joseph. He couldn't participate half-assed—he had to take this seriously and not screw this up for her.

He left the dining room and relaxed on the sofa. He searched on his phone and read more about the celebration. Carolina had said at the end there would be music and dancing and food.

He clicked on a video from last year's Las Posadas in Santa Maria. Carolina caught his eye immediately. She hadn't played Mary but instead was dressed in an elaborate, frilly, bright purple Ballet Folklórico costume adorned with multicolored ribbons. She held her skirt out wide and tapped to the music, a series of intricate steps that Enrique couldn't follow, waving her dress like it was a fan. Though many of the other dancers had partners, Carolina danced solo. But she smiled wider and brighter than the other girls, pure joy on her face.

It was how Enrique thought Ramón looked when he was playing mariachi music, or how Julieta looked when she was cooking.

What gave Enrique that joy? Gardening, for sure . . . but was that enough? He liked yoga and loved surfing but didn't really have a creative pursuit. Even Jaime had photography. Maybe Enrique should take up a new hobby. He let his mind wander as the music played on.

Thirty minutes later, Tiburón finished the robe. He stood and grandly shook out the garment, which Enrique threw on over the top of his T-shirt and board shorts. He walked over to the nautical rope-encased mirror and glanced at himself.

"This is great, Tib. You're really talented."

Tiburón grinned. "That I am. I've been sketching some designs I want to do. Real stuff. From our culture."

"What are you doing working at Las Pescas? You should make and sell your clothes."

His eyes lit up. "I want to, man, but it's not that easy. I need inventory, a website, models."

"Jaime's a model. And I can build you a website."

Tiburón craned his neck, causing the shark tattoo to snarl. "I don't need no handouts. I've been saving up."

"It wouldn't be a handout. I can be an investor."

Tiburón's posture softened. "Thanks, bro." Tiburón hugged Enrique, which for some reason Enrique thought was as binding as a handshake.

"And besides that,"—he shook Tiburón's hand—"we're family."

CHAPTER SIX

arolina secured the baby bump to her belly, then slipped her white top with blue trim over her head. Her skirt hung low on her hips. Wow, the pressure on her stomach and hips was super uncomfortable. How could Mamá possibly have endured ten pregnancies?

Mamá helped affix the traditional headdress onto her hair. The stale scent of smoke and mothballs overtook Carolina, and the rough fabric irritated her skin. But none of those inconveniences mattered.

What an honor it was to be chosen to play Mary in this year's Las Posadas. And it was even more of a blessing that a Joseph had literally shown up on her doorstep. That had to be a sign, or even a miracle.

The church that she had grown up in was small but ornate. The paint on the walls was chipped and the pews were wobbly. But she had been baptized, received her First Communion, and been confirmed here. This place was her home. When she was a girl, she dreamed of walking down the aisle here, but many years ago she had stopped being able to envision herself as a bride.

She glanced at the clock hanging on the wall between all the Jesus sculptures. It was four in the afternoon. Enrique would be here soon.

Or would he?

A chill swept over her. Maybe he'd been just joking about playing Joseph. Why on earth would a handsome, rich man want to waste a day of his beach vacation in Montecito walking around her small town with her, pretending to seek shelter? Had he been a good Catholic, then *maybe* she could understand him thinking that joining her could be his duty, but he'd readily admitted that he wasn't practicing.

And being a devout Catholic was a requirement by her father for any man who wanted to date her.

Luckily, she wasn't interested in him. At all.

But God worked in mysterious ways—she would not judge His reasons for sending Enrique to her, whatever they were. It was simply His intention to provide her a Joseph.

She just hoped Enrique honored his word.

Blanca entered the church. While Carolina and her mother always dressed modestly, Blanca was again pushing the limits. Her white cotton top was low-cut, showing off her breasts, and her skirt was too tight. Carolina could read her sister like a book—Blanca was definitely hoping that Tiburón showed up.

Mamá's jaw clenched. "Blanca! We're in God's house. Cover yourself."

Blanca twirled her hair. "What's wrong with this outfit? Besides, I don't have anything else."

Mamá pulled a cardigan from her oversized purse and tossed it to Blanca. "Now you do."

Blanca let the garment fall to the floor. Her eyes met Mamá's. After a brief stare-off, which Mamá clearly won with her intimidating gaze, Blanca picked up the sweater and put it on. She scanned the room. "Enrique's not here yet? Do you think he will come?"

I checked the clock again. "I don't know. Maybe it was some type of joke."

Mamá shook her head. "It was no joke. It was divine. You have to believe."

Carolina wanted to have faith and trust Enrique's word, but she didn't know the guy. What she *did* know was that she'd often been the butt of jokes growing up. Boys pretended to be interested in her but really only wanted beautiful Blanca, and she couldn't even blame them. Blanca was a dead ringer for Selena. Her stomach was flat, her hair was long and shiny, her lips were full, and she had a dazzling smile. Carolina's hair could best be described as a frizzy mess, her body was soft and curvy, and she had no upper lip. The lifetime of rejection stung, for sure. What kind of man would ever be interested in Carolina when her younger sister was so captivating?

She hated to think like that—that her worth was somehow contingent on her looks—but at twenty-three, she was approaching old maid status in her culture and community. Though she wasn't seeking a suitor, it would be nice, for once in her life, to meet a man who was interested in *her*, not just using Carolina to get to her younger sister.

Or, as probably in Enrique's case, to monopolize her farm.

"Well, if he doesn't show up, we won't have a Joseph. It will be fine." Her chest tightened. It would not be fine. She would be the first Mary in the history of Las Posadas in Santa Maria not to have a Joseph. Everyone would laugh at her. She could hear the mean-girl bullies now. *Poor Carolina couldn't even get some guy to agree to walk with her.* And these mean-girls were now women, married women. Most of them never left Santa Maria and never would. Carolina wished sometimes she could go somewhere new and start over.

Deep voices filled the hall from beyond the door. Footsteps rang out in the church. Then the door flew open.

Enrique stood there in a long brown robe, his hair loose, clutching a cane.

Whoa.

Though the robe was loose, his muscular chest bulged through a white undershirt. He winked, and she turned her head to see if Blanca was standing behind her. But Blanca was standing next to Mamá and not in Enrique's line of vision. When Carolina finally regained the nerves to look at him again, he was still staring at her.

Ugh, why did he have to be so hot? She was in a church playing the Virgin Mary. She shouldn't be having lascivious thoughts about this sexy man. Well, at least Father Juan was leading the procession. When the night was over, he could march her straight to confession. Really, who sins while playing the Virgin Mary?

Carolina wouldn't be the only one sinning tonight. Blanca was licking her lower lip and her pupils were dilated. But her little sister wasn't looking at Enrique; she was staring at the three other men.

Standing right behind Enrique were his two brothers and the primo with the shark tattoo—dressed in long cloaks with crowns on their heads.

Carolina couldn't help herself. She burst out laughing.

Ay, Dios mío! They were dressed as Melchior, Caspar, and Balthazar, the Three Kings. Three Kings Day wasn't until January sixth, but Carolina was already excited for that part of her holiday celebrations. These Montez men would most certainly not still be in town to find the baby Jesus hidden in the Rosca de Reyes sweet bread. And that was in the best interest of all, because if one of them found it, he would have to host a tamale party for Día de la Candelaria in February.

What sort of tamales would the Taco Kings cook? Would Enrique get in the kitchen and whip up some sort of feast?

Ay, stop! Why was she thinking about February?

Blanca walked over to the men. Jaime stroked his red velvet cape. "Nice outfits, gentlemen. Where did you get them on such short notice?"

Tiburón puffed out his chest, his green cloak the grandest of all. It even had a faux-fur trim. "I made them last night."

Tiburón turned his attention to Mamá. "My name is Tiburón Garcia, by the way. Mucho gusto, Señora Flores." Mamá cautiously extended her hand and Tiburón kissed it.

Well played, dude. But it's not going to work. Blanca can't date.

Mamá politely returned the greeting. "Mucho gusto, Señor Garcia. Welcome to our church."

Blanca's eyes widened, and she eased close to Tiburón. Then she dramatically tossed her hair. "You *made* them? These are so gorgeous. Are you a tailor?"

Tiburón swallowed and shifted his gaze. His voice lowered. "I'll be whatever you want me to be."

Blanca not so coyly batted her eyelashes. "Wow. I'm impressed. I sew, too. And design. Maybe we can collaborate sometime?"

Tiburón flashed a hopeful grin. "It's a date."

¡Ay, Dios mío! It was most certainly not a date.

Mamá broke up their moment as she walked over to inspect the outfits. Her eyes lit up as she studied the seams. "Good work. But we had clothes for Joseph. And we normally don't have Wise Men for this celebration. You didn't need to go to all this trouble."

Tiburón spoke confidently. "I know that you normally don't have the Three Kings, but we thought we'd shake it up. As for the costumes, I wanted to add some flair." Tiburón looked around the room. "Where's his donkey?"

Enrique shook his head. Ramón shifted nervously on his feet and scratched at the costume, and Jaime kept his gaze straight out the window, with a blank look on his face. Yup. His brothers wanted to be anywhere but here. But all she needed was Enrique—his brothers didn't have to participate. At least Tiburón seemed happy.

Enrique took a step closer. The scent of cedar mixed with cloves filled the air between them. His dark eyes met hers.

Carolina wobbled, and Enrique grabbed her arm.

"Sorry," she muttered. "It must be the bump. I'm off-balance."

He grinned. "Well, you're glowing. Who's the lucky man?"

"God. Thanks for agreeing to raise this baby as your own."

Enrique laughed, and she joined him.

He brushed a lock of hair out of her face. "I hope this isn't inappropriate, and please tell me if I'm out of line . . ."

Her breath hitched the tiniest bit.

"When you say whatever you intend to, I'll let you know."

With another dazzling smile, his dimples appeared. "You look beautiful tonight."

Carolina's skin tingled, her mind racing about what it would be like to kiss him as she tried to compose a thought. He must be playing her. Surely, he was flirting to convince her to strike a deal with his company.

But just on the off chance he wasn't, she decided to not call him out. Yet.

"Thank you. And that was fine. I mean, not offensive," she stammered. "Sorry, I'm just nervous." She paused. "I mean about Las Posadas. Not you." Gosh, why did she talk? "I mean—"

He offered his arm. "You're adorable. Okay, wifey. Let's go. And you promised me a donkey."

Carolina liked his playful nature. "He's out here, José. Follow me." She led him alone to the back of the church and into the courtyard where there was a beautiful manger scene all set up and, in a nearby pen, the donkey.

Enrique walked over to the animal and petted him. The donkey brayed. "What's his name?"

"Spice. There's a Clydesdale stable a few miles away. They lend him to the church every year. He's great and the kids love him."

"Cool." He paused and then turned to gaze into her eyes. The church lights illuminated his face. "Hey, Carolina . . . I'm sorry about yesterday. I didn't mean to bombard you and demand a meeting. We only came because I thought you'd agreed. Forgive me."

Her cold heart melted a bit. "I'm sorry I was so rude to you. I wasn't expecting you. But I'm curious—why are you so fascinated with my farm? There are plenty of farms around here who would be more than happy to partner with you. Spell it out for me. What exactly do you want?"

Without hesitation, he spoke in a firm tone. "I want to partner with ethical operations."

A metallic taste pooled in her mouth. He just didn't get it. Sure, partnering with her farm might help him sleep better at night, but it wouldn't improve the lives of the campesinos at the farms he currently utilized. If anything, it might hurt them, as they could be out of jobs.

But it wasn't her responsibility to educate him. He would have to come to this realization himself. Without her help.

"Got it. But like I said, we are at full capacity and aren't looking for any other restaurants. We don't have the bandwidth to take on more accounts. I'm sorry you wasted your time."

"I didn't waste my time." He leaned closer. A frisson of heat raced through her body. "I'm not just interested in the farm—I'm interested in you."

She gulped and her mouth became moist. "What? Why?"

"I read some articles about you. How you use innovative hydroponics. Your progress on sustainable farming. How you make sure your employees have access to health care. How you worked nights. How you excelled in school, danced, and still farmed alongside your parents. How you commuted back and forth during school to make sure you could still help out." He licked his lower lip. "You inspire me. And I like to surround myself with people I admire."

Was she in a dream? This handsome man was throwing out compliments like she dispersed fertilizer. He was smiling at her. Staring at her. He had called her beautiful. He seemed to be interested in her not just as the owner of a farm, but as a woman.

A drop of mist from the sky fell on her skin, waking her up from her fantasy. Oh no, was it going to rain tonight? She prayed the weather wouldn't ruin her night.

He took a step closer to her, their breath commingling in the air.

No, no, this was too intense already. She took a big step back.

Her guard went up. Way up. This smooth-talking millionaire couldn't possibly want her. He was a playboy. She had seen pictures of him online, shirtless on a yacht with bikini-clad models and influencers to his left and right, front and back.

Girls who looked like Blanca, not her.

Nope. Not having it. He was flattering her. He had to want something.

She was confident in her intellectual prowess and her business skills, but she was realistic about her place in society, her place in her family, and her place as a woman. She wasn't a natural beauty like Blanca or a faux fox like some of the girls she saw online with plastic surgery and identical sculpted features.

This man could not be trusted.

He was a devil in Joseph's clothing.

CHAPTER SEVEN

C arolina turned away from him, not responding to what he'd just said. Her loose hair cascaded over her shoulders and framed her pretty face. "We need to go inside. Father Juan and the rest of the carolers will be here shortly."

"Got it. Let's go." Enrique followed Carolina back into the church, a safe distance behind her to give her space.

Carolina had stood close to him a few seconds ago, her body softening toward him. Her skin glistened under the courtyard lights. But then her body had stiffened, and her tone had changed. Had he said something wrong? Maybe he'd overstepped again with his compliments. But he had meant every word.

Enrique had never really had any trouble communicating with women. He didn't like to play games and was always open with his feelings and honest about his intentions. Though he had spent the last few years casually dating, he never led women on. He hadn't asked for any sort of relationship with Carolina and wasn't even sure if she wanted to date him. He had just told her how much he admired her.

Oh well, he couldn't worry about it now. He had Las Posadas to lead.

Back inside the church, he found Ramón and Jaime talking to each other, and Rosa, Linda, and Julieta sitting together in a pew. Tiburón was chatting with Blanca. Enrique chuckled, admiring his friend's pursuit of her.

Enrique looked around the church, a place where he had never felt comfortable. This one was opulent, but a tad intense. There were several bronze statues of Jesus on the walls and some dramatic religious art depicting the Virgin Mary and the Last Supper. Enrique felt guilty and he wasn't even sure why. It was nothing like the casual beachside church he often passed and had been to several times in Pacific Beach, which had a big sign out front that said "Saints, Sinners, and Surfers Welcome." People attended services in bikinis and board shorts. That house of the holy was definitely more his vibe.

He looked over at Carolina, who was praying by the altar. She was obviously devout—she was playing the Virgin Mary, for God's sake. Then again, he was playing Joseph. Surely there had to have been a man who was better suited for the role.

Ramón had left Jaime and caught Enrique's arm. "You owe me big-time for this Three Kings getup. It wasn't even necessary! I still can't believe you agreed to play Joseph for this woman."

"Not for her—for the business, Ramón. For us." Enrique smirked. "And besides, you've done crazier things. You proposed with an entire mariachi band. And didn't you serenade Julieta with old-school Spanish ballads in a garden the night you met?"

Ramón turned up his hands. "Fine. You got me. I don't know *what* happened the night she and I met. Maybe it was the costumes or the atmosphere or the holiday . . . but I was so drawn to her. I suppose I'm a romantic."

Enrique turned and studied the gorgeous woman at the altar, her head still bowed in prayer, her long lashes fanning over her cheeks. It almost felt like he couldn't look away. There was something about her . . . maybe in another time, another place, he could have asked her on a date. She was smart, beautiful, and strong—everything he admired in a woman.

But you need her for her business acumen, not another notch in your belt.

"You don't like this girl, do you?" Ramón asked, as if reading his mind.

Enrique shook his head. "No. Carolina's pretty and smart, but she has a life and business up here, and I love San Diego. It would never work."

"Right, it wouldn't. She's also religious, and her family is very traditional." Ramón pointed to her, still in the corner, clutching her rosary beads. Or counting them? Maybe it was some prayer. Enrique had no clue. "And you, José, are not."

"Well, that's not a deal breaker. I'm Catholic."

"Right. So am I. And Julieta is having me go to all of these classes so we can get married in the Catholic Church. It's a complete nightmare." He gave a wry smile. "I want to elope, but she won't even discuss it. But, happy wife, happy life." He pointed to Julieta, who was kneeling in a pew, praying.

"The classes can't be too bad. We did CCD."

"Yeah, and I don't remember shit. I doubt you do, either. Name a saint, Rico Suave."

A saint? The first thing that came to him was that old movie his father used to love called *The Saint*, starring Val Kilmer.

His mind searched. He had to know at least one holy figure.

Finally, a name popped in his head. "St. Francis of Assisi."

Ramón laughed. "You only know that one because he's the patron saint of animals and the priest at our high school blessed our dog."

Buddy, the designer Bernedoodle that their father bought them, was such a great dog. But Ramón was right—Enrique wasn't religious at all.

"You win. But I'm not trying to date her. She's attractive. I'm intrigued by her. Impressed. But I'm just doing Las Posadas as a favor, and I think it's cool to learn about how other Mexicans celebrate Christmas. Julieta wanted to celebrate anyway. You should thank me." Enrique had to be honest with himself—it wasn't just a favor. He wanted to get the farm contract. "And I hope to at least have one good conversation with her about her farm. Then we can enjoy our holiday."

"Famous last words. Be careful, man. You don't want to hurt her—she looks pretty innocent."

Enrique studied her, the way her lips moved softly as she murmured in prayer, the womanly shape of her hips as she knelt. "You just think that because she's dressed like the Virgin Mary."

Ramón shook his head. "Nope. From what I know about Señor Flores, she's probably super sheltered. Though Blanca seems ready to break free."

A lump grew in Enrique's throat. He knew Ramón was likely right.

Jaime approached them. "When is this shit going to start, anyway?"

Ramón's face contorted. "I don't know. Relax, man. Do you have somewhere to be? It's not late yet."

"So what if I do?" Jaime pointed at Ramón's face.

Enrique stepped in between his brothers. "Come on, let's not fight in a church. What's wrong, Jaime?"

Jaime sneered. "I'm just sick of both of you always telling me what to do. I'm afraid to look at Blanca the wrong way after you went off on me about not hitting on one of the Flores girls, but Tiburón can be all over her and you don't say a word. You can rope us into this nightmare during my holiday break just so you can convince some *other* stupid farm to grow our food? Bullshit."

Ramón smirked. "Break from what exactly? Making TikToks?"

Jaime stepped into Ramón's space; his chest puffed up for a fight. Great. Two of the three Wise Men were about to rumble. In a church. On the night they were celebrating Las Posadas.

Enrique moved between them again, then glared at Ramón. "Let's drop it, okay?" He turned his attention to Jaime. "You're right about us giving you a hard time. I'll stop doing that. You aren't interested in Blanca, though, are you? Tiburón is crushing on her."

They all turned and stared at Tiburón, who was sitting next to Blanca in a pew with a Bible in his hand. She was looking up at him and smiling.

"Nah, man. I'm taking a break from women."

Enrique stifled a laugh. "I'm sorry I roped you into this. I'll make it up to you."

Tiburón got up and joined them.

Enrique punched his shoulder. "How's it going with Blanca? She seems super into you."

Tiburón shook his head. "Well, she likes me, but that's not the problem. She's not allowed to date."

Enrique's face contorted. "What? Why?"

"Because her dad has this dumbass rule that she can't date until Carolina dates."

Enrique's jaw dropped. "That's insane. Sorry, man."

A twinkle formed in Tiburón's eye. "Well, if you wanted to help me out, you could go out with Carolina so I could date Blanca."

Oh hell no. Enrique was not going to be roped into some old-school Shakespearean farce and hurt Carolina's feelings. "What is this? *The Taming of the Shrew*? No, man. That's fucked-up. I like Carolina, but we're too different."

Tiburón pleaded. "Think about it. For me."

"What a fucking mess." Jaime was right. This trip *was* a nightmare. This whole scheme to come up here for the holidays had backfired. Carolina wasn't remotely interested in partnering with the Montez Group, Tiburón was getting his hopes set on Blanca, but he'd have to jump through some insane misogynistic hoops just to date her, and now Enrique was being asked to fake date Carolina so Tiburón could pursue Blanca. This trip had become much more difficult than Enrique expected. His family should be at one of the hip seafood restaurants in the area, where they could be dining on smoked fish tacos, drinking sangria, and celebrating the holidays the way they always did—with good music and plenty of alcohol.

Ramón patted Enrique on the shoulder. "Don't worry about it. Julieta is thrilled to go to the procession tonight. She loves these things. So, you got points with her. And thus, with me."

Jaime nodded. "Rosa thinks it's pretty cool, too. Let's just get it over with so we can enjoy our vacation."

Enrique was grateful that he was still as close as ever to his brothers. He'd worried that once Ramón was engaged to Julieta, he would drift away.

Even so, having Linda as a surrogate mother during the holidays was bittersweet. He missed his mother, even though they had a difficult relationship. And hell, he missed his papá. They'd barely spoken since Ramón had ousted him from the company. It was the right decision, but Enrique still wished he could have a family as close as Julieta's. Or as close as Carolina's seemed to be.

"I'll go see what's happening." He walked back over to his pregnant bride, who was sitting in the pew, reading the Bible.

"So, what are the rules?"

Her face wrinkled. "Rules?"

"Yes. The rules. For Las Posadas. I've never done this before."

"No rules, really. We walk next to each other. Everyone behind us will sing songs. It's fun. Just stay close to me, and I'll cue you."

"Okay. I'm looking forward to it." He exhaled. "You're lucky, you know that?"

Her head tilted. "Oh really? Why?"

"Because you're so young and have already achieved your goal of taking over the farm your family worked at. You have a firm purpose." *Something I wish I had.*

She stroked her hair. "Oh. The decision to buy the farm was easy for me. It has been our home, and I wanted to make sure the other workers were taken care of. When the old owner decided to sell it, I had to save it. I grew up there."

Enrique gazed into her eyes. "That's very honorable."

"Thanks. I didn't just do it to be honorable, though. I did it for my family. Everything I do is for them." She paused and leaned closer to Enrique, frowning. "So much so that I don't know where they end, and I begin."

"I hear you. My family is everything to me, too."

She smiled and squeezed his hand. They may have been vastly different, but Carolina and Enrique had one thing in common—they would both do anything for their families.

An older man in a sweeping brown robe and a white belt sailed into the room, commanding a sense of peace.

He beckoned toward Enrique's bride. "Carolina, we will begin in a moment."

"Baby," Carolina called, and a little girl ran over to her. "Enrique, this is my sister, Sofía, but we call her Baby. She is the angel who will lead the procession."

She looked so adorable in her white gown with the sparkly halo attached to her head. "Hi, Enrique." She turned to Carolina. "Blanca's right! He is cute."

Enrique laughed.

Carolina rolled her eyes. "Don't mind her. She's just excited to be playing the angel."

Father Juan gathered them together, and the rest of the parishioners soon joined the group, as they would walk behind Carolina and Enrique.

Carolina's gaze swept outside.

Enrique leaned over to her. "What is it?"

She pursed her lips. "My father. He's not here. He was supposed to come right after work. He never misses Las Posadas."

"I'm sure he will be here soon. I can't wait to meet him." He was looking forward to meeting Carolina's father so he could eventually speak to him about partnering with the farm. Though now, Señor Flores would probably grill Enrique about his intentions toward Carolina. Her father might mistake Enrique volunteering to play Joseph as an interest in dating his eldest daughter, which it most certainly wasn't.

Just then, Mrs. Flores's cell phone rang. She answered, walking outside the chapel. A few moments later, she ran back into the church.

"¡Cari!" Her breath sounded labored.

Carolina ran over to her mother, with Enrique in tow. "Mamá, what is it?"

"It's Papá!" she cried. "He collapsed. He's in the hospital."

CHAPTER EIGHT

⁂

Carolina clutched her fake baby bump. Her dress felt impossibly hot, as if she would suffocate at any moment. She had to go to Papá.

Blanca, Adela, and Eva gathered around Mamá and exited the church to talk on the steps. The brisk night air did little to ease Carolina's panic.

This was her worst nightmare. He had seemed off lately. She knew she should've taken him to urgent care last night when his cough had sounded bad, instead of waiting for an appointment. How foolish she was. Selfish, even. She had been so wrapped up in work and Las Posadas that she'd neglected her own father. He worked way too hard and refused to take any time off.

That was it. She was going to put her foot down. She didn't need him on the farm anymore. She would force him to retire, but he was stubborn like she was.

Blanca spoke first. "What happened, Mamá?"

"He'd just ended his day and was coming in to get a glass of water when he collapsed outside the office. Luckily, Rogelio was with him and rushed him to the hospital. Papá says he is feeling okay now, but they are checking on him."

Thank God his foreman was there, or who knows what could have happened. Carolina nodded, her lip quivering, and turned to Enrique. "I have to leave."

"Of course. I hope he's okay."

Carolina tugged on Mamá's sleeve. "Let's go right now!"

Mamá shook her head. "No, there's no point in all of us rushing over there just yet. They don't know what is wrong with him. I will go." She grasped her daughter's shoulders. "There is nothing you can do but wait and pray. Mija, he would want you to participate in Las Posadas tonight. You should honor your commitment to God."

What was her mom saying? She couldn't possibly go on with tonight's festivities, not while Papá was in the hospital. "No. I need to be there for him."

"And what good will that do? I'll tell you. Nada. You will just stress us both out. Papá is with good doctors now. His fate is in God's hands. And God wants you to do Las Posadas. He didn't send you a Joseph only for you to not walk. Everyone should pray for Papá together. That is what we need." Mamá hugged Carolina, Blanca, Adela, and Eva.

"Blanca, watch your sisters, and don't tell the younger ones what's going on just yet. I will call you when I hear any news."

Her mother kissed her elder daughters goodbye, then raced out of the church.

Carolina just stood there, hands pressed to the bump that constricted her stomach. She didn't want to do Las Posadas anymore. She just wanted to be with her father. Yes, of course he was strict, but he was still the daddy she'd looked up to since she was a child. The man who'd taught her to tie her shoelaces. The first man to ever buy her flowers.

Enrique had been the second.

A tear pricked at her eye. *Dammit.*

Carolina reentered the church with Enrique.

"Hey, are you okay?"

She shook her head. "No." She choked back a sob.

He put a cautious arm around her shoulders. "I'm so sorry about your father."

"I appreciate that."

He took her hand. The warmth from his palm comforted her. "Let's get through this night, and you can go to him."

Carolina looked up at this thoughtful man. This couldn't all be an act for the farm, could it?

"Thanks. You're right. On with the show." She shook her head to compose herself, and her veil fell to the ground.

"Here, let me help you."

He picked it up and turned to fasten the veil on top of her head. As he stood in front of her, the heat of his breath warmed her neck. Shivers ran down her spine. Their lips were so close they almost touched.

Baby ran over to them, and Enrique stepped back. Carolina smiled through her pain when she saw her. When Sofía was born, Carolina felt a special bond toward her—the eldest and the youngest. Carolina had helped so much to raise her, it was as if she was almost her own child. At only five, Baby was so sweet and innocent. Her long black hair was braided into two long plaits.

Carolina knelt down and hugged Baby. "You are the prettiest angel I have ever seen."

Her brown eyes lit up. "Thank you. Why did Mamá have to leave? Where is Papá?"

Carolina swallowed the lump in her throat. "They had something very important to do, but I'm going to send them pictures and a video."

Baby nodded vigorously. Carolina clutched her hand and stood up to face Enrique. "I'm ready."

He linked his arm with hers and walked her over to the priest.

Father Juan was dressed for the occasion in an old-school Franciscan habit.

"Padre Juan, my father is in the hospital. Will you pray for him?"

He placed his hand on her shoulder. "Of course, mija."

"Thank you, Padre. But could you not use his name in prayer? I don't want the community to know about this until we find out what is wrong with him." She pointed to Baby now skipping happily toward the front of the group and laughing with their sister Victoria. "And some of my sisters don't know what's happening."

"I understand. I will not say his name."

"I appreciate that."

Father Juan led Carolina, Enrique, and Baby to the church steps. A parishioner brought the donkey from the back of the church and handed him to Enrique, who grabbed the reins. Ramón, Julieta, Linda, Jaime, Rosa, Tiburón, and Blanca followed behind them. Outside, a crowd of at least a hundred people had already gathered for the journey. They were carrying candles, which illuminated the night.

Christmas trees were in the shopwindows and bright red bows were wrapped on every streetlight. It was all so beautiful and glorious. She just wished her father were there to see.

Father Juan addressed his congregation. "Before we walk tonight, I would like us to join in prayer for everyone's journey tonight. We also have a sick member of our congregation who needs our prayers. Let us pray."

Carolina nodded and Enrique followed suit. Their hands brushed as she moved to pray, and he gently laced their fingers together. He squeezed hers.

Her heart raced.

Father Juan spoke. "Beloved St. Padre Pio, who shared in Christ's suffering in a special way through the stigmata, you especially loved the sick and infirm. Through your intercession before the throne of God, may we be healed in body and soul, particularly in regard to our dear loved one."

"Amen," the crowd responded in unison.

Warmth filled Carolina's chest. Padre Pio was her favorite saint and was known for healing the sick. He could heal Papá. Carolina was grateful that Father Juan had chosen him to pray to.

"Tonight, we will start our pilgrimage for shelter. Representing the Virgin Mary is our own Carolina Flores."

People began to clap, but Carolina was in no mood for applause.

"And we have a guest to play Joseph. Please welcome Enrique Montez. And he's even brought along some Wise Men to help with our journey."

Enrique waved, a suave look on his face. "Hi, everyone. I'm honored to be here. I'll be honest, it's my first Las Posadas. But I'm excited to participate in your tradition. Thanks for welcoming me."

Carolina watched the eyes of the crowd, which consisted of almost every prominent family in Santa Maria, rake over Enrique. Carolina was locally famous in her hometown, and everything she did was scrutinized. A girl she'd gone to high school with whispered to another former classmate, then looked at her phone. Their mouths both dropped in unison, and then they both pointed at Carolina.

Probably wondering what Enrique is doing with me.

No, no! Carolina pushed that intrusive, self-deprecating thought out of her head. She was awesome. Smart, kind, and resourceful. And she even felt pretty tonight, despite being dressed as a pregnant

Virgin—make that *the* pregnant Virgin. Enrique should be thrilled to be with her.

But there was still a doubt.

Her throat burned, but she had bigger things to worry about than idle gossip and mocking. She had only enough energy to focus on getting through the night and going to her father.

Father Juan took a step onto the street. "Let us begin." He led the choir in Spanish hymns.

Enrique walked silently beside her, still holding her hand. He probably didn't know the songs, but that was okay. She enjoyed his calming presence near her.

After a few blocks, they arrived at the first home, which was decorated with Christmas lights and a pop-up nativity scene. The parishioners sang a song to ask for shelter, and the homeowners sang back that they could not be allowed in.

Enrique strutted down the street as if he had played Joseph for many years. Carolina clung proudly to his side, enjoying this happy moment on her dark night. The donkey trotted alongside them, with a brief stop to munch on an apple offered to him by someone in the procession.

At the next house, they were again denied shelter.

Lanterns lined the streets, guiding their way. Papel picado hung overhead as the parishioners caroled and held candles. The magic of the season filled the air, or maybe that was the scent of the cinnamon from the Ponche Navideño that Carolina could already smell.

A few more homes denied them. Finally, they arrived at the last house of the night. They were welcomed in and embraced.

"Looks like these guys have room in the stable," Enrique joked.

Carolina laughed. "You did a great job."

A huge feast of tamales, enchiladas, tacos, and pozole awaited them. Carolina was so nauseous that she didn't want to eat. She sat on a bench as Enrique left to get some food. A woman handed Carolina some hot Ponche Navideño. The fruity drink was laced with cinnamon and rum. She took a sip of the beverage to warm up, then Enrique brought her a warm chocolate-filled concha, her favorite sweet pastry. He sat next to her and placed his hand on her back.

"Thanks." She took a bite and wiped the sugar off her lips before checking her phone. No word from her mother.

The celebration was now in full swing. Mariachis played music and people were dancing in the backyard. Father Juan handed Enrique a stick to break the seven-point star piñata, which represented the seven deadly sins. Carolina stood up and blindfolded Enrique, and he swung at the object as the crowd cheered him on.

He smacked it once and Carolina focused on his bicep. Those arms. What would they feel like wrapped around her body?

Another huge hit but still no luck. Finally, he destroyed the star, and the kids rushed beneath it to collect the candy. Enrique shoved up his blindfold and scrambled out of the way before he could be knocked off-balance by some ravenous kids. Carolina couldn't help it—she began to laugh as she quietly explained the tradition. "The star represented the seven sins; you conquered it and were rewarded with blessings, or in this case, candy."

He grinned. "I had to conquer sin? So, the priest could tell I was a sinner?"

Carolina smiled for the first time since Las Posadas began. "Father Juan can read people."

A lady handed Enrique his own glass of ponche, which he quickly downed. "This stuff is good."

"Glad you like it. So, what did you think of your first Las Posadas?"

"I loved it." He grinned. "It's amazing to see all these people out here celebrating the holiday. I normally just stay home." He spoke with a bit of sadness.

"That's too bad. We always have a big celebration with our family and cousins and aunts and uncles. But it's nice to enjoy Las Posadas with everyone in the community." She paused. This man had been so great to her, and he didn't even know her. She needed to acknowledge him. She touched his arm. "Sorry I've been so standoffish to you. It's been a rough night. You seem really kind."

He shook his head. "Don't worry about it at all. I'm sorry about your dad. And I'm having fun."

She grinned. Carolina had participated in so many Las Posadas, but this one really struck her, and it wasn't just because her father was sick. This journey—asking for shelter and being denied—was the journey of so many in her community. Las Posadas was so pertinent to many Latinos in America today. And here Enrique was, ready to work with her farm. He had connections and so much money—their partnership could change the lives of so many.

She took another sip of her ponche just as her phone finally pinged. She looked down and read a text from her mom.

Mamá: Papá is awake. The doctor says he had a blood clot in his lung.

Her hand trembled. "I have to go. My father is awake. He had a blood clot in his lung. I can't believe it . . . he doesn't even smoke." But he *had* worked in the fields all of his life. Those pesticides probably caused this.

"I'm so sorry. Is he going to be okay?"

She threw up her hands. "I don't know. Good night."

She was turning to walk away when Enrique reached for her hand. "Wait, I'll go with you. Let me drive you."

"No. It's okay. I have a car."

"You're too upset to drive. I can take you. We took two cars here—my family can ride with Ramón."

She considered refusing, but he was right. She was shaken up.

And Enrique had been . . . He'd been more than nice. He'd been such a big help tonight. And he'd made her smile—it had been a long time since a man had done that.

Would it really hurt to let him go with her? To let him keep her company?

"Okay. Thank you."

He took out his phone. "Where is he?"

"Santa Maria General." He tapped on his phone as she got up to find Blanca.

Blanca was under a tree, chatting with Tiburón while a few of their younger sisters ate candy nearby.

"Blanca, can you make sure everyone gets home? Papá is awake. He has a blood clot in his lung. I'm going to head over there."

"Is that curable?"

"I don't know." And she didn't. At that point, she was completely helpless.

"Okay. Text me. Of course I'll watch the girls. And I'll get the donkey back to the church."

"I'll help," offered Tiburón.

"Thanks." Carolina hugged her sister and nodded at Tiburón. The two sisters were so different and fought often, but ultimately, Blanca was Carolina's best friend. She told Blanca everything and couldn't imagine what it would be like not to have Blanca in her life.

Enrique approached Carolina. "Let's go." Enrique took Carolina's hand and they walked to his Tesla SUV. And even though Las Posadas were over, and they were no longer "husband and wife," his hand felt natural around hers.

They didn't talk for much of the ride. Carolina was too nervous and upset to engage in trivial conversation.

Finally, they arrived at the hospital and exited the car, making their way to the front entrance.

Enrique brushed a lock of hair off her shoulder, his brow furrowed. "Do you want me to stay out here?"

She shook her head without thinking twice. "No. Please come with me." She didn't want to do this alone.

Enrique and Carolina walked into the hospital and talked to a nurse. She escorted them down a long hallway to the room.

When she entered, Carolina took one look at Papá, hooked up to the machines, and gasped.

It was even worse than she had feared.

The stark white walls and harsh fluorescent lights made his normally dark skin look pale, and the room smelled like bleach. His chest heaved and his labored breathing echoed through the room. Mamá sat by his side, clutching his hand.

His eyes opened slowly. "Mija."

Carolina rushed toward him, grabbed his free hand.

"Papá! You're awake."

Papá dropped Mamá's hand, squeezed Carolina's fingers, looked around the room—and smiled. It was the biggest, widest smile she'd seen from him in a long time. His eyes flickered with life as he pointed at Enrique. "Mija." Papá pointed at Enrique. "Quién es él? Tu novio?"

Her cheeks burned. Carolina wanted to crawl under the hospital bed to shield herself from embarrassment. She couldn't believe her father had asked her if Enrique was her boyfriend. In front of him, no less. Carolina prayed Enrique didn't understand Spanish. But even if he wasn't fluent, *novio* was a common word.

But she studied Papá . . . He looked so happy, seeing her with Enrique. He would not be happy to discover that he was a Montez. Though Carolina knew she could convince him that Enrique was a good guy. Papá was so desperate to marry her off, he shouldn't care who the guy was.

All her father had ever wanted was for Carolina to find love. How could she disappoint him now, when his health was failing? She didn't want to make him upset, especially now, and Enrique had been so cool with Las Posadas . . .

Why would he mind if she told a white lie to make her father happy?

Forgive me, Father, for the lie I'm about to tell.

"Sí, Papá. His name is Enrique."

Chapter Nine

*N*ovio?

Enrique was the first to admit that his Spanish sucked. His parents didn't speak any Spanish in their home, since his father wasn't taught it as a kid. Ramón had made it a point to reclaim his culture in college and had even attended a summer language school in Cuernavaca, Mexico, where he had intensive one-on-one Spanish six hours a day, five days a week. Enrique and Jaime had gone as well, but instead of learning *español*, they'd cut class and spent their nights partying at the discos and their weekends jetting off to Acapulco to catch some rays and women, much to the dismay of their host families, who had opened up their homes to the Montez brothers.

Enrique took Latin in high school because he liked Roman mythology. As for his Spanish, he couldn't roll his r's, and even though he could scrape by in his ancestral tongue, he almost had a panic attack every time he tried to have a conversation about anything other than tacos.

But he was certain that he knew the word *novio*.

Boyfriend.

Carolina had just lied to her father and told him that Enrique was her boyfriend. He most certainly was not. They hadn't gone on a date. They hadn't slept together. Hell, they hadn't even kissed!

His body temperature rose. Was there air-conditioning in this room?

Carolina turned to look up at him. Her bottom lip was shaking, a pleading look on her face.

And her father's eyes were welled with tears.

They looked like happy tears.

Great. Now this sick, possibly dying man thought Enrique was dating his eldest daughter. He noticed they were still dressed as Joseph and the Virgin Mary. It was almost funny . . . but he wasn't laughing.

Enrique had two choices. He could play along with it for now, and deal with Carolina later. Or he could take off and let her face the aftermath alone.

But the latter option seemed cruel. She was clearly devastated, her father was ill, and it was the holiday season. Plus, if he fake dated Carolina, then Tiburón would be able to actually date Blanca. And maybe, if he played along with her lie, she would let him spend time on her farm to learn about her agricultural techniques and gain more knowledge about farmworkers' rights.

And maybe, just maybe, she would agree to provide produce for their restaurants.

Alright. He'd play along. What was the harm?

He walked over and extended his hand to her father. "Mucho gusto, Señor Flores. I'm Enrique Montez."

Carolina mouthed a thank-you. But he wasn't going to let her off the hook that easy. He needed to talk with her later.

Victor Flores struggled to push himself up and shake Enrique's hand. The monitor by the bedside started beeping—his heart rate was elevated. "So nice to meet you, young man. Though I'm afraid Carolina has told me nothing about you. And since you failed to ask permission from me to date my daughter in the first place, I have some questions."

Mamá nudged Papá's hand. "Be nice. You don't want to scare him away."

Enrique pursed his lips. Even if he *had* decided to date Carolina, he would never imagine he had to ask permission from her father. They were both adults.

"He was going to ask permission tonight at Las Posadas, but you weren't there." Carolina sat on the bed and handed her father a glass of water from the bedside table. "And you can get to know him later, Papá. For now, let's focus on how you are feeling."

He sipped the water. "I'm great. They gave me some good medicine. But I don't want to talk about my illness." His gaze narrowed intimidatingly. "I want to learn about the first and only man to capture your heart."

A look of horror washed over Carolina's face. "Please don't work yourself up, Papá. Where's your doctor?"

"I don't know where the doctor is. Nor do I care. I want to know about him." He pointed stubbornly at Enrique. "So, tell me about yourself, son. Where did you two meet?"

Carolina's voice was trembling. "Papá, actually . . . Well, the thing is—"

Enrique quickly took her hand and squeezed it.

With his attention back on Señor Flores, Enrique spoke loudly. "Well, sir, it's a long story. I read a profile about her in the paper and admired her commitment to her family and farmworkers' rights. We connected over email and have been getting to know each other for the past few months. She invited me up to see your family's farm to teach me about sustainable farming. Then she asked me to play Joseph in Las Posadas. I've never participated in the holiday before but was happy to help." He paused and stared into her brown eyes. "I quickly realized how kind and loving she is. I intended to ask your permission to date her tonight, but since you weren't there, she invited me to come here to meet you at the hospital. And . . . here we are. To be clear, we have not had a formal date yet."

She beamed at him. "Yes, Papá. It's very new, which is why I hadn't mentioned him to you. I had planned for you to meet tonight at Las Posadas."

Señor Flores sat up straight in his bed. "Are you Catholic?"

Ugh, why does this keep coming up? "Yes, sir."

"Good. Good. And what is it that you do for a living? My daughter is a top farm owner."

It was adorable how proud her father was of Carolina. Enrique slowly opened his mouth to spew the parts of his resumé that would impress Señor Flores the most, but Carolina spoke first.

"You know about Enrique. Enrique Montez. As in, the Taco King Montezes."

Señor Flores's jaw dropped, and his expression turned from hopeful into a scowl. "Yes, I know about you and your family. You're one of the playboy princes to your father's empire." He wagged a finger at his daughter. "I met his father—that snake—years ago, mija. He treated me like dirt. He is not a good man. Your boyfriend is not from a good family. This is over. Permission denied."

Great. Enrique wasn't even dating Carolina and her father already didn't approve of their relationship, fake or real.

Enrique should just take this as an opportunity to end this ridiculous charade. He could walk out of this room now, never visit her farm, and spend the rest of his Christmas break surfing. He definitely didn't feel the need to defend his family's honor.

"Papá, I don't know his father, but I have read about him. I, too, had preconceived notions about the Montez family based on his father's actions. So much so that I didn't even want to meet with Enrique when he first emailed me."

She paused, then smiled at Enrique. "But in the little time that I have known Enrique, he has been nothing but a complete gentleman. He volunteered to help me with Las Posadas, he comforted me when he found out you were sick, and he even accompanied me here to see you in the hospital. Why don't you get to know him before you pass judgment? He should not be punished for the sins of his father. It's not very Christlike, especially during this time of year."

Whoa. She really thought that?

Enrique had spent the last year defending his father ad nauseam to so many people. Everyone—businessmen and potential partners alike—constantly judged him because of his father. It was refreshing to be defended for once.

Her father looked at Enrique and then back at his daughter, then back at Enrique again. Victor's eyes focused on Enrique from head to toe. He muttered something in Spanish to his wife, who said something back. Finally, he let out a heavy huff and a reluctant smile crossed his face.

"Fair enough. I will give you a chance, but I have not made up my mind yet. My daughter does make a good point. Besides, you must be pretty special for her to even consider making you her boyfriend— she's never dated anyone before."

Never dated anyone? Like *ever*? Why? She was twenty-three! And beautiful.

Enrique pushed his questions aside to compile his thoughts. "I've never met a woman like her."

Carolina didn't know anything about Enrique and was basing her opinions on him on the limited conversations they'd had in the two times they'd met. Enrique wasn't a jerk; he *had* been kind to her. His nanny had raised him to be a gentleman.

Still, what Enrique had said was true. He'd never met a woman like Carolina. She was headstrong, compassionate, and loyal. And sexy. Her doe eyes melted him.

But she didn't seem to like him or his family's business at all. And they didn't even live in the same county. He wasn't the right man for her.

The wool from his ridiculous robe scratched his skin. It had been a long day, and all Enrique wanted to do was go back to the vacation home, which was an hour away from inland Santa Maria, take off this costume, jump into a hot shower, and call it a night. This whole trip had been weird enough already. "Well, it was nice to meet you, Señor Flores, but I should give you all some privacy. I hope you feel better and get to go home soon."

"Me too. I'd like to invite you over for dinner when I'm released. My wife is a great cook." Señor Flores paused and lowered his head in shame. "I'm not sure if you know this yet, but I need to be honest with you. Much to my grave disappointment, Carolina doesn't cook and doesn't even want to be a housewife. At all. I think you should be aware of her shortcomings in case this changes your opinion of her and you choose not to continue your relationship."

Carolina clenched her fists. "Papá!"

"It's true! You burn tortillas. He should know these things as your boyfriend. What kind of man wants a woman who can't cook?"

Enrique looked at the older man lying in the hospital bed, his face so animated despite the lack of color in his cheeks. He didn't want to anger Señor Flores, but he wouldn't tolerate him talking about Carolina like that.

Enrique looked at him directly. "I do." Was Señor Flores actually this traditional? It was unfathomable to Enrique. They lived in

America and his daughter was a college-educated farm owner, who he seemed truly proud of otherwise. Why did he care if she couldn't cook?

Señor Flores's mouth gaped. "It doesn't bother you? A woman should cook for her husband and raise their children. And a man should provide."

If Enrique was really interested in dating Carolina, her lack of cooking prowess would be the least of his concerns. "I don't care if she can cook. I'm happy to make food for both of us. I'm an excellent chef." Enrique puffed out his chest a little.

"You . . . cook?" Señor Flores asked, deep lines crossing his brow.

"I do. My nanny taught me when I was a boy, all the traditional recipes—tamales, pozole, enchiladas, whatever Carolina wants to eat. In fact, I'd be happy to prepare dinner for *you*. Good night, Señor Flores. I hope you get better."

Her father's eyes bugged out. Ha. Served him right. His daughter's worth had nothing to do with her ability to cook. Enrique loved strong, powerful women. His future wife would be more than welcome to devote herself to a career if that was what she wanted to do. Enrique would be happy to be a stay-at-home soccer dad.

He turned and walked to the doorway.

"I'll be right back, Papá. I'd like to walk Enrique out." Carolina's shoes tapped on the linoleum behind him.

They walked in silence through the corridors, passing the nurses' station. Enrique refused to make a scene.

As soon as they were outside of the hospital, Carolina grabbed Enrique's arm. "I'm so sorry about that. I don't know what I was thinking!"

Enrique shook his head. "It's fine, I—"

"No." She squeezed his arm tighter, stepped closer until there was barely a whisper of space between them. "You don't understand. I've never had a relationship, ever. But he looked so happy when he thought you were my boyfriend . . . I just thought I would let him believe it for a while since he isn't feeling well. It was careless and selfish of me. I never meant to rope you into this. You must think I'm so pathetic."

"No, I don't. I think you're adorable." Enrique leaned closer. "But I don't lie, babe."

Her eyes widened at the word *babe*. "I understand that. I'm so sorry." Carolina looked down at the ground, then glanced back up at him, a plaintive expression on her face. "But could you just play along while you are in town? Please? Until Christmas? Then we can say we broke up and this never happened." She paused and pinched his arm. "You can even blame it on my lack of cooking and cleaning. That way, my father will totally be on your side."

"I'd laugh, but that's not funny. How could he think your lack of kitchen skill means anything to a man?" Enrique asked, his brow furrowed.

"He just does." Carolina dropped his arm. Her gazed fixed on one of the mountains lining the horizon in the distance. "I don't think he believes that anyone would ever want me. I mean, why would they? I'm too ambitious, would make a horrible housewife, and I'm not as pretty as Blanca."

His gut wrenched. Did she really believe that? He lifted up her chin with his hand. "You're beautiful, Carolina. Plenty of men would be lucky to date you. You're incredible."

She looked away; her cheeks flushed. "You don't have to say that."

"I know I don't." He took her hand and gazed into her eyes. "But I mean it. I'd ask you on a date myself, but we don't live near each other, and I'm hoping we can work together. Mixing business with pleasure is never a good idea. I wouldn't want to start something I couldn't finish."

Enrique hated long-distance relationships. He'd attempted it once with a college girlfriend, and it had been a disaster. Carolina's life was firmly in Santa Maria, and Enrique loved San Diego. It would never work.

"I agree. That would be really hard." Her voice sounded a bit somber. "But I wouldn't have said yes anyway. I don't want to date. Growing up with my father, I've dealt with enough misogyny for a lifetime."

Enrique's stomach tensed. He ignored the unreasonable sting he felt after her casual rejection and focused on what she was actually saying. It was sad to learn that most of the men she knew were like that. "Well, I'm nothing like your father. Quite the opposite, in fact. You don't have to date anyone if you don't want to, but not all men are like him."

"The ones I meet are," she said quietly.

"Well, then you need to meet different ones. Your dad is a trip. Is he for real? He can't possibly be *that* traditional." Meeting her family had been like stepping back in time.

She laughed. "Oh yes, he can. You would be shocked. I technically shouldn't even be talking with you alone without a chaperone. If I don't go back in a few minutes, he might rip out the breathing tubes and come find me."

Enrique scratched his chin. Surely, she was exaggerating. "Seriously?"

"Seriously." She paused and looked up at him. "So will you help me?"

He tilted his head. "I could. But what's in it for me?"

She gulped. "I'll at least consider your proposal for my farm, but I can't promise anything. That decision will be based on business. I can also tell you everything about my farm. I can give you a tour and teach you about hydroponics. Educate you further about farmworkers' rights."

Enrique wanted all those things. That was why he'd come here.

But . . . staring at Carolina in the moonlight made him want something else.

Maybe he could try to show her father how amazing his daughter was. That she had worth even if she would never be a housewife. That she was kind, loyal, intelligent, and ambitious.

And better yet, help Carolina realize how incredible she was. Not just as a successful farm owner, but as a woman.

And as an added bonus, his boy Tiburón would have a chance at dating Blanca.

"I'll take that deal. But I want one more thing."

She shifted on her feet. "Then what do you want?"

He brushed a lock of hair out of her face. "A kiss."

Her jaw dropped and she swallowed hard. "What? Why? This is a fake relationship. You said you don't do long distance anyway."

"I know. I don't. But I like you. You're funny. And spunky. And sassy. And I think you like me, too, or you wouldn't have told your dad I was your boyfriend. Or defended me to him. And I just want to spend some time with you. I'll be a perfect gentleman. But if you don't want to, I'll back off. I'll be your fake boyfriend whether you kiss me or not."

His hand grazed the small of her back, the tension between them almost magnetic as he continued, "But I hope you will."

She licked her lower lip, and her breath faltered. "You're not wrong. I like you. You're kind. And you're weirdly sweet. And . . ." Her gaze fixed on his mouth, then flicked back to his eyes. "You have amazing lips."

"So do you," he replied, and stroked a lock of her hair off her face.

He grinned and leaned into her. "Kiss me, mi amor."

CHAPTER TEN

Kiss him? He wanted her to kiss him?

But he didn't know her embarrassing truth. She didn't just play a virgin in Las Posadas; she was one in real life.

And even worse—she'd never been kissed.

She felt exactly like what all those mean-girls taunted her about in high school when she spent all her time studying. A weirdo who no guy would ever like. Why would this ruggedly handsome, rich, and kind man even want to kiss her? She had been rude to him when they'd met and refused to talk to him about her farm. Then she'd topped off her awful behavior by lying to her father about the nature of their relationship without telling Enrique first.

But he was still here.

Warmth flushed over her. She wanted him to kiss her. To feel his lips on hers, to taste his mouth.

To be his, if only for a moment in time.

"I'm nervous." Should she tell him? After all her lies, he deserved to know at least something that was truthful. "I've never been kissed before."

His jaw dropped, but he quickly closed it and smiled. "I'm happy to be your first."

She looked up at him, his long, dark hair falling into his face. Her heartbeat raced. "I'm afraid I'll be bad."

His gaze raked over her body. "That's not even possible."

She wanted to sink into the ground with her humiliation, almost wishing this night had never happened.

But there was no snide or mocking expression on his face. Just a twinkle in his eyes.

"But I don't want to pressure you. You have to tell me if you want me to kiss you."

They stood in the hospital courtyard, under the buzzing fluorescent lights of a multistory parking lot. This was definitely not where she'd imagined her first kiss would take place.

But if she didn't seize this moment, it might not come again.

She placed her hand on his chest. "Bésame, Enrique."

He grinned and pulled her closer. "I thought you'd never ask."

She closed her eyes, waiting for him, nerves racing through her body. His hands cupped her face, then his mouth covered hers.

His lips were sweet and gentle. As their mouths moved softly against each other, her heart swelled. Oh, this . . . this was divine.

His tongue gently pushed against her lips as if it wanted to gain entry. She had assumed that this would've been a quick, obligatory lips-only kiss, but she was pleasantly surprised she was wrong. She wanted more, more of him, more of his heat. She opened her mouth for him, and *damn*. He tasted like the rum from the ponche, and he smelled like freshly chopped firewood. Adrenaline pulsed through her body as he explored her mouth and pressed his hard body against her soft one. She was still wearing that stupid pillowy baby bump, and she just wanted to rip it off and get even closer to him.

The kiss made her core ache with longing for more intimacy. After all of the years imagining what her first kiss would be like, who it would be with, and if it would ever even happen, the moment was here and now. And it was delicious.

Too soon, he thumbed her chin and slowly pulled away from her.

Her chest caved. He was probably thinking what a horrible kisser she was. That there was a very good reason no one had ever wanted to kiss her before now.

There was something fundamentally unattractive and unappealing about her, she was sure of it. Her father had always said that she needed to be more ladylike. That was definitely part of it. She was too shrewd, too opinionated, too just inherently unlikable. Which was perfect for business, an area she never doubted herself in, but just the thought of dimming herself for a man made her feel helpless.

"I'm sorry." She looked at the ground, feeling her cheeks burn in embarrassment.

"For what? Don't be. I'm not." He smiled and ran a hand through his hair. "It was great. I'd like to do it again."

Again? Well, maybe—

No. No. Another kiss was a bad idea. One kiss had been fine to ease the tension between them. And quite frankly, it was a relief to finally get it over with, to not be that weirdo woman who had never been kissed.

Another kiss was definitely out of the question. She'd almost lost her sense of self in that kiss. She couldn't risk it again.

But there was one problem.

She'd liked the kiss. Actually, she'd loved the kiss. She wanted to kiss him again and again. She wanted him to want to kiss her back.

And not just on her lips. She would let Enrique kiss her neck, sprinkling even more kisses on her breasts, and maybe even down her body, in between her legs. A shiver passed over her.

Yes, she was a virgin, but it wasn't exactly by choice. She most certainly was not saving herself for marriage, an institute she had no desire to partake in. Her virginity was not a prize for a future husband.

Maybe she wanted to have sex. Hell, a lot of sex.

Enrique would be great in bed. In fact, he'd be a perfect guy to take her virginity. Because then he would go back to San Diego, and she would never have to see him again. He wouldn't be able to break her heart because she would know from the beginning that there was no happily ever after for them.

But Carolina reminded herself that though the kiss might have been real, their relationship was completely fake. He had been a gentleman ever since she'd met him and had not ratted her out on her awful behavior in front of her father.

And now she had roped this gentleman, who probably gave her this kiss out of pity, into a fake relationship with her. She didn't need to go around fooling herself into thinking she could ever have something so out of reach.

She needed to do what she did best—take control. "I think maybe we should set some ground rules for this arrangement."

He laughed out loud. "You're giving me rules, babe? You told your father that I was your boyfriend, and now you want to tell me how this is going to go? That's not how it's going to work."

Oh no. What had she done? What if his gentlemanly behavior had been some sort of act? He had asked for a kiss, which was one thing, but what if he expected her to sleep with him? Sure, she had *just* entertained the thought of losing her virginity, but that was on her terms, not his. She wasn't going to trade sex as some sort of payment for this ruse.

She stood strongly and stared him down. "I-I'm not going to sleep with you just because you are pretending to be my boyfriend." Even if he was kind of handsome. And that *kiss* . . .

But a kiss did not a good man make.

If Carolina slept with him, it would be because she wanted to, for fun, even to finally lose her V-card, but definitely not because she owed it to him. She didn't owe anything to anyone. Her home and the farm were paid in full.

He touched her chin with his thumb. "Hey, wait. Relax. I'm not like that at all. I would never, ever pressure you to do something you don't want with me. There's nothing sexier than enthusiastic consent. I wouldn't have even kissed you if you hadn't agreed to."

His words soothed her soul and took the edge off her nerves. Ay, she was such a mess. She had just completely freaked out for no reason. She did believe he was a kind man. A good man.

She shook her head to clear it, and the world around them started turning again. A patient was wheeled in from an ambulance by paramedics, while doctors shouted orders over the sirens.

This was definitely not the most romantic spot.

"Okay. Sorry, I overreacted. I do that a lot."

"You're just passionate." He grinned. "Look, we don't need rules. I'll pretend to be your boyfriend until I leave town after Christmas, and then we'll just go our separate ways." He leaned in closer and cupped her face as if he was going in for another kiss. "Just promise me one thing—don't tell him I dumped you because you can't cook. I refuse to feed into more of his ridiculous ideas about women. Deal?"

Swoon. His words were even better than a kiss. He was so dreamy. And progressive. Nothing like the guys she knew around here. "Deal."

He released her from his embrace and reached out his hand to shake hers, as if this was some sort of business agreement, which, technically, it was.

She shook his hand.

He pulled her toward him again with a quick tug and a lopsided grin, and Carolina let out a surprised laugh before his mouth took hers. Another kiss! Two in one night. Her heart raced so fast. Was this normal? Maybe she was having a heart attack? At least she was in front of the hospital. She should get her chest scanned while she was here, just for good measure.

And her head checked, too.

He pulled away, and her heart sank. She was doomed. She had only met him a day ago, and she was already developing feelings for him. She liked him. She was attracted to him. And a kiss or two certainly was not a big deal to Enrique.

He had probably kissed thousands of girls.

He reached into his pocket and grabbed his phone. "I'm going to head home. Unless you want me to stick around."

She shook her head. She needed to focus on Papá and not on this tangled web she had just woven herself. "No, I'm great. Thanks for asking." She paused. Papá had asked Enrique over to dinner. If he was released from the hospital, he would be upset if Enrique didn't come over. "So, if Papá gets released in the next few days . . . are you free for dinner? I'm not sure what the doctor's orders are yet. I'll text you when I have an update."

He smirked. "Do *you* want me to come over for dinner, or are you just asking me for your father?"

She shrugged her shoulders. "Both. But if you can't, I understand."

"I'll be there. Give me your number, babe."

Babe. There was that word again. Did he call every woman babe? She liked the term. What should she call him? Dude? Honey? Amor?

Ay! She was hopeless. She didn't even know how to talk to this man, or any man, for that matter.

"Sure, baby." Oh my God! Cringe. She sounded like such an idiot. Why did she talk? At least he winked at her when she said it, so maybe she'd pulled it off.

They exchanged numbers. Carolina shivered in the evening breeze, and Enrique put his arm around her shoulders as he reached his other hand into a pocket on his robe and pulled out his car keys.

"Good night, babe." He brushed a final sweet kiss on her cheek, then she turned her head and their lips met. Again.

This time, she was more prepared, even comfortable exploring a bit. She tangled her hands in his hair, grazed her fingers down his neck. Her heart danced, heady with lust.

They broke from the kiss. Carolina couldn't look away from this man. He was so handsome in the gentle moonlight. She barely noticed the other people milling around the entrance to the hospital—

Wait.

Was that *Blanca*?

Oh no. Blanca would know about the fake relationship soon enough, but Carolina had wanted to keep the kiss to herself just for a little longer.

Her younger sister rushed up from the car park, a little jig in her step and eyes wide.

Carolina covered her mouth and took a step back from Enrique, who just stood there with a sheepish grin on his face.

"Good night, ladies. See you soon for dinner. And hope your dad gets better." Enrique waved to the slack-jawed Blanca and winked at Carolina, and then entered his vehicle.

"Ay, Dios mío! Carolina Yvonne Flores! I saw that! He kissed you!!! Oh my God! Are you dating him?! Wait—" A look of realization washed over her. "This means I can finally date. I could kiss you myself!"

Carolina gave her a shaky thumbs-up. Blanca was right. She could date now. Her father couldn't go back on his word.

This would be a good thing. It was absolutely ridiculous that her father prevented his twenty-one-year-old daughter from dating because Carolina hadn't wanted to date. It was misogynistic and controlling. If Carolina's lie had brought her father some momentary happiness and allowed Blanca to break free from that ludicrous rule, then it was worth it.

Enrique was right. She needed to start calling her father out on his misogyny, but that was easier said than done.

"You're correct. You can." Carolina raised her hand to high-five Blanca, but Blanca wrapped her arms around Carolina and kissed her on the cheek.

"I love you so much. Thank you. Oh my God. But forget about me. Tell me everything! What happened with Enrique? What was the kiss like? OMG, that's your first kiss ever! Are you in love?"

Carolina grinned. She motioned Blanca over to a small bench in front of the hospital. She was a bit dizzy, probably from all that kissing.

She clasped her sister's hand. "Yes, he's the only guy I've ever kissed. You know that. It was amazing. Like, it was sweet at first, but then more forceful. My heart raced, and he smelled so good. I was completely overwhelmed."

"You are so lucky! I'm so happy for you! So, are you guys together now?"

Carolina had lied enough tonight. She had to tell the truth—at least to her sister. "Well, it's not what it seems. He accompanied me to the hospital, and when we walked into the room, Papá asked if he was my boyfriend."

Blanca's eyes bugged. "Oh my God, you did not. Tell me you didn't lie to Papá."

"Says the girl who lied to Enrique and impersonated me in an email."

Blanca tossed her hair dramatically. "Whatever, I stand by that decision."

Carolina bit her lower lip. "I did. Papá looked so happy, Blanca! And he's sick. I didn't want to tell him no. So, I said yes."

Blanca shook her head. "And Enrique went along with the lie?"

"He did, shockingly. But Papá started being a jerk about Enrique's dad, so I shut him down. Papá then informed Enrique that I couldn't cook and said he would understand if Enrique didn't want to date me."

Blanca rolled her eyes. "Dad is the worst. He thinks our only purpose in life is to serve men. It's so gross. I want my man to serve *me*."

Carolina grinned. "I know, right? Enrique was so cool about it and even stood up for me. He said that he didn't care at all that I don't cook. That he would be happy to cook for me. Can you believe it?"

"I hate you right now. He's so perfect. When's the wedding?"

Carolina sighed and sank further into the hard metal seat. "This is fake, remember? He lives far away, and we would never actually work out. But Papá did invite him for dinner when he gets out."

"Can he bring Tiburón? He's so hot."

Carolina rolled her eyes. "Blanca, we both know that Papá would never accept Tiburón with his tattoos."

Blanca gulped and lowered her voice, almost as if she were worried their father would somehow hear. "I know. And it's not just the tattoos. He told me tonight that he became super religious . . . while he was in prison!"

"Prison? Yeah, no, forget it."

Blanca shook her head. "But he's a changed man. I just want Papá to give him a chance. He wants to settle down and have kids someday."

Papá would never approve. Ever.

"Well, good luck. You really like him?"

"Yes, I do. He's really sweet and cool." She looked at the night sky, dreamily. Blanca always pursued these hot guys—behind Papá's back, of course. But none of them wanted to settle down, get married, and start a family. Unlike Carolina, Blanca wanted to be a mother and a housewife. She loved children and wanted a big family. But still, she always went for the hot, bad-boy player. "Anyway, tell me more about Enrique. Tell me more about the kiss?"

"I shouldn't. It's best I forget it." Carolina sighed.

Blanca dramatically shook her head. "Nope. I want details."

"Fine. He asked me to kiss him. I thought he was just joking, but he was serious. And he wouldn't kiss me until I agreed to. It was . . . amazing." The excitement in her voice dropped as reality set in. "But I think he was just in the moment. Let's be real—he's probably kissed thousands of women, and I've only kissed him. And this was after I had pretty much forced him to be in a fake relationship with me."

"Well, I wouldn't worry about it. He likes you for sure. Just enjoy this time with him until he leaves. If it's meant to be, it's meant to be. If not, there are other fish in the sea."

Easy for Blanca to say. She had a new crush every week.

Carolina didn't. She almost never liked anyone.

But she was starting to think that she liked Enrique.

Chapter Eleven

Enrique could still taste Carolina on his lips, but regret hung heavily in his soul. Not for the kiss; no, definitely not. He'd enjoyed her hot little mouth. But he hadn't realized that she'd never been kissed before.

And now he felt guilty for taking that moment from her if he had no intention of starting a real relationship with her.

It was her first kiss.

Not that it didn't mean anything to him. He felt a spark between them. And there was something else. Something deeper.

But Enrique rarely stopped at a kiss. Kisses for him usually began the night, not ended it. He couldn't remember a time when he'd just enjoyed the simplicity of a first kiss.

It made him want more.

Ugh, Ramón was right. Enrique should've been more careful with Carolina.

But it was too late now. What was done was done. And it hadn't completely been his fault. She had trapped him into a fake relationship. And now he had the possibility of partnering with her farm. And Tiburón could pursue Blanca. After Christmas, Enrique would return to San Diego, and she would go back to her life.

He arrived back at the vacation home. Ramón, Julieta, Tiburón, Jaime, and Rosa were gathered around the firepit on the deck. Enrique greeted them, grabbed a beer, then sat in a bright blue Adirondack chair and took a swig.

Jaime threw a twig at him. "Hey, José, you can change now."

Enrique looked down at himself and realized he remained wrapped in scratchy brown wool. "Yeah, I forgot I was even still wearing this. It's been a long night."

Julieta swiveled her chair closer to his. "Las Posadas was fun. Different than the other ones I've been to. This one was smaller and less opulent and had more of a traditional vibe, probably because it is such a small town. I liked it. What did you think?"

"It was cool. But Carolina was a wreck."

Rosa warmed her hands up over the fire. "Really? Why?"

"Her dad was supposed to be there, but he ended up in the hospital. He has a blood clot in his lung." Her father looked like a man who'd lived a hard life. Anyone who spent their years tending to crops hadn't had an easy road.

Rosa shuddered, despite the heat. "Oh no, that's awful. He must have been the member of the congregation we said prayers for earlier."

"Perhaps it's from working the fields," Enrique mused. Now that was a real reason to consider sustainable farming—not just so he could achieve a green-star rating on their restaurants, but to truly make a difference on an individual scale.

To save someone's life.

Maybe that was why Carolina was so passionate about environmentally friendly products and creating a safe work environment—

she'd seen the effect that dangerous working conditions could have on people firsthand.

Tiburón stoked the fire with a stick. "That sucks, man. I worry about my tío. That's exactly what happened to him—respiratory issues from the fields."

"Yeah, I worry, too." He turned to Ramón and Jaime. "We should visit Tío Jorge."

Jaime's brow raised. "Yeah. We haven't seen him since we were boys."

Ramón nodded. "It's been way too long."

Julieta shook her head. "Field workers have so many medical problems. Many of their children have health problems also."

"Yeah. Carolina has worked in the fields her entire life, too." He paused. He didn't know if he wanted his family all up in his business, but he could really use some advice. "I took her to the hospital after the party to see her father . . . and he thought I was her boyfriend. He actually asked her if I was, and she said yes."

Ramón spit out his beer. "And you corrected her, right?" He looked at Enrique, who shook his head slowly. "Enrique, Señor Flores thinks you're dating Carolina? What were you thinking?"

Enrique exhaled. "I know. Then Señor Flores started grilling me. He basically thinks I'm scum because of Dad. It was all so fucked-up."

Jaime exhaled, blowing up his bangs. "Maybe you should've taken your own advice about not dating one of Señor Flores's daughters."

Enrique threw up his hands. "Hey, this wasn't my fault. *She* was the one who said I was her boyfriend, not me."

Rosa's brow furrowed. "Why would she say that?"

"Her dad is sick, and she's never had a boyfriend. Carolina's parents don't think she'll ever find love. He looked so happy when he thought that I was dating her, so she didn't want to correct him."

Tiburón let out a bellowing laugh. "You're screwed, bro. But hey, at least now I can score with Blanca. Thanks, dude."

Julieta bit her lip.

Enrique noticed and couldn't resist. "What are you thinking, Julieta?"

"I mean, I can't say that I blame Señor Flores for being mad about who you are because of your dad. Your father has done some shady-ass stuff. It's not your fault at all, but I get where he's coming from."

She wasn't wrong. For years, his father had cut corners, gentrified neighborhoods, and lowballed produce providers. Enrique understood Señor Flores's concerns. "Yeah, I do, too. But it was still messed up. Carolina stood up for me, which was cool. Once we left the room, she apologized. She felt awful."

Ramón put his head in his hands. "Man, and I thought the beginning of my relationship with Julieta was a mess."

"It was a mess." Julieta pinched Ramón, then sat on his lap and they kissed.

Enrique groaned. "Well, it was. But look at you two now."

Ramón nodded. "Enrique, you're not going to keep up this charade, are you?"

"Maybe I will, at least through Christmas like I promised. What harm could come from it?"

Jaime threw up his hands. "Are you kidding? The man is on his deathbed!"

"He didn't seem that bad."

Ramón pulled on Enrique's costume. "He has a pulmonary embolism. This clot could be fatal."

Enrique clenched his fists. Fuck. This was so screwed up. "I promised her I would pretend to be her boyfriend until Christmas."

Ramón laughed. "Fine then. But don't get seriously involved with her. If she's never had a boyfriend, you'll break her heart."

Ugh. "Too late. I kissed her. And it was her *first* kiss. Like ever."

Rosa's eyes bugged. "Ay, Dios mío, Enrique. Why? Don't you get it? She's from a super traditional Mexican Catholic family. And you went along with it when her father assumed you were her boyfriend? He's probably planning the wedding now, and if she felt something when you two kissed, she might be, too."

Tiburón chuckled. "Sounds good to me. Let's make it a double wedding. I'll marry Blanca. She's a smokeshow."

Ramón stood up.

"Alright. That's enough for one night. I'm going to bed. Julieta is forcing me to go salsa dancing tomorrow, so I need to rest up."

Now it was Enrique's turn to laugh.

"Man, you're so whipped," Jaime teased.

Ramón ignored him and turned to Enrique. "Please don't mess around with Carolina. It would be cruel. She's not like the girls you normally date. That kiss probably meant the world to her. While to you, it was just another night."

Ouch. But Ramón was right. The fake relationship was one thing. Enrique knew deep down that he probably shouldn't have kissed her.

Julieta also said good night and followed Ramón into the house. Jaime went inside to make a snack, and Rosa followed him in, plopping on the sofa to watch some television.

Enrique was grateful to be alone with Tiburón. They were both relaxing in the quiet of the night, watching the waves roll in the distance, the flames from the fire dancing against the inky black sky.

After a while, Enrique broke the silence. "You really like Blanca?"

"Yeah, man. I do. She's beautiful."

"I've known you for a while now, Tib. I've never seen you so into a girl."

"Well, I haven't been. I want to start fresh, you know? I'm not ashamed of my past, but I want to get away from it. And I love it up here," he said, gesturing to the sandy dunes stretching out before them, ghostly white in the moonlight. "I'm not saying I'd marry Blanca tomorrow—but I really like this place. I could see myself moving nearby and settling down. I just want a nice life. I don't need a lot of money like you all have. I just want a house, and a sweet wife, and a dozen children."

Enrique laughed. "Just a dozen, eh?"

"I love kids. Girls down in San Diego, they don't want the simple life. I had a lot of time to sit with myself and think about what it is I want, and I could see myself here."

"How do you know Blanca does?"

"Because she told me so. Tonight. And if we got to know each other a little better, and she is half the woman I believe she is . . . Bro, I would spoil the shit out of her if she would give me a chance."

Wow. Tiburón had it all figured out. And he wasn't afraid of commitment. "It's cool that you know what you want. I thought I did, but now I'm not so sure." He paused. Now was as good a time as any to ask the one question that was still burning on his mind. "Hey, so . . . what were you in prison for?"

Tiburón exhaled. "Stupid shit. I was a dumb kid. Totally lost. I got into a gang. Was trying to be cool, but I was just a punk. I got caught breaking into a building. I stayed in good graces with the gang to get through prison but vowed that if I got out, I'd be a changed man. And I've been honest ever since."

That was awesome, how he'd turned his life around. Enrique hated to admit it, but just a few years ago, he would've judged Tiburón for his past and probably not even given him a chance. And now, Enrique considered Tiburón to be one of his closest friends. "I admire you, man. And honestly, Blanca would be lucky to have you."

"Thanks, bro. That means a lot to me." He gave a wry smile and tipped the neck of his bottle of beer toward Enrique. "You know, I didn't like you at first, but we're cool. I thought you were a douche."

He smiled. "I didn't like you, either. I thought you were a thug." While Enrique and Carolina's fauxmance was going to end no matter what, Tiburón might actually have a chance with Blanca. Why shouldn't Enrique help his buddy get his girl? And if Tiburón was by his side, maybe it would prevent Enrique from kissing Carolina again. "Hey, do you want to go with me to dinner at Carolina's house—if he's out of the hospital soon?"

"Thought you'd never ask. But bro, I like Blanca. I want to get to know her. If you're just messing around with Carolina, you should be direct with her. Like now. You don't want to dishonor her or her family."

Enrique winced. "I'm not going to dishonor her. We aren't living in the nineteenth century."

Tiburón popped his knuckles and shook his head. "You don't get it, do you? Her parents are old-school. Blanca told me she wasn't allowed to date until Carolina did."

"Well, that's no longer a problem now."

"With that crazy-ass rule, I can guarantee you that her father will expect a traditional courtship. You may be allowed in the home with family present, but you won't be able to be alone with her. I once dated this chick, and her dad came at me with a shotgun because he caught us alone in her bedroom. I'm not fooling around with you, dog. This is how it's done."

Enrique didn't want to believe Tiburón, but based on the way Señor Flores had behaved tonight, he did.

But it didn't matter anyway.

He told himself he wasn't going to get involved, and he wasn't going to go any further with Carolina.

He was playing with fire. This had just been a work thing, but the way he'd felt when they'd kissed . . . well, that had been something.

He hadn't given her false hope that they could be more, because they couldn't. His life was in San Diego, and her life was here.

Plus, he would never agree to play by her father's misogynistic rules. They were harmful to women, and Enrique would have no part in them.

The problem was, he had already agreed to pretend to date her. He had no idea what her father expected of him at the dinner he had to attend once Señor Flores was released from the hospital.

But Enrique was certain he wouldn't be able to abide by her father's rules or keep his mouth shut the next time he saw Carolina's father treat her like a possession.

Chapter Twelve

Carolina sat in a chair in her parents' bedroom as her mother brushed her long black hair. She almost never had any reason to style it, but when Mamá grabbed the curling iron, Carolina knew she meant business.

Getting dolled up was so foreign to Carolina—she was so used to having her hair pulled tightly off her face in a bun so she could work in the fields, that she had no idea what her mamá had in store for her.

It had been three days since her father was discharged from the hospital. Luckily, the doctors had caught the blood clot in time, and he didn't need surgery.

Carolina regretted lying to her father, but she hadn't regretted the kiss. And Enrique might not have kissed her if it wasn't for those stupid, careless words. So, her lie had been worth it.

And after ruminating on the situation for the last few days, she had decided that despite the mistruth, this fake relationship was perfect. She could have a holiday fling with this hot man and then never have to see him again. There was no chance of falling deeply in love, and even better, no chance of a long-term relationship where she lost all her independence. Carolina had spent a lifetime trying to stand up to her father; she didn't want to ever have to answer to another man. Better yet, Blanca would be allowed to date. Carolina wanted her little sister to be happy.

Mamá looked at Carolina and beamed with pride. "Mija. Why did you not tell me that he asked you to be his girlfriend? God sent him to you not only to play Joseph but also to be your future husband. What a blessing."

Oh God. Here we go. "Why is it so important to you and Papá that I get married? Blanca is dying to get married. Focus on her. Why can't I just be a happy-go-lucky solterona?"

Mamá curled the iron tighter, straining the hair against Carolina's scalp.

"Please, Carolina. Why do you want to be an old maid like your father's sister?"

"Why not? Tía Luísa has a great life." Her aunt lived in Barrio Logan, a small Mexican neighborhood in San Diego, with four rescue dogs and three cats. Wait—Julieta's restaurant was in Barrio Logan—did her Tía Luísa know her? Or the Montezes? Carolina made a mental note to ask. Either way, Tía Luísa didn't have to cook or clean for anyone but herself and her pets, and she could come and go as she pleased. It sounded like a dream. Sometimes, when the chatter of all the women in her house drove her crazy, Carolina wished she could escape to her aunt's and not tell a soul where she was going. It would be pure bliss.

But Tía Luísa didn't have an easy road to this life. She had been ostracized from her family for many years. When she was younger and unmarried, she spent the night with a man. Carolina's abuelo kicked her out of the house and forbade the rest of the family from seeing her. Carolina's papá warned all his daughters that the same fate awaited them should they ever do something so stupid.

But Carolina would never defy her papá's rules like that.

Mamá waved the hot rod toward Carolina. "Stop. Papá will hear you. I think he's willed himself to live only to be able to walk you down the aisle."

Carolina rolled her eyes. This was not the first time she'd been the recipient of one of her mother's famous guilt trips.

Though, her words did the trick. Anxiety surged through her. "Did you ever think that one of the reasons I never wanted to date or get married was because Papá is so controlling? He wouldn't let Blanca date until I did, even though she is an adult. Adela is an adult, too. I mean, he even warned Enrique that I don't cook in case he wanted to bail. Who *does* that? Is that my only worth? Cooking for my husband?" The hot iron scalded Carolina's neck. "Ouch!"

"Lo siento. It was an accident." Mamá made the sign of the cross. "But there is nothing wrong with a woman taking care of her familia, including her husband. I don't know where we went wrong with you."

Carolina sneered at her mother's words. But Carolina knew exactly where they went wrong. When Papá had finally accepted that he wasn't having a son, he'd taught Carolina about the farm. And she'd loved it. She had always been a tomboy. When she was a child, there was nothing she'd have rather done than play in the dirt, while Blanca was dressing up dolls, hosting tea parties, and daydreaming about her future husband.

Carolina had crushes on boys growing up, but they were never interested in her. She wasn't unattractive; she just hadn't ever focused on her appearance. She spent her lunchtime at calculator club rather than hanging out with the boys on the quad, and then she came home right after school to work until dark. All she'd wanted growing up was a better life for herself to make her parents' sacrifices worth it.

And she had done that. By herself. She didn't need a man. Though Enrique didn't seem to be controlling or misogynistic like her father, she was sure he had to be a player; he was too smooth. This was nothing more than a holiday hookup for him.

And it could be the same for her.

Which was why she was counting the minutes until he came over.

As if he could hear her thoughts, her phone pinged.

Enrique: Do you mind if I bring Tiburón?

She didn't mind at all. But Papá would be so rude to a man with tattoos like that.

Maybe that would be a way to end this charade once and for all? Papá would be a jerk to Tiburón and Enrique would stand up for him, like he stood up for her when Papá declared her a poor prospect as a housewife. Then everyone would get angry, and the men would just leave. Soon after, Papá would no doubt realize that he'd pushed Carolina's potential husband out the door and maybe even see the error of his ways, and then Carolina would be free. She wouldn't have to date. She could live her life as a farm owner, buy her own place, keep her own company, and be happy. Alone.

But there was only one problem with that idea.

She wouldn't get to kiss Enrique ever again.

Still, it had to be for the best.

Carolina: Sure. Tiburón can come.

Enrique: Great. See you soon, babe.

Babe . . . *Was* she his babe? Did she want to be?

"Done." Her mom fluffed her hair. "You look beautiful."

Carolina looked up in the mirror for the first time and gasped. She was made up as if she would be dancing Ballet Folklórico, but the free hair was a game changer. Instead of a tight knot on the crown of her head, her hair cascaded down her back. Who knew she had so much volume?

"Gracias, Mamá."

Mamá embraced her and then went to the kitchen.

Carolina put on her clothes, a modest green dress—formfitting and flattering. The soft fabric caressed her skin instead of scratching it.

Gone were the dirty pants and muddy shoes. She *felt* beautiful, a feeling she wasn't used to experiencing.

Carolina left her parents' room and headed to the front of the house to peek out the curtains. Carolina's sisters were all lurking in the yard, eager to greet Enrique. Adela, at nineteen, led the pack. The youngest girls were playing with a dollhouse on the steps while Eva was on lookout for the car.

Poor Enrique—he had no clue what he was in for. He definitely could use Tiburón for support.

Blanca emerged from their shared bedroom into the living room.

Wow. If Tiburón had a crush on her before, he would lose his mind when he saw her tonight. She was wearing a tight-fitting dress that highlighted her curves while technically remaining full coverage.

"Tiburón is coming. Enrique just texted." Carolina tugged the curtain closed just in case he saw her. She couldn't be caught eagerly waiting at the window like a desperate housewife.

Blanca gave a sly smile. "Oh, I know. He just texted me. Hence the outfit." But then the happiness fell off her face. "But Papá will hate him." Blanca slumped into a green velvet chair.

"Maybe Papá will give him a chance."

Blanca shook her head. "No way. Even if you marry Enrique, Papá would never let me go out with a man like Tiburón."

Carolina turned to her sister. "Papá needs to stop judging people. Tiburón could be a wonderful man. Maybe Papá will see that tonight. It's what's inside that counts."

"I hope so. I want to have his babies."

Ay, Dios mío. Carolina rolled her eyes.

For all Carolina's protests about getting married, she did think it would be nice to have a partner in life. Someone who was supportive and cared about her. It had been so hard to go through college feeling disconnected emotionally. She had her friends and family, of course. But she would've loved having someone to go hiking with on the weekends or even to see a movie with sometimes.

Papá walked into the living room, a bit unsteady on his feet. Though his skin was sallow, and his breathing was still labored, he was wearing his best suit and his shoes were shined.

Carolina was doomed. He was probably under some sort of delusion that Enrique was about to ask for her hand in marriage.

In some regions of Mexico, courtships were done differently. The young man had to get the father's blessing to date her. Then he would be invited to the home, like Enrique had been tonight. All dates would take place in the house with other people present. The couple might find a few stolen moments alone on the property, if they were lucky. From there, an engagement would quickly follow—after the man had asked the father for the daughter's hand in marriage. And the suitor had to bring gifts to the father just to pose the question. Sometimes he would bring baskets of fruit and bread, a candle to light before the Virgin of Guadalupe, food, or even a live animal in exchange for permission to marry. If the father denied him, it was game over. If he approved, the suitor would plan an elaborate proposal for his future bride and repeat these gifts on the wedding day as some sort of a dowry.

It was fast. Romantic.

And totally unrealistic—especially considering the man in question wasn't even her real boyfriend.

"Papá, how are you feeling?"

He grinned. "Never better. The doctor says I've made a miraculous recovery."

Carolina wasn't so sure. Knowing Papá, he would've signed himself out of the hospital, even if the doctor had given him a grim prognosis. His greatest wish was to see his eldest daughter married. "Even so, I've been doing some research. I've called to get you on a waiting list with a specialist in Santa Barbara. He's doing amazing work in this field, and—"

"No, no, no." Papá held his hand out like a stop sign, then sat in his favorite leather reclining chair, but his knees wobbled as he did, belying his lack of strength. "Tonight is not about my health. Can we instead focus on this miracle of miracles? My daughter has a boyfriend."

"Well, yes, but—"

"What a great night it will be." His voice was filled with anticipation, which made Carolina feel even worse. He kissed her hand and twirled her around like he used to when she was a little girl. "You look so beautiful. Just like your mother."

"Gracias, Papá."

His eyes softened. "I remember courting her. How nervous I was. But I was sure she was the one for me." He lowered his voice. "I heard this man's affection for you in his voice. The way he defended you to me. Brave. I admire that about him."

Enrique *did* seem to be impressed by her. "It was sweet, wasn't it? But please don't embarrass me like that again. I know I may not be what many men would want as a wife, but I have value."

He pulled her into an embrace and kissed the top of her head. "Of course, mija. I'm sorry I said that. Your papá is from a different generation. But please know I'm proud of you. You remind me of myself. Any man would be lucky to have you as his wife."

A lump grew in her throat. Those were the words she'd always wanted to hear. Did he really think that? Or was he just on a high from the anticipation of the night? She wanted her father to support her and love her unconditionally. Maybe there was hope for changing his ways.

Baby ran through the door to join Carolina and her papá in the living room.

"They're here! A big SUV just turned into the driveway. I can't believe Cari finally has a boyfriend! I'm going to be a flower girl!"

Ay. Carolina put her head in her hands.

The rest of the sisters raced inside.

"Take your places!" Adela yelled, like she was directing a play.

The women dispersed themselves among the brightly colored blankets and worn pleather couches.

The doorbell rang. Carolina's toes tingled.

Mamá appeared from the kitchen. She was wearing the diamond cross Carolina had bought her for Mother's Day.

Carolina took a deep breath, said a quick prayer, and opened the door.

Her heart leapt into her throat when she saw Enrique, clutching a big bouquet of roses and a box of chocolates. He was wearing a blue pin-striped suit with a handkerchief in the chest pocket, and his hair shone under the porch light.

His bright, dazzling smile made him look like a movie star.

Tiburón stood next to him, dressed nicely in a black suit. He was also carrying a bouquet and a cake box. And he was wearing a turtleneck—no tattoo in sight.

Smart move.

Enrique handed Carolina the roses and kissed her on the cheek.

"Thank you. Welcome to our home." She whispered in his ear, "You didn't have to do all this."

He grinned and whispered back, "Carolina, I don't ever do anything I don't want to do. It was my pleasure." Heat flashed in his eyes. She felt like the most beautiful woman in the world under his gaze.

He lowered his voice. "You look incredible in that dress."

Chapter Thirteen

No matter how many times he tried to look away, Enrique couldn't stop staring at Carolina.

Her long black hair was curled, wisps of it framing her face. A few loose strands rested on her breasts. Her bright green dress showed off an incredible body. Her waist was tiny, and her hips were wide—a perfect knockout hourglass figure. But most importantly, she was strong. Her body was crafted from hard labor. It was insanely erotic. So many women in San Diego were too skinny and had so much filler that they all looked like they were airbrushed, but Carolina was a natural beauty.

Meanwhile, Tiburón was fawning all over Blanca, who, like her sister, was also a stunner. Blanca was batting her eyelashes at Tiburón.

Tiburón didn't waste any time enacting the carefully thought-out plan he'd already mentioned to Enrique. He was going to go all out to win Señor Flores's approval.

First step was to butter him up.

Tiburón greeted Señor Flores. "Mucho gusto, Señor Flores. My name is Tiburón Garcia. I would like to court your daughter, Blanca."

Enrique stifled a laugh, and Tiburón gave him a pointed stare.

Señor Flores sized him up. "I wasn't expecting another suitor tonight. But I'm impressed that you asked my permission *before* dating my daughter." Señor Flores glared at Enrique.

Nice passive-aggressive dig, dude. Enrique hadn't done anything wrong. Had he known he was supposed to ask Carolina's father's permission to date her, he still wouldn't have because the whole thing was sexist. And Enrique had never even decided to date her. All he'd agreed to do was be her Joseph. And now he was courting this girl like it was the 1950s.

Even worse, it looked to Señor Flores as if Enrique were intentionally disrespecting him. This whole thing was all so fucked-up.

Tiburón dating Blanca was a different situation. He worked at Las Pescas, but that wasn't his calling; he didn't have a career he loved in San Diego. He could move up here and work with his uncle. Or finally start his dream of opening a clothing line.

For Enrique, it wasn't that simple. Sure, he was attracted to Carolina, and he admired the hell out of her. They also had similar interests in farming. But Enrique had a life he loved in San Diego, and he didn't want to rush into a courtship. Even though he was attracted to her, they were too different, from opposite worlds.

Enrique couldn't imagine a life spent going to church every Sunday, or worse—not being able to use birth control if she were as devout a Catholic as she seemed. He shivered. There was a reason he'd stopped practicing his religion when he was old enough to make that choice. It just seemed so hypocritical. He had close friends who were gay, and he couldn't rationalize worshipping at an altar where they weren't accepted. Organized religion just wasn't for him.

But he would fulfill his promise to Carolina. And at the very least, by agreeing to date her, Tiburón had the chance to woo Blanca.

Enrique was surrounded by women everywhere—on the sofa, standing in the doorway, sitting at the dining table. All of Carolina's sisters were dressed nicely. And staring at Enrique. He felt like a caged lion in the zoo.

Tiburón sat next to Señor Flores on the sofa, gabbing away in Spanish. Another shortcoming for Enrique in this situation. He understood a few words here and there, but they were talking too rapidly for him to understand any more.

Enrique always felt like an outsider when he visited his more traditional Mexican friends and their families. There were inside jokes and cultural traditions that he had never experienced firsthand. Like Las Posadas and Lotería night and . . . hell, pretty much anything outside of Taco Tuesday and Cinco de Mayo. When he was younger, he desperately wanted to fit in with his friends and his cousins. But no matter what he did or how hard he tried, he never felt Mexican enough.

Not that he didn't recognize his privilege. He did. It was painfully obvious that his father's wealth had afforded him and his brothers so many opportunities. Advantages that he hadn't earned himself.

Sweat beaded on his forehead.

He'd initially arranged this trip to Santa Maria to try to stand on his own, contribute to the family business in a meaningful way, and become his own man. And now, he stood in Carolina's home, lying to her father and feeling supremely uncomfortable.

He felt like a fraud. What was he doing there?

Carolina reached out and grabbed his hand. "Are you okay? You look a bit pale."

He loosened his tie. "Honestly, I'm uncomfortable."

She nodded. "Wait just a second." She raced into the kitchen and came back with a glass of water. "Here, drink this."

Enrique downed the water. But no sooner than he had drunk the last drop, her father stood up and walked toward him.

Time to face the firing squad.

"So, Enrique, what are your intentions toward my daughter?"

Enrique gulped. "I, um, I don't have any."

Behind Señor Flores, Tiburón shook his head quickly. Wrong answer.

Señor Flores's eyes bulged. "You don't have any intentions toward her? Why are you here then, wasting my time?"

Enrique pulled at his collar and scanned the room. Everyone's eyes were on him still, as if they were waiting for his next move.

"I didn't mean that. I mean, I would like to get to know her."

Señor Flores narrowed his gaze at Enrique. Then Señor Flores let out a huff, or possibly a wheeze, and returned his attention to Tiburón. Good move, old man.

Enrique didn't want to be rude, but he needed to get out of there.

Carolina touched his shoulder. A jolt of electricity shot through his body. "Would you like to get some fresh air? I can show you the farm."

He placed the glass on the wooden coffee table. "I'd love that."

She took Enrique by the hand and led him to the front door. "Papá, I'm going to show Enrique the farm."

Papá looked up from his intense conversation with Tiburón. "Alone?"

"Yes, alone. He's a farmer."

Her father scowled. "Take Adela with you."

"Papá! I don't need to be chaperoned. And certainly not by my nineteen-year-old sister. We're going for a walk, on my property, not sneaking off. I walk with adult men on this farm every day!"

Her father opened his mouth to say something, but Carolina stood and pulled Enrique out of the house. "Quick. Let's go before he comes after us."

The cool air was a welcome change from that stuffy house. "You really aren't allowed to be alone with me?"

"It's nothing personal. I'm not allowed to be alone with *any* man outside of business. And he is dead serious."

"For real?"

"Unfortunately."

"So, you're not allowed to date?" They walked toward a grove of citrus trees.

"I am. This *is* a date." She paused and took a deep breath. "My first one."

Enrique sighed and put his hands on his head. This was the weirdest shit ever. Was he on some hidden-camera-type show? He couldn't possibly fathom that this was actually how people still lived. Tiburón was completely right—her family was super traditional.

He focused on the sunset over the horizon—the golden sky melting in with the snowcapped mountains. He took a moment to breathe slowly and try to center himself.

This was what he needed. Just some time out on the land. After escaping that awkward start to the night, he didn't even care about seeing the farm, though he still wanted to learn more about this place. But for now, all he wanted was to get away from her house and that suffocating feeling that everyone was judging him.

"Do you want to take a tractor or walk?"

"Let's just walk."

He took her hand out of gentlemanly habit, and they walked out of her driveway and started their stroll in a row of garlic, the pungent scent filling the air. Grape vines contrasted with nascent strawberry plants, which would probably be ready to harvest this spring. This farm was massive.

Normally, Enrique loved staring out at the ocean from his home in La Jolla, but the view of all these plants as far as his eyes could see almost seemed better. The round artichoke globes reminded him of the undulating waves in the ocean. Wind blew the leaves of the garlic plants, which varied in size.

And all this magnificent greenery fed people throughout California.

After a few strides, Enrique squeezed her hand. "Thanks for getting me out of there. I wasn't trying to be rude, but I was super uncomfortable."

"Oh, please don't apologize. I'm the one who should be groveling to you. I got you into this mess. At least Tiburón seems to not mind this courtship dance."

"He's fine with it. His family is more traditional anyway. He's looking for someone to start a relationship with, and he's certainly attracted to her. I hope they hit it off. He's a great guy and wants to settle down with a woman who wants a big family."

"Then they're a perfect match. All Blanca wants to do is get married and have babies. Though I sometimes wonder if it's just because she's desperate to leave the house. Can't say that I blame her."

He paused and turned to her. "You bought this farm yourself, right?"

"Yup. And the house."

Enrique scrunched his face. "Why don't you just move out and get your own place?"

She turned her palm up. "Because I'm Mexican."

"What does that have to do with it? So am I."

Carolina laughed. "I can't leave the home unless I'm married. Papá would flip." Her voice turned somber. "It is what it is."

Enrique's mind was blown. "I don't get it. I don't. This is all yours." He gestured to the sprawling land ahead of them. "If they are going to treat you like this, why stay? I love my family, but I would never let them control me like that."

She turned away from him and kept walking.

"Well, that's a privilege you have. I just haven't had the reason to stand up to my parents. It was never worth the fight. I have never wanted to date anyone before, and it has never gotten so bad at home that I wanted to leave and humiliate my parents."

Right. Enrique wanted nothing to do with enabling this toxic situation.

"This is just too much. I'm sorry, Carolina. I don't know if I can do this."

She bit her lip and swallowed. "It's okay. I understand. I'm sorry again. You can go home. I'll be fine."

"Hey, stop. That's not what I meant." He grinned and leaned in to kiss her cheek and reassure her. "That's not what I was saying. *This* I like. Being here, alone with you. But in the house, with all your sisters everywhere, Tiburón and your dad speaking Spanish . . . I don't know. Maybe it's my anxiety. I just didn't feel comfortable."

"Do you speak any Spanish?"

"Not really. My parents didn't use it around the house because my grandfather didn't speak Spanish to my dad. He wanted his kids to be American and not face discrimination. My brother Ramón speaks it very well, but he's always been good at school and languages. And, well . . . everything. He studied it at Stanford and Harvard, and we even went to a language school in Mexico, but Jaime and I never picked it up." He sighed. "I just never got the hang of it, you know? It became kind of like a complex for me. My cousins used to make fun of me when I tried, and then in high school and college, my friends would speak Spanish in front of me, and I felt excluded. I've wanted to learn, but it's just never come easy."

She placed her hand on his back. "I'm sorry. That must be rough. It was my first language. I learned English in kindergarten. And by watching *Sesame Street*. But my parents barely spoke English back then. I was their translator for years."

He grinned and put his arm around her. "Well, maybe you can be mine."

"I'd like that." She leaned into his chest, the warmth of her body against his sending his pulse racing. This was nice. He liked spending time with her. But he wasn't ready to declare his intentions to her father. Especially since he didn't have a clue what his intentions were or if he had any.

He turned to face her, pulling her close. "Carolina—this full traditional courtship scenario isn't really my thing."

She gulped and turned her head away from him. "Got it."

"Babe, no, that's not what I meant, either."

She looked back at him; her eyes hopeful. "What did you mean?"

"I'm here until Christmas is over. I like you. I like spending time with you. I do want to learn about your farm. And I like being alone with you out here. Can we just hang out and have fun for the holidays? I don't want to lead you on. I *will* be returning to San Diego. But I'd also like to get to know you better."

She pursed her lips. "I'd like that, too. But, like I said, my dad is super strict. We can see each other here at the farm. As for hanging out alone, I can try to get away, but it will be sneaking around."

"I don't want to create conflict with your family, but I'll take any time with you I can get."

"You say the sweetest things," she murmured, color in her cheeks. She rose on her tiptoes, her lips so full, so close to his.

"I guess you bring it out in me," he said, and as the sunset glistened on her lips, he leaned in and, like a thief, stole just one sweet kiss. Her hands roped around his shoulders, sending a tingle down his spine.

Enrique claimed her, devouring her sweetness. His lips trailed down from her lips to her sweet neck. Carolina gasped.

She slowly broke from him with a sly grin on her face.

"What, beautiful?"

"I just never thought I'd like kissing so much."

He smirked. "We're just getting started, babe."

Chapter Fourteen

Carolina's pulse raced and nerves filled the pit of her stomach at Enrique's words. "Lucky me."

The second those words left her mouth, guilt crashed over her. Her entire life, she had been conditioned to be a good girl, whatever that meant.

She was a great *woman*. She was kind, hardworking, and ambitious. And that was all that should matter. But none of those attributes mattered in the good girl games. She was expected to remain a virgin until her wedding night, though Carolina didn't even know if she wanted to get married. Having an intimate relationship with someone appealed to her, but marriage? Not so much. Her father was so controlling, and her mother deferred to him. That was not the type of life Carolina wanted.

Though she was a virgin and had only had her first kiss a few days ago, she couldn't stop thinking of Enrique's touch.

But sleeping with Enrique could be a supremely bad idea. What if she liked it as much as she liked his kisses? What if she loved it?

Would she become hopelessly attached to whoever took her virginity? Or even worse, become addicted to Enrique's touch and then be crushed when he ultimately left her? If the way Enrique kissed her was any indication of his sexual prowess, that was an entirely realistic possibility.

But she welcomed the idea of becoming more intimate with Enrique. Imagining his hands caressing her body stoked a fire inside of her.

His hand cradled the back of her neck as he drew her into yet another kiss. She couldn't get enough of this man. He smelled like pine and passion, and she was drunk on his taste.

A tractor rumbled in the distance. She forced herself to pull away from Enrique. "Did you hear that? My father probably sent out a search party for us."

Enrique gave a mirthless laugh and turned to walk back. "What is he, a California Ranger?"

She chuckled. "You're funny. I like you."

He reached for her hand. "I like you, too. So, what do you like to do for fun?"

Her face crinkled. "What's fun?" she asked sarcastically.

"When you have time off."

She laughed. "I never have time off. But I used to like to dance."

"Oh, that's cool." He grinned, then narrowed his eyes at her. "Then let me take you dancing."

Imagining Enrique holding her in his strong arms as they danced the night away was too good to be true. "When?"

"Like, now. Tonight. After dinner."

Carolina shook her head. "Nope. That's definitely out of the question. My dad wouldn't allow it."

Enrique exhaled and turned to her. "This isn't my place and all, and I don't want to make assumptions about your life, but you deserve to be happy. Everything I know about you and have read about you makes me certain that you have sacrificed everything and worked so hard so your parents could have this security. But you have to live for yourself, too."

"You're right." His words hit her like a punch to the chest. A vision of her future flashed before her. Her younger sisters would be married with their own families and Carolina would still be taking care of her parents, which she didn't mind at all. But she *did* want to be independent.

Carolina dreamed of owning a small cottage near the beach where, on her rare days off, she could grab a book and read alone at an oceanfront café.

She would still work hard on the farm, and she could never see her life without her family, and she wanted to make time for dancing . . . but maybe she could also find time to experience all the things she was missing.

Like friends she wasn't related to.

And maybe even a man.

She had been waiting for her life to start. How much longer should she put her own happiness aside for the benefit of her family?

"We need to head back."

They slowly walked through the front door. Tiburón was still sitting next to her father, who cast a suspicious glance at Enrique, and Carolina met his eyes.

"Glad that you finally decided to join us." He glared at his eldest daughter. "Carolina, get in the kitchen and help your mother."

She didn't exactly want to leave Enrique alone with her father, but she also didn't want to anger him further.

"Yes, Papá."

She gave Enrique a look over her shoulder and scurried into the kitchen, where Mamá and Blanca were gossiping while putting the finishing garnishes on the enchiladas.

A sprig of cilantro flew out of Mamá's hand as she twirled toward her. "Carolina! Where did you go?"

"Just for a walk." Time to change the subject. She lowered her voice. "Blanca, what do you think of Tiburón?"

Her lips widened in a big smile. "Oh, I adore him. He's so kind, and sweet and funny. Even Papá likes him. He was impressed by how respectful he is."

Carolina grabbed the plates from the cupboard and brought them to the counter. "So, you think you will date him?"

Blanca nodded and sprinkled queso fresco on top of the enchiladas. "I do—if Papá gives him his approval. Tiburón is the best. Look!" She flashed her wrist at Carolina, revealing a shiny, fancy bracelet. Were those diamonds? "He brought me a bracelet. I mean, guys have given me gifts before, but they never asked Papá for permission to date me. He told Papá that he's ready to settle down, and he's looking for a wife! Can you believe that? He wants a big family. I told him I love babies."

Carolina pursed her lips. Blanca was already planning her future with this stranger. "I'm happy for you—really, I am. And Enrique says Tiburón is a great guy. But, Blanca, you don't even know him. Like, at all. Are you sure this is what you want?"

Mamá slapped Carolina's hand. "Don't. Don't scare your sister off. Not everyone is like you, mija. Some women want to get married and have children. Compatible goals and upbringings are the most important elements of a happy marriage."

Carolina scoffed. "What about love?"

Mamá turned her palms up. "What about love? I married your papá at eighteen. I didn't know anything about him, but my papá liked him. Your papá promised to take care of me, and he has. It wasn't always easy, especially when you were young. But our commitment to each other and to God was all we needed."

Nothing about that sounded romantic. She was grateful her parents had a good marriage, but she wanted passion, a spark.

And she already felt one with Enrique.

Too bad whatever chemistry they had would only last until he left for San Diego.

"Tiburón is a good man. He told Papá about how he has turned his life around and how he loves kids. He played with all your sisters." Mamá lowered her eyes. "Which is more than I can say for that novio of yours, who wasn't even respectful enough to ask your papá first for the chance to date you, before he asked you. And he didn't even try to talk to your father or siblings. He ran out of the house the first chance he got."

Rage seethed inside Carolina. Her parents thought Enrique was a jerk, which couldn't be further from the truth. If anyone was a jerk, it was Carolina, who'd forced Enrique into this Shakespearean farce.

But now, he was her faux novio. And that made her happy for now. Why did she always have to focus on the future?

"That's not what happened, Mamá, and it's not fair for you to judge Enrique. He wasn't raised like us. Tiburón seems to better understand our customs, but Enrique is third-generation—he told me he didn't even speak Spanish because *his* grandfather, who came from Mexico, wanted his kids to be American. I studied this at college. It's generational trauma."

Mamá shook her head. "Don't start with your sociological, woke nonsense. It's about respect."

"No, Mamá, it's not. Enrique doesn't see me as Papá's property. He sees me as a strong, independent woman." She pulled her shoulders back and stood tall. That was who she wanted to be—if only she could always act that way.

"You better not get any funny ideas, mija. I stand by your father on this. You aren't to be alone with that man again. I will forgive you for taking off with him tonight, because he did initially come up here to inquire about the farm, but we have a reputation to uphold. I will not stand for you soiling your father's name and possibly preventing your sisters from later finding men."

Wow.

Enrique was right. If nothing changed, she was always going to be stuck in this controlling and oppressive household.

But what could she do?

She could grab the serving dish of enchiladas her mother had prepared and force Enrique to endure an awkward, interrogative dinner with her family when they weren't even in a relationship.

Or she could rebel. Like a tempestuous teenager.

All she ever focused on was work. What were her personal goals? Securing a husband sure as hell wasn't one of them. Or watching Blanca start planning a future with a guy she barely knew.

Carolina closed her eyes and inhaled a calming breath, then slowly let it out. Did she have the courage to stand up to her parents?

And if not now, then when?

She'd known this day was coming for months—years, even. She had to break free from her parents, to stand up to them and be herself. She kept putting it off . . . but was there ever going to be a better time than this?

At least there was finally something new in her life—Enrique was in town. She was dying to get to know him better beyond the watchful eyes of her parents. And she wanted to go dancing. Being swept up in his arms and salsa dancing the night away sounded like a dream.

But it was slipping away.

I can do this. Deep breath. Pull off the Band-Aid.

Three . . . two . . . one . . .

Showtime.

"Mamá. I have spent my entire life doing what is right. I went to church every Sunday, I worked in the fields, I got straight A's in school, I went to college and commuted home to save on bills and preserve my reputation, and I even raised enough money to buy the farm so I could take care of the family. But now, I want some freedom because I've earned it. I don't want to be courted and married to some man I don't even know if I'm compatible with. I don't even know if I want to get married. Ever. It's fine if Blanca feels comfortable preserving this tradition—but I don't. Not even if it makes you happy."

Mamá's eyes bugged, and she yelled at her eldest daughter. "You will not disrespect me in my house!"

Carolina laughed. "Well, it's *my* house, actually. But that's fine. I don't need it."

Blanca's jaw dropped. "Cari! Stop."

"No. I should've done this years ago." Carolina turned and walked toward the living room.

"Carolina! Get back here at once!" her mom called out, but she didn't respond.

Enrique was sitting at the dining room table, wringing his hands, his forehead wrinkled, his fists clenched.

Her father had him cornered. "So, Enrique, do you see yourself married in the next year?"

Being interrogated by Papá was something Carolina wouldn't wish on her worst enemy.

"Enrique, let's go."

Enrique's brows raised as he stood. "Where?"

Carolina looked at her father, then back to Enrique, then back to her father. She had created this fake relationship as a ruse to keep her family happy. What she was about to do would instead possibly tear them apart—but it had to be done. Enrique had made her want things she hadn't really wanted with another man before.

There was no going back. The time was now.

"Out on a real date."

CHAPTER FIFTEEN

Enrique wasn't exactly sure what was going on, but he was grateful to leave Carolina's house sooner rather than later. He looked back at her father, who was screaming from the table at his daughter.

"Carolina Yvonne Flores! I forbid you to leave the house! I don't know what happened, but you will not make a scene in front of our guests. I raised you better than this."

Carolina grabbed her purse as she made a dash for the door. "I'm not eloping, Papá. I won't even be out late. I'm just going out for the evening. I deserve it. Don't wait up."

"Carolina, come back here at once!" he shouted from his seat at the table, but she kept moving.

Alrighty then.

Enrique gulped. "It was nice to meet you all. Hope to come back soon. Have a great night." Enrique didn't know what else to say.

He glanced at Tiburón, who just shook his head. "Tiburón, I'll be back to give you a ride home. I don't think we'll be out long."

Tiburón laughed. "Sure you won't."

Enrique clutched Carolina's hand as they walked out the door. Once they were outside, Carolina's chest heaved, and tears streamed down her face.

"Are you okay? What happened?"

Her mascara was smeared. "Can we just get out of here?"

"Sure thing, babe."

He opened the door of his SUV for her, and then got into the driver's side. "Where to?"

"Anywhere. I just want to be normal for the night."

Enrique admired Carolina's bravery standing up to her father. Hell, he still hadn't stood up to his own father. Ramón had always handled their conflicts, while Enrique tried to remain neutral. That was the role he assumed as the middle child.

She clearly needed to take her mind off her family—he wanted to take her somewhere fantastic, worthy of the turmoil she had just been through.

But Carolina's spending time with him now clearly had more to do with her independence from her family than her affection for Enrique, who she didn't really know.

Anticipation built in Enrique. Usually, he just met a girl on an app or in a bar. They would flirt and then go back to his house to hook up. Sometimes they would see each other again, but it would often end before it even really got started, since Enrique had not been interested in developing a relationship.

But this time, it seemed different. He had already spent some time with Carolina, and they hadn't been intimate yet. It was . . . nice.

Maybe some of Señor Flores's rules on dating weren't the worst thing in the world. They ensured that both partners were committed to dating seriously. Enrique wasn't ready to have a chaperone, but slowing things down, keeping dates out of the bedroom—that might be a better way forward. That way, an emotional relationship was established first. The hookup culture that was all too familiar to Enrique made him almost numb to deeper feelings. That didn't mean he wanted to propose to a woman he didn't know, but he could see the benefits of courting someone with no distraction of sex to overwhelm his perceptions of the relationship.

But he was done thinking about long-term decisions. For tonight, he would plan a great date.

Dancing it was.

Julieta had dragged Ramón to the local salsa club the other night, and Julieta had recommended that the others check it out if they had a chance. Enrique entered the address on his navigation. It was an hour away, and he did have to bring her back home, but he wanted to take her somewhere really special and impress her.

"I know just the place." He reached over and placed his hand on her luscious bare thigh. "Dinner and dancing."

She exhaled. "I really appreciate you dealing with all this drama. I'm so sorry."

"Carolina, I admire you. I mean, I came up here in the first place because you intrigued me, but seeing you stand up to your family was really brave. And I know it must've been hard for you."

She gasped, then her mouth turned into a smile. "You're really great. Nothing like I thought you'd be."

"What did you think I'd be like?"

"Arrogant. Cocky. Entitled based on your wealth. After we met, I googled you and your family and read some articles. I'm sorry I judged you."

"Don't mention it. I'm not perfect, Carolina. Far from it. But I'm trying to be a better man."

"A better man? What do you mean?" Carolina asked, then her eyes widened. "Did you go to prison, too?"

"No!" Enrique laughed. "But I was just pretty wild for a while." He studied her face—her teeth clenched. Maybe he should explain so her mind didn't come up with crazy ideas of his hedonism. "Nothing too serious—I dated many women, partied around the world, drank heavily, just had a good time. Honestly, I enjoyed it but it left me feeling empty. That's one of the reasons I wanted to come up here and meet you. I loved your story. I just really wanted to be around someone who was passionate about what they did for a living—and damn good at it, too."

"That means a lot to me. I didn't think anyone would ever see those pictures of me in my graduation gown sitting in the fields when Blanca posted them on her Instagram, but they went viral. Next thing I knew, I had reporters contacting me. I was reluctant at first to speak to them, but I wanted to bring awareness to the plight of farmworkers." She laced her fingers with his.

Enrique's hand tingled from her touch. At one point, Carolina looked down at her phone and turned it off. Ugh. He couldn't even imagine what kind of messages her family was leaving her.

They spent the rest of the ride in comfortable silence. Enrique wanted to give her time to process what had just happened with her family.

They pulled into a seafood restaurant next to the salsa club. A valet took the car. Young couples milled around the velvet rope in front of the club, waiting for their turn to get in. Carolina leaned against Enrique, and he put his arm around her.

The waitress guided them to a table with two chairs close together and a panoramic view of the ocean, the waves crashing against the rocks below. What a contrast from the dinner at the Flores house. Clean white tablecloths and a bouquet of flowers dressed each table.

But Carolina was the most breathtaking part of this scene. As if a weight had already been lifted off of her, her smile grew radiant, and she relaxed into the night.

Carolina gulped down a glass of water as soon as they sat down.

Enrique ordered champagne to start the evening, which the waiter brought a few minutes later.

Enrique lifted his glass. "A toast! To my beautiful date, who is such an inspiring woman, and to all the many incredible things she's accomplished. I'm very lucky to be here with you."

Carolina raised her own glass and clinked it with his. Her eyes filled with tears. "This is already such a special night. I know it must seem silly, but I never go out. I don't ever celebrate my hard work. Thank you."

She leaned over the table and kissed him softly.

It was the first kiss she'd initiated; it felt good to know that she desired him.

He tugged at his collar. "You're welcome. I'm happy to show you a good time. But I feel bad. Like I came into your life and blew up your world. That wasn't my intention."

She clasped her hands together. "Oh, this isn't your fault at all. In fact, you have opened my eyes to so many things. I didn't quite realize it, but I'd been unhappy for some time. I'm successful professionally, but I live for my family. I've been afraid all my life to stand up to them . . . but I'm not afraid anymore." She perused the cocktail list.

"I love that you're not afraid. But are you worried what will happen when I take you home?"

"No. They'll deal. Can we not talk about them for the rest of the night? This is my first date ever, and I just want to enjoy it." She licked her lower lip. "And get to know you."

"Absolutely."

The waitress came and Enrique ordered a dirty martini and Carolina asked for a margarita. He ordered calamari as a starter and the steak and lobster tail as his entrée. Carolina chose the jalapeño cheese corn fritters and shrimp pasta.

Gently, he eased his arm around her shoulders. She nestled into his chest and fit him perfectly. There was a certain ease being around her. Had he really only met her a few days ago?

Carolina looked up at him. "I did enjoy walking with you at Las Posadas. I feel bad that I was so distracted about my father."

"Don't. I had a great time."

The waitress brought their appetizers. Enrique squeezed lemon juice on the calamari and drenched it in the spicy aioli. The crunch from the breading was perfectly crispy.

"So, enough about me. Tell me more about yourself. What exactly do you do for the Montez Group?"

Enrique took a sip of water and pondered how exactly to answer this question. "Well, I love to cook, actually. I wanted to go to culinary school, but my father wanted me to attend college." Enrique regretted not going after what he loved, but it had all worked out. "There, I found my passion in farming. I have a small farm in Encinitas that we use for the test kitchen. I grow rare herbs."

"Oh, that's so cool. Which ones?"

"Hoja santa. Epazote. Achiote."

She stroked his hand. "Oh—that's so great. I don't grow those. I'd love to see your farm."

"I can't wait to show you. But yeah, so for work, I mainly secure the produce, do contracts with the farmers. It's not that exciting, and I'm bored. But that's part of the reason I wanted to meet you and work with you. I wanted to be more hands-on, make a difference."

She batted her eyelashes at him. "I think it's so great that you really want to be part of the solution."

Their entrées arrived, and Carolina marveled at the beautiful plates of rich food.

She twirled her pasta. "This is so fabulous. I'm having such a great time; thank you again."

He winked. "Anytime, sunshine."

They finished their dinners and shared a Mexican-chocolate lava cake. The dark sweetness oozed on the plate and the vanilla ice cream cooled the heat.

After Enrique paid, he took her hand and led her outside to the dance club entrance. He tipped the bouncer, and they went inside.

Bright lights cut the floor like lightsabers and dance music blared from the speakers. Girls did shots at the bar as men vied for their attention. It was so loud that Enrique had to raise his voice so Carolina could hear him.

"Would you like to dance?" He held out a hand.

"I'd love to! Can you salsa?"

He grinned. "Yeah. I can. My mother forced me into cotillion classes at Mr. Benjamin's in La Jolla, and I was a chambelán at many quinceañeras. In college, I took some ballroom and Latin lessons."

"Well, aren't you the Renaissance man." He laughed and pulled her into a dance hold. The bass from the music vibrated into the floor. Carolina came alive with the movement. She swayed back and forth, swinging her hips and twirling in his arms. Enrique grabbed her by the waist and spun her around a few times. She placed her hand on his chest, which sent a jolt through his body.

She was so damn sexy. His hand lowered to her incredible ass.

Enrique leaned in and kissed her on the neck. "You're so hot, babe."

She grinned and tossed back her hair in a quick dip before he swept her close again. Enrique imagined she would look just like this in bed—carefree, passionate, and wild.

He whispered into her ear, "I'm so glad you told your father I was your boyfriend."

"I am, too. And I'm glad Blanca tricked us, or we never would've met." She kissed him right on the dance floor for the whole club to see. Her hot tongue darted into his mouth. Feeling her tight, sexy body against his was almost too much to bear.

She pulled away, breathless. "I never want this night to end."

CHAPTER SIXTEEN

Carolina and Enrique danced until her feet ached. This night had already been one of the best in her life. Free from the responsibility of her family, Carolina was in control. Her hair was frizzy and wild, but she didn't care—with Enrique, she felt like the most beautiful girl in the world.

Carolina downed a final shot of tequila. Enrique put his arm around her and led her out of the club.

He grinned, the sweat dripping from his forehead. "Did you have fun?"

"I had the best time. I can't believe that as much as I love dancing, I've never danced just to let loose. I was always practicing or performing."

"You have to do something daily that brings you joy. I do yoga and I surf. Even when I'm having a bad day, taking that time for myself recenters me."

She paused and caressed his face. "How did you get so wise?"

He chuckled. "I was just unhappy for a long time. Especially last year, after our family received so much hate online because of my father's terrible decisions. I went to therapy and tried to deal with my emotions." He paused. "It's not my place to say, but maybe you should try it."

Her nose wrinkled. "What? Yoga and surfing?"

"Well, those too. But I was talking about therapy. It could help you deal with the tools to communicate with your family."

Carolina nodded but couldn't even fathom going to therapy and talking to someone about her family. They would probably judge Papá too harshly and not understand where he was coming from. He was raised in another country and had never adapted to this one's customs. Yes, there was a fine line between being traditional and abusive, but Carolina prayed that she could make Papá see the errors in his ways.

But if things got really bad, maybe she would consider it.

When they'd reached the parking lot, Enrique pinned her against the side of his SUV and kissed her passionately. His hands ran down her curves, and this time, Carolina was more emboldened and touched him as well. His hard chest, his toned bicep. Her hand grazed his belt. Did she dare? She stroked the waistband of his pants and he let out a groan. She could feel every inch of his body pressed against hers, hard and strong.

This was the feeling that her friends in college had talked about. The lust, the longing, the desire. She finally understood why her father didn't want her to go out alone with a guy. It wasn't just her father's reputation or honor—once she'd had a taste of what he considered sin, she wouldn't be able to stop.

And he'd be right.

But this wasn't about her father, her mother, or her family anymore. This was about Carolina. She wanted to be free and live life on her terms.

They stumbled into the SUV. Carolina looked at her phone. It was one in the morning—and there were twenty missed calls from her father.

Dammit.

"Do you want me to take you home?"

Fear coiled in her belly. "That's probably a supremely bad idea." But spending the night with him was a worse one. His chiseled jawline made such a handsome silhouette in the moonlight. Carolina had the fleeting desire to lose her virginity in the back of his SUV but resisted the temptation. Since she had waited so long, she wanted it to be special, more intentional. She didn't have to be married, or in love; he didn't even have to be her real boyfriend.

She just wanted to be one hundred percent sure and have no regrets. Acting out of passion and rebellion was never a good idea. "But I'll have to face him sometime. So yes, please take me home."

But she didn't want to be responsible and go home, especially since she would certainly face the firing squad. What if she were a different woman, raised by a different family? Would she spend the night having hot sex with Enrique?

Yes, please!

But no. She wasn't ready for that type of intimacy . . . yet.

What would it be like to live on her own and do whatever she wanted?

She decided right then that she was going to find out.

But not tonight. She'd had enough rebellion for one day.

After a long ride, Enrique finally drove down the gravel road that led to her house.

"Stop here." She didn't want him to drive any farther, because she could almost guarantee her family would be watching from the window.

"Why? They already know I'm with you."

She placed her hand on his shoulder. "Because I need to do this alone."

He exhaled. "Fine. I texted Tiburón—he left hours ago in an Uber, so it's just your family." He stopped the car and cut the lights. "Hey, if you need me, call. I'm not going to try to pretend to understand your relationship with your family, but you did nothing wrong tonight. You don't deserve to be berated for going on a date."

A lump grew in her throat. "I know. You're right. But being right doesn't change the fact that this is my family, and I knew their rules." Carolina leaned over and gave him a sweet kiss. "Thank you for tonight."

"You're welcome. Can I see you again before I leave?"

She grinned. "Of course. Actually, would you like to come over the day after tomorrow? In the daytime, I mean. Not for another interrogation by my family. I can show you the farm for real. That is why you came up to Santa Maria in the first place, right?"

His eyes lit up. "I'd love that. It really was. I want to do better. But Carolina, it's not just about the farm anymore. I like spending time with you."

"I like spending time with you, too."

He gave her a chaste kiss, most likely because they were near her home, and then got out of his SUV and opened her door.

She hugged him goodbye. Oh, those muscles. "I'll see you on Monday, okay? Get here at five a.m. We start work early."

"Sounds—early. But good." He winked. "Good night, babe." He walked back around to the driver's seat, and when she turned around for a final glance, he was still watching her.

Once she was on the porch, the tires scattered the gravel as he pulled away, and the taillights disappeared in the distance.

Carolina took a deep breath.

She put her key in the door and opened it.

Her father and mother sat next to each other on the couch, matching scowls on their faces. Blanca was on the recliner, her face animated, clearly waiting for the train wreck to commence. Carolina was surprised that she hadn't made herself popcorn. Her parents didn't say a word as Carolina slowly locked the door behind her, put her keys down, and took her shoes off before turning to her family.

The stonewalling was killer, so Carolina decided to get the first words in. "I know what you're going to say, but I am telling you that you are overreacting. I just went dancing. That is all. That is what normal American women do. I have abided by your rules my entire life, but I'm an adult. I've been a grown-up for a long time, actually, and I've decided that I am entitled to some freedom."

Her father opened his mouth, but instead of words, a wheezy cough came out. Carolina's chest ached at the sound; she was heartbroken and concerned about his health, but she wasn't going to use that as an excuse to continue to live under his thumb.

Mamá tensed up her shoulders and spoke for them both. "No, Carolina. You are not entitled to anything. Yes, you may technically own this house, but in our culture, the father is always the head of the household. He deserves respect. You humiliated him tonight. In front of Blanca's suitor, Tiburón. He probably thinks we raised wild women!"

"Tiburón? The ex-convict? You're worried about what he thinks?" Blanca shot Carolina a look, and she felt a quick sting of guilt for being cruel toward Enrique's cousin, but Carolina held firm.

Papá spoke. "You watch your mouth about him. Unlike your date, Tiburón showed us nothing but respect. He answered all my questions without any attitude and declared his intentions toward Blanca. He is interested in starting a serious relationship with an eye toward marriage."

This was unbelievable. "I did not humiliate you! I simply went on a date with a man I like. One date. He took me out to a lovely dinner and then we went dancing. And you know what? It was the best night of my life."

Her mother couldn't let it go. "Well, you will not live in this house defying our rules."

Carolina's throat tightened. "Well, if you want to play that game, this is technically *my* house. I bought it. And I'm going to do whatever I want."

Blanca let out an audible gasp as Mamá clutched her chest and Papá's eyes bugged out.

Carolina's heart dropped. Maybe she had pushed too far. Yes, it was her house, but she would never kick her family out.

Ever.

But she still could leave . . .

She paused, wondering if she should further engage. Ultimately, she decided she was better off removing herself. "I'm going to go to bed."

Neither of her parents said another word. Carolina scurried down the hall as Blanca raced after her.

When she reached their bedroom door, Carolina held her hand up like a stop sign. "Don't start, Blanca. I don't want to hear it."

Blanca clutched Carolina's wrist.

"Well, I'm going to say it. What are you doing? Look, I'm thrilled you stood up to Papá. We both know he's ridiculous. Insane, even. But Cari, he's not going to change. Ever. You know this. I know this."

Carolina did know this. She closed the door behind her, collapsing on her bed, and Blanca sat next to her. At least they had some privacy in this house, after all the girls being stuffed like strawberries in a packing crate for years. Blanca and Carolina were so excited to have their own space. They had painted the room lavender, and Blanca crocheted some blankets to make the space comfortable. It was cute, cozy, and completely theirs.

"I agree. But what are my options? Live here until I die or wed a stranger? I don't want to get married, Blanca. Ever. I could never, ever be controlled by another man."

"Not all men are like Papá. You know that. Enrique's not like that. Tiburón told me that Enrique is super chill."

"Fine. You're right. But Enrique and I aren't about to enter any long-term relationship. He made it very clear that this fling of ours has a start date and an end date. His life is in San Diego, and mine is here. Period. End of story."

Blanca placed her hands on Carolina's shoulders and forced her sister to look at her. "No. You don't know that. Not end of story. You both could fall madly in love. He could change his whole world for you. It happens all the time."

Carolina gulped. "Yeah, for girls like you, not me."

Blanca slapped Carolina's leg. "Stop. You're amazing. Enrique would be a moron not to fall in love with you."

Carolina rubbed the mark on her leg from her sister. The momentary sting was almost worth Blanca's support. "Fine. Even if that were a possibility, we're still worlds apart. Culturally, spiritually. I know you think love is a fairy tale, but that's not how the world works."

Blanca rolled her eyes. "True love conquers all. I believe that. You are so amazing. Any man would be lucky to have you. That's why I answered his email. He clearly admired you. And I knew that there was a possibility that he would see what I see in you. A beautiful, intelligent, kick-ass woman."

And with her sister's words, Carolina burst into tears. Maybe it was from the tequila shots, or the romantic night she shared with Enrique after the emotional manipulation of her parents, or a culmination of the entire night. But for once in Carolina's life, she not only believed that she was worthy of romance and love, but she admitted to herself that she wanted it.

It was just too bad that the one person she was interested in was completely unavailable.

Chapter Seventeen

On Monday, Enrique woke at dawn and headed to her farm. Nerves twirled inside of him. He reminded himself that this was what he had come here to do—see her farm, learn from her, and most importantly, convince her to partner with the Montez Group.

His mind raced. What was he doing? It had started innocently enough. He'd emailed her, he thought she'd invited him up, and so he'd made plans. He'd thought that she would've shown him the farm and either accepted his proposal of a working relationship or not. Then he would've celebrated Christmas with his family and been back in San Diego by New Year's.

Though he already knew she was beautiful, and he admired her before he met her, he never intended to hit on her. Or kiss her.

Or catch feelings.

And now he couldn't think of anything but her. After seeing the way her body had moved on that dance floor—he imagined the way she would move in bed. Though he was certain she was a virgin, and he was wary of being her first.

Many men made it a goal to sleep with a virgin, but Enrique wasn't one of them. He never judged a girl on her past, whether she had many lovers or none, but he understood the commitment that sex meant to some women. Enrique didn't even want to consider sleeping with Carolina unless he was certain they were in a serious relationship. The weight of being her first lover and then leaving her might be too much to bear. And the alternative—staying? Why was he thinking about that possibility anyway? That was definitely out of the question because there was no future for them. This was a holiday fling—no more, no less. He loved his life in San Diego, and she was deeply rooted in her community. She owned and operated a farm— she would probably never consider abandoning it, nor should she have to.

And why was he even assuming that Carolina would want to sleep with him? What a cocky jerk. This poor woman just wanted to go on a normal date, and he was thinking like some sex-crazed idiot. Enrique hated himself sometimes for the way his testosterone clouded his judgment.

Enrique blasted the music, trying to push away visions of a naked Carolina riding him as he sucked on her nipples until he made her come.

Fuck.

Enrique turned his attention to the road ahead as he approached the farm. For as far as he could see, rows of green plants extended skyward with pale strawberries glistening in the morning sun like light pink sapphires.

He pulled into the driveway, parking behind a tractor next to the farm entrance.

And then he saw her, standing there waiting for him.

Wow.

He had expected her to be wearing working-style clothes like she had the first night she met him, but instead she was wearing a wide-brimmed straw hat that covered her cascading curls and an off-shoulder white dress with red hearts on it.

She. Was. Breathtaking.

Carolina skipped toward him. "Hola." She kissed him on the cheek, and the straw of her hat brushed against his head.

"Hola." He wrapped his arms around her waist. "¿Qué tal? What happened with your parents when you went inside?"

"Yelling. But they are giving me the silent treatment. I haven't pushed it. I think they are hoping that it was a onetime rebellion and it won't happen again."

Enrique grinned. "Well, was it? One time?"

She bit her lower lip and cocked her head, her hair swinging around even under the hat. "Why? Are you asking me on another date?"

"Maybe I am." But Enrique didn't want to ask her out again just yet. He had to be certain that he wasn't leading her on. Their fake romance was over—clearly there was no benefit for it to continue, as Enrique was certain that her father despised him.

If Enrique was going to date Carolina and deal with all the obstacles that might follow, it would be for real.

She gave him a wry smile. Hopefully, she wasn't hurt by his teasing. She walked them over to a man standing near a huge industrial plowing machine.

"Enrique, this is Manuel. Manny is going to show you the ropes this morning."

Enrique paused. "I thought you were going to take me around the farm? I have a bunch of questions for you specifically."

Carolina's lips spread into a wide smile. "Enrique, I grew up in these fields. I picked berries in the hot sun until my skin burned and I would collapse from exhaustion. But somewhere along the way, I fell in love with the fertile soil. The pride from growing the produce that ends up on tables. As I got older, I kept digging into the dirt until my fingers bled. Now it's your turn. You want to learn about my farm, about *me*? This is where you start. I'll see you later."

And with that, she turned and walked away.

Fuck. This was not how Enrique had expected his day to go.

But a wave of guilt washed over him at his own disappointment. He was painfully aware of his privilege. He needed to be out here laboring with other farmers to truly understand what farm life was like, if he could ever hope to be a fair owner.

Why had he never done this before? This was a great way to find out firsthand about the real challenges farm employees faced, his included.

Manny spoke to him in Spanish. Despite Enrique's best efforts, he didn't understand him at all.

"Yo no entiendo," Enrique eked out. God, what a nightmare.

Manny nodded. He led Enrique to a row of strawberries, handed him a box, and wordlessly showed him how to pick the fruit.

Enrique crouched down. Manny's hands worked the crops like a machine. Enrique, however, was slow and awkward. As he looked out on the endless harvest, he tried to imagine what his life would be like if he had been born on the other side of the border. He was twenty-eight. Would he have had a wife and family to support by now? Would he have decided to cross in hope of a better life for them?

Manny was kind and patient with Enrique. For the next few hours, they picked. Then, as the sun rose hot on their backs, Manny finally signaled to Enrique that it was time to take a break. He reached into his lunch box and gave Enrique a bottle of water and split a chorizo burrito with him.

And it tasted better than any he had ever eaten. Was it because he was famished and so grateful for a warm meal? The foil it had been wrapped in was still hot to the touch and the chorizo was spicy and the beans were mouthwateringly delicious.

Lunch break ended as quickly as it came, and it was back to work. But this time, Manny escorted him out of the fields to a windowless building, where many female workers were packing fruit into boxes. At first, Enrique thought that this would be easier than picking the fruit, but he was sorely mistaken. The ladies were fast as their hands moved across the strawberries, sorting the good ones from the bad. At least the small warehouse had air-conditioning. Did the warehouses on the farms the Montez Group contracted with have proper ventilation? How did he not know the answer to that question? What a jerk.

After returning to the farm several hours later, this time to focus on artichokes, Enrique was spent. Those sharp little leaves hurt when they stabbed into his hand. He loved eating these little globes—grilled with garlic in between their leaves, paired with a lemon aioli. But he had never once realized how hard it was to pluck these prickly monsters from the ground.

Carolina eventually walked toward them; her skin glistened in the afternoon sun.

When he saw her, Enrique ran and hugged her like he was a Marine returning from war and she was his loyal wife back home. Her laugh melted some of the ache in his arms. She was a bright spot after a hard day's work.

"How'd you do?"

Enrique wiped the sweat off his face. "I'm not going to lie. That is some difficult work. I get why you wanted me to pick the fields first before talking about partnering with you—I needed to see how truly arduous this was. I'm just mad at myself for never actually working in the farms before."

She nodded at him; her eyes were bright. "Well, why would you have? You've never had to work if you didn't want to. When I read your email after Blanca showed me her reply, all I could think about was how entitled you were. A rich man from a successful company reaches out to a small farm and insists they give him a full tour, share their trade secrets, and partner with them? I couldn't imagine it."

He winced. "Yeah, I guess it was pretty arrogant of me."

"It was, but it's okay. You said you wanted to partner with an ethical farm, and that's all well and good. But that isn't the only point, Enrique. Your company is currently contracted with other farms that don't treat their farmworkers well. You need to fix those places. Those workers need you. You asked for my help, but you don't need it. You are smart and you have resources. Talk to the workers; listen to their complaints; provide them medical care. Get to know these people by spending a day on their farm every few months. And if the farms you work with don't comply, then don't work with them. And for fuck's sake, learn Spanish."

Enrique winced at her direct honesty. "You're right. I was looking for a quick fix. I'd heard that you treat your workers well, and I thought partnering with your farm and imitating whatever systems you had in place for your team would alleviate my guilt. But the only real way to evoke change is to operate from the ground up. Thank you for helping me realize this."

She grinned. "You're welcome."

He took her hand. "But it isn't true that it was just for the farm alone. After I read your article, I felt almost called to meet you. I've read lots of success stories featuring women, but I didn't drop everything to find any of them. I guess I wanted to feel more of what you invoked for me in that article. A sense of purpose."

She gleamed. "Well, I'm happy that I inspired you. I know you came up here to see the farm, and I've barely shown you any of it. Is there anything else you'd like to learn about my farm? What do you really want to know?"

Enrique exhaled. He had been running over this very thing in his head.

"I'll be honest . . . I don't want to make excuses, but I feel clueless when it comes to creating a safe and healthy environment for my farmworkers. Where would I even start? My father has always been about profit, focused on one thing—the money. But when he bought up a block in Barrio Logan, everything changed for us. We were just going to turn Julieta's restaurant into another one of our locations and replace the other local establishments with chains and box stores. But Ramón started dating Julieta, and then we all became part of her wonderful and humble family. Ultimately, Ramón gave stock from the company to Linda to preserve the neighborhood and its character, and now she owns the block. But something shifted inside of me, as well. I don't want to be rich, entitled, and clueless anymore. I don't want to just go through life explaining away every unethical and problematic thing our company does to justify margins. I want to be better than that."

Carolina brushed his shoulder. "Enrique, that's beautiful. *You're* beautiful. I love that you are trying to do the right thing, and I know it's hard. The previous owner of this farm treated us like shit. We all worked awful hours, were exposed to dangerous pesticides, and had no access to health care. Many of the people who work on these farms don't have any choice. They are here illegally; they don't speak English. What are they going to do? Tell the authorities? No. They'd get deported."

"I get that. They have no voice."

"That's right. We need people like you with both power and integrity to spark change. I'm only one farm owner, but with your wealth and reach, you could make a real impact. There is an entire subset of hardworking people who do this to provide a better life for their families back in Mexico. So, you want to be good and fair? You need to pay everyone a living wage to support them and their loved ones. You need to provide access to affordable housing. You need to not use harmful pesticides. You need to regularly provide them with medical care. Set up a tent on your farm and have doctors and nurses available—free and confidential."

"I know. There's so much to do. I don't even know where to begin."

"Start with one thing at a time. I feel like you know everything I'm telling you. Nothing I'm saying is new information in this industry. I know it's hard to do the right thing. You *will* lose money. A lot of it. Your profit margins will drop. You won't produce as many crops. The labor will be slightly more expensive. There are all sorts of barriers. But your company is huge. If you do this, you will set an example for the rest of the fast-food empires to follow."

Enrique exhaled like the wind had been knocked out of him. She was right; this all seemed so obvious now. But Enrique realized that he needed someone to make this so clear to him. He needed someone to believe in him, to listen to him. Support him. And someone to tell him that what he'd done in the past, though wrong, could be forgiven.

Someone like Carolina.

"Carolina, I've done so many things wrong in my life. I know you think I'm a good, respectful man, but I'm not. I'll be honest with you. I'm a slacker. Ramón always has worked his tail off, and I've ridden on his coattails. But the *worst* thing I ever did was not care. I never gave our workers or their conditions a second thought, not in the farms we contract with or in our restaurants. I bought into my dad's narrative that they were lucky to have jobs."

"It's never too late to grow. And to seek forgiveness."

"Thanks for everything." He paused. There was something about

Carolina that brought out the best in him. And he would never for-give himself if he ruined the chance of having a relationship with her. "So, about that date I mentioned earlier . . . Have you ever been to Carmel-by-the-Sea for Christmas?"

She licked her lower lip and tilted her head. "No, actually. But it's almost three hours away."

"I know. I was thinking we could go up there tomorrow. We can stroll through some art galleries, go shopping, have lunch. And look at the lights in the evening."

She paused. "Like spend the night? I can't do that. My father would flip."

Enrique shook his head. "No. We can just get up early and make it a day trip."

"Oh. Well, that sounds fun. Sure."

He wrapped his arms around this gorgeous woman and kissed her. "Then it's a date."

Chapter Eighteen

On Tuesday morning, Carolina suffered through yet another silent meal in her household. Her parents hadn't mentioned anything else about the other night that she had been out dancing. Her father was at a doctor's appointment, so Carolina only had to tolerate her mother.

Even so, the tension was excruciating.

"Mamá, pass the orange juice."

Her mother kept her gaze at the wall.

"Mamá! Pásame el jugo de naranja! Por favor!"

Mamá didn't move. Finally, Blanca stood up and reached over their mother to give the beverage to her sister. Carolina poured it from the carafe into her glass and downed it—the sweet and tart citrus was so refreshing; it was almost worth the humiliation she had to endure to drink it.

When would this nightmare end?

The rumble from an SUV engine echoed through the thin walls of the house.

Enrique had arrived.

Well, clearly, the drama would not end today.

He was under strict orders to remain in his vehicle—Carolina had already told him by text to wait in the Tesla.

It was time to escape.

Carolina excused herself from the table, not that anyone would miss her presence, and peeked out from the curtain in the living room.

After the way her parents had been treating her, they didn't deserve an explanation. But Carolina decided to try to be the better person and show them some respect.

"Mamá. Enrique and I are going to Carmel for the day to see the Christmas decorations. I'll be back later tonight."

Mamá pointed a wooden spoon at her that was covered in scrambled eggs. "Carolina Yvonne!"

"Oh?" Carolina laughed. "You can talk? I thought you lost your voice."

"Don't mock me, mija. Siéntate."

"I'm not sitting down. You won't even have a conversation with me, and now I should sit here while you yell at me for my own decisions? No. I'm leaving."

Mamá's face scrunched, and Blanca's eyes widened in horror. "Look. I know you like him, and we might forgive your behavior the other night, as a onetime courtesy. We don't want you to get hurt."

Carolina felt a softening in her chest. Her parents were looking out for her in their own way. But even so, their stonewalling was unacceptable. "I'm not going to get hurt, Mamá."

"I don't know about that. He doesn't even *live* here. What do you think is going to happen in the future?" Mamá asked, propping her elbow on the table.

"Nothing. I think nothing is going to happen in the future. And that's fine. We are getting to know each other now."

"Mr. Right Now is Mr. No Future."

Carolina didn't even bother to respond.

Mamá narrowed her gaze. "Don't be home too late. I mean it, don't push your luck."

"I won't. I'm aware that my curfew is eleven." She kissed Mamá on the cheek and rushed out to Enrique's SUV.

"Hey, sunshine." Enrique greeted her with a kiss and a coffee. The latte was as warm and sweet as he was. What syrup was that? Caramel? Ha—that would be a fun prelude to this day.

"Hola." She squeezed his thigh. Being in the car with him felt so normal.

He headed north, away from her family and toward freedom.

Carolina couldn't wait to see the Christmas decorations. She was grateful to have the company, and to spend more time with Enrique, but even if he weren't here, this was a perfect way to spend the day. Why did she never make time to do things for herself? This wasn't even her parents' fault—she could've taken Blanca and Adela.

Carolina needed to better prioritize her self-care.

She looked over at Enrique, confidently driving his SUV. This was his vacation, and she hadn't even asked about his family. Ugh, she had been so wrapped up in her own drama, she wasn't taking the time to get to know him.

"How's your family? I still can't believe they all came way out here because you wanted to meet me." She turned down the air-conditioning for her side of the SUV. There was also a booty warmer. This Tesla was fancy.

He smirked. "They're good. Well, it's just my brothers here and Julieta's family—her mother, Linda, and her cousins, Tiburón and Rosa. Actually, they all wanted to invite you over for Christmas Eve."

She shook her head. She could never miss celebrating Nochebuena with her family. "Oh, that's sweet of them. But I'll be with mine." Though the way things were going, she wasn't even sure if that was true. She considered for a second inviting him over but decided against it. They were not in a serious relationship. It wouldn't be appropriate. And it would give her father even more wrong ideas about them.

"What about your parents? They aren't here with you?"

His face tensed. "My mom is in Italy, actually. On a cruise with her boyfriend. My father, he's alone in La Jolla. We had a pretty big falling-out. Well, mostly he and Ramón did."

"Ah, that's so sad." She hoped that she would always remain close to her family no matter what choices she made. That they would never reject her like she'd feared they would the other night.

Like she feared now.

Enrique continued toward Carmel on Highway One, the most beautiful stretch of freeway with priceless views. The waves crashed against the rocks, and magnificent trees towered in the north. Carolina almost never took the time to stop and marvel at the ocean. Why was her entire life consumed by work and family? Where was the joy? She almost never left Santa Maria.

She touched Enrique's arm. He'd already learned so much about her life, but she didn't know much about his. "So, what's your life like down in San Diego?"

"Honestly, it's pretty laid-back. I live with Jaime. We wake up early to surf, and afterward I get in a workout or a run. I usually have something to do for work—I'll either go to the test kitchen or visit my small farm. Then I often hang out with Jaime and my friends, and we go out somewhere at night, like a new restaurant or a rooftop bar or catch a Padres game."

"Wow. That sounds like a great life." Carolina wanted to get out of her comfort zone and try new things herself, but it almost felt too easy. Did he do any community service? What about extended family? Like aunts and uncles? He had to have a big extended family—he was Mexican! Carolina wanted to pry but held herself back.

"I can't complain. What about you?"

She laughed. "Nothing like your life. I wake at five to go to the fields alongside our workers, but I'm usually checking the irrigation or the soil or the plants. I don't pick as much produce as I used to, but I will help out if we are short. Then I do some paperwork, which I hate, so Blanca does most of that. Sometimes I take a quick siesta. And then I'm back out on the fields. I go to a church group on Wednesdays, and I used to practice with my dance troupe a few nights each week, but I had to stop dancing last year because I was too busy with the farm. I attend Mass on Sunday. Any free time I have, I spend with my family. I help my younger sisters with homework, take them to their own lessons, and just play with them."

"You're amazing, you know that, right?" He leaned over and kissed her when they were briefly stopped for some road construction. "I'd love for you to visit me in San Diego someday."

She pursed her lips and remained silent. The best she could force out was a head nod. Elation burst in her chest for him mentioning some type of future with her, but fear resided right next to that emotion. He had specifically said that he did not want a long-distance relationship. Had that changed? If so, what did she want?

And what if she did fall for him? Badly? Like head over heels obsessed with him, checking her cell phone at all hours of the night waiting for texts from him obsessed? She had no idea how she would actually handle her emotions in a relationship. What if she lost her mind?

All she knew was that meeting him had given her feelings and glimpses of dreams that she didn't even know she had. She didn't want him to go.

But she had no choice. He was leaving; she was staying in Santa Maria.

A few hours later, they arrived in Carmel-by-the-Sea. Enrique parked several blocks away from the town square in front of the cutest storybook cottage. The thatched roof and pastel pink shingles made Carolina feel like she was in her own fairy tale.

Maybe she was.

Enrique took her hand and led her down the wide, sandy-colored cobblestone streets toward downtown. The streetlights were wrapped with Christmas bows, and the store windows were decorated with fake snow, bright lights, and holly.

He pointed at a brown brick building. "Let's go in here really quick."

It was the city hall. What did they need there? A marriage license? Ha—definitely not.

They walked in. A lady with gray hair and bright pink lipstick greeted them. "How can I help you?"

Enrique grinned at the woman. "We're here to get her a license for high heels."

Carolina laughed. "What? I always thought that was an urban myth!"

The lady shook her head. "No. It isn't. It's actually against municipal code to wear high heels without a license in our town. Not that it's seriously enforced these days, but the law is the law. What's your name, darling?"

"Carolina Yvonne Flores." She paused and looked at her boring, sensible tennis shoes. She hadn't wanted to overdress for the date, and now she felt foolish. "But I don't need a license. I don't have any heels."

Enrique winked at her. "Yet."

Oh, this man.

The woman filled out a big certificate and presented it to Carolina. "Thank you."

"You're welcome." She nodded at them and shuffled back to her seat behind the desk.

He led her outside. Carolina pulled on Enrique's arm and kissed his cheek.

"How did you know about that? You've brought another woman here, haven't you?" She gave him a playful side-eye.

He shook his head. "Yes, I have. My mom."

"Ah, that's so sweet."

"Now let's get you some heels."

She looked down again at her sensible walking shoes. "Oh, I'm fine. Really. I don't need anything."

"Come on, babe. You may not need them, but I'd love to buy something nice for you. Maybe some shoes you can dance in? And we could find you a dress to match."

"I suppose we can take a look." Carolina never shopped for new clothes, ever, unless she needed a new pair of Dickies for work. Blanca had all the pretty dresses in the world, but Carolina didn't have anyplace to wear nice outfits other than Mass. Carolina never splurged on herself. With the exception of a modest dress for church and sturdy dance shoes for practice, what was the point in buying clothes that she would rarely wear?

They strolled hand in hand through the shops and finally stopped at a boutique. But it wasn't just any boutique. This place was high-end. Chanel purses beckoned. Blanca would have passed out.

But Carolina wasn't Blanca. Carolina's stomach clenched. She didn't like luxury stores. She felt like a lone garlic bulb in a field of strawberry bushes.

There were rows and rows of pretty dresses, sexy shoes, and shiny jewelry. The clothes were even arranged in a rainbow ombre pattern from scarlet red to deep purple. It was like being trapped inside one of those home organizing shows that Mamá watched. Guau, her mother would love to have a closet that looked like this store.

"Get whatever you want." Enrique touched her shoulders, causing Carolina to shiver.

She examined herself in the full-length mirror next to a rack of sunglasses.

Carolina was wearing a plain white T-shirt and a long skirt that fell to her ankles. "I'm okay. It's a waste of money."

"Well, I'm paying, and I don't think it's a waste." He brushed the hair off her face. "You look gorgeous to me no matter what you wear. But indulge a little."

She pointed to a sundress with bright yellow lemons on it. "That's cute. I love lemons." Ay, Dios mío! Carolina cringed. She sounded like a fool. It was like Baby's "I carried a watermelon" line in *Dirty Dancing*. Why was she so awkward?

"You'd look stunning in that." Enrique signaled to a woman who worked there.

A saleswoman walked over to them from the back of the shop. She quickly and professionally assessed Carolina's body and then picked one of the bright dresses off the rack. "This should fit you. Shall I put it in a room for you, miss?"

"Sure." Carolina followed her right to the dressing room. The dark hair on her arms stood at full attention and her heart raced. Nerves and anticipation swirled through her—this whole day seemed like a fantasy, but it was tough for her to just live in the moment.

She undressed and slipped the dress over her head. The soft fabric caressed her body, accentuating her curves. She stared at her figure in the mirror. She looked . . . sexy. Carolina had never seen herself as sensual, but in this dress, in the soft, warm glow of the dressing room lights, she was a knockout.

The saleswoman had also placed some bright red pumps in the room. Carolina loved high heels and never had a problem walking in them, because she had spent so many years dancing with the Ballet Folklórico. Carolina's eyes practically bugged out of her head when she saw their bottoms, and she stroked the red soles—they were Louboutins, an identifying detail she knew about from Blanca's endless fashion magazines. Blanca dreamed of owning a pair one day. She would be so jealous. Luckily, they were the same size, so Carolina would let Blanca borrow them.

There was only one problem with Carolina's outfit—her underwear didn't work with the dress. Her broad, wide bra elastics showed under the thin spaghetti straps, and her panties were too dark.

She leaned out of the curtain. "Ma'am."

The saleslady walked back over to her. "Can I get you something else?"

"Yes. A bra and some panties." Carolina told the lady her sizes, and the lady went around the corner, returning later with an adorable matching yellow lace bra and thong.

A thong.

Her face crinkled. "Do you have anything with, uh, fuller coverage?"

"Of course, dear. But not in the yellow. Do you want to match the bra?"

Carolina did want to match the bra. It was such a cute set. She exhaled, stepping out of her comfort zone and into the lingerie.

She again looked at herself in the mirror. She practically couldn't recognize herself—a gorgeous young woman on a romantic day trip with a man whom she really liked.

She emerged from the room.

Enrique's eyes traveled seductively all over her body. "Wow."

He motioned for her to turn.

She twirled around, and even added a little dance kick. She felt like a princess.

He pulled her close and kissed her. "You're a smokeshow, Carolina."

She hadn't heard that term before. She didn't understand his SoCal surfer boy slang, and he couldn't comprehend her Spanish. But they shared one language that needed no translating.

Amor.

CHAPTER NINETEEN

Carolina looked stunning in her new dress and sexy high heels. Her legs were toned and tan. The way her hips swayed when she walked down the street caused him to literally salivate. But Enrique knew this "relationship" had been nothing but an unlabeled whirlwind. And things that started fast, ended fast.

What did he want? He was attracted to her, and by the way she grinned at him and acted nervous around him, he could tell she was enamored with him, but that wasn't enough. They didn't live near each other. They had different lifestyles, different ideas on everything from religion to relationships. While she was currently challenging her ideas about tradition and family, deep down, Enrique couldn't shake the thought that their lifestyles were too incompatible, and he would never ask her to choose between himself and her family.

But this was becoming more than just a hookup.

He was crushing on her, but with so many things stacked against them, his gut was telling him that this would go horribly wrong. Was he possibly considering a long-distance relationship? He knew how difficult and painful the distance would make their connection.

And, even worse, if this ended now, she had already created a rift in her close-knit family because of him, though clearly it wasn't just about their relationship—she was asserting healthy boundaries. Even so, he didn't want to be responsible for creating drama.

Enrique pushed his confusing thoughts away and focused on the day ahead.

"Are you hungry? What would you like to eat?"

She gave a sly smile. "Anything—but Mexican." Enrique laughed. He was such a cliché—Mexican food was his favorite type of food, but he, too, wanted something different after indulging in Julieta and Linda's nonstop cooking.

They looked at a few dining options, and Carolina picked a quaint French restaurant for lunch where she ordered the salade Niçoise and Enrique had steak frites.

Carolina swirled her blood orange soda in her glass and made direct eye contact with Enrique. "So, Enrique, do you date a lot?"

Enrique gulped down his own glass and cleared his throat. "Honestly, I used to. But not much lately."

She leaned forward. "Why? What has changed?"

He hated to be put on the spot. But clearly, she was trying to see what his intentions were. What were they, anyway?

"Well, I mean I was meeting women on apps."

She winced and his gut clenched.

She brushed her hair out of her face. "I understand. That's what people do nowadays. I'm not judging. I just have never understood that. How do you know if you have anything in common with some-one by a picture?"

Enrique stifled a laugh. Because he hadn't cared if he had any-thing in common with these women. They were hookups—plain and simple. He translated his thoughts into a more palatable answer. "I agree. You can't. I mean, there are profiles and personality questions that help, but it's usually based on physical attraction."

She nodded. "And you never found any nice women on the apps?"

Was she really that naive or just testing him?

"I'll be honest—I wasn't really trying to get to know them." Her face fell. Back in for the save. "I wasn't looking for anything serious—back then."

"And now?" Her fork pierced an olive, and she popped it into her mouth. Her full lips were so tempting.

"Now, I'm open to any and all possibilities." He pulled at his shirt. Was the heater on? Enrique considered diverting her attention to a new topic, but he had some questions of his own. "And what about you? Why have you never dated?"

Her eyes glazed. "Just too busy with work and school."

Enrique reached across the table and held her hand. "Nope. That's not just it. Your parents are clearly dying to marry you off—to someone other than me, but that's beside the point—and you'd do anything for them, so if you truly wanted to, you would. Even if you were busy. So, what's the real reason?"

She turned her attention back to him, then looked down toward her feet. Her voice softened. "You're right. I could say that it was that I never met anyone I liked, and I guess that's partially true, but I never really looked, either."

Enrique wasn't going to let this go. He was incredibly curious about why this beautiful woman had never wanted to date anyone other than him. "Because . . . ?"

"I don't know."

Enrique knew he shouldn't push. She didn't know, and that was fine. But he was dying to understand her. And more importantly, figure out if she was just using him to rebel or actually liked him as a person. "That's fine if you don't. I'm sorry, I don't mean to press. You're hard to read sometimes, and I'm just trying to figure you out."

Her fists clenched. "Okay, fine. I guess it's that I just never saw myself married or as someone's wife, and, in my family, dating leads to marriage. Hookups aren't acceptable."

"You *can* date someone and not marry them. Marriage shouldn't even be on the table for a long time." Two years at least, in his opinion. Enrique was shocked at how soon Ramón proposed to Julieta, but they were happy. Who was Enrique to judge?

"I know, I do. In a perfect world, that makes sense. In my family, it doesn't. Marriage to me represents a loss of independence. I don't want to be some man's property—go directly from my father's iron fist to my husband's."

A bitter taste filled Enrique's mouth. It was so tragic that not only Carolina but other women still felt this way today.

"I'm really sorry, Carolina. For the record, I don't see marriage like that. In a perfect world, it's a partnership between equals. Not that I know what I'm talking about—my divorced parents haven't been a great example of marriage." Uh, open mouth, insert foot. This whole conversation had been a disaster.

Time to change the subject. He moved their exchange into safer territory—"So tell me more about your sisters; how many are there?"—and he was thankful she followed his lead.

Enrique noted to himself that he needed to be damn sure he wasn't playing any games with Carolina.

After they dined, they strolled into a gallery featuring a local artist. She bought a piece of landscape artwork depicting a field of bright strawberries, which she refused to let him pay for, and he picked out some New Age spiritual books.

It was a breezy and beautiful day, minus the awkwardly intense lunch conversation. She laughed at his silly jokes, and he enjoyed showing her around one of his favorite towns.

Finally, the sun began to set, illuminating the sky with a stunning orange hue. It was time to see the Christmas lights. Enrique grasped her hand, and they weaved in and out of the streets, stopping at the charming cottages. One house had transformed into a life-size gingerbread house—the owner had added fake giant, colorful gumdrops to the yard and even blanketed the roof in faux snow.

Carolina's eyes widened. "Wow! That's so cool!"

Enrique leaned over and gave her a soft kiss. What a fun day.

But unfortunately, their date was almost over. Enrique had to take her home.

Exhausted after a day of sightseeing, they finally grabbed some coffee at a local café.

Carolina sipped on her peppermint latte and snacked on a cookie.

Enrique looked at his own watch. "Babe, it's eight. Do you want to go back home? The clouds are moving in quickly and it's supposed to rain later, so we should probably hit the road."

"I don't want to leave." She pursed her lips. "I'd love to stay all night, but I can't."

"Yeah, that would be great. But maybe we could come back again sometime." *Like next year.*

Where had that thought come from? He was supposed to be only wanting one week. But things with Carolina were rapidly progressing.

"That would be great." She smiled.

"Let's go," he said, leaving a generous tip on the table.

He pulled out Carolina's chair, gave her a kiss, and walked her back to the car. He looked over his shoulder, pulled out onto the road, and drove out of downtown.

The rain drizzled down nonstop, and the traffic was backed up for miles.

If he was with any other girl, he would've asked her to spend the night in Carmel-by-the-Sea with him and then head back tomorrow. But he had sparked enough tension with her father—the last thing he wanted to do was add fuel to the flame.

After an hour of almost no movement stuck behind a truck with a broken bumper, Carolina was biting her nails and tapping on her phone.

Enrique checked his phone for a weather update. "Hey, sorry about this. I checked the forecast before we left. There was only a slight chance of rain. We'll give it twenty more minutes."

"It's okay. It's not your fault. Blanca says it's storming at home, too."

Another twenty minutes turned into an hour. The rain came down heavier, and there was even a brief bout of hail, the rocklike ice pounding on the windshield.

Then a navigation alert came across his vehicle.

Warning. Flash Flooding. Roads Closed Ahead.

Oh fuck.

This was supremely bad.

Carolina's lip quivered as she frantically typed on her phone. "It says they closed the road out of here. We won't be able to get home."

Stay calm, Enrique. "I can just turn around and we can go back on the main freeway."

She pulled up a map on her phone and showed it to Enrique. "But that will take five more hours, and in these conditions? Is that even safe?"

Enrique took a deep breath. "Carolina, I promised I'd take you home, and I meant that. I will."

She shook her head. "No. This is insane. The only reason you are trying to get me home is because of my father, right?"

"Pretty much." Enrique ran his hand through his hair.

"Well, staying the night is the only logical option."

"I could get us a room here. Or two rooms of course, if you like. But I really don't want to make any more trouble for you."

Carolina's hands shook. "You've been a perfect gentleman since I've met you. I don't think your intention was to trap me in an unexpected storm and force me to spend the night with you. But I suspect my parents are going to assume this was our plan and the reason you wanted to take a day trip with me."

Enrique's stomach churned. How awful. "Carolina, I would never."

"I know you wouldn't. I do. But I need to call them."

She dialed home. "Mamá. I know—

"Yes, we're caught in the storm, the One is closed—

"Yes, we can go around, but Mamá, we won't be home until almost morning.

"It's not safe—I should stay here—"

He watched Carolina's eyes widen as she listened to her mother on the phone, her mouth a perfect O. "What? No, of course not. How could you even say that—are you serious right now?"

Enrique's stomach churned.

"You've got to be kidding. I am spending the night here for my safety and Enrique's. It's not like that, and you know it! You're being ridiculous.

"Fine, Mamá. Whatever you say. Who cares about my reputation anyway—I don't want to get married. Bye." She hung up, tears streaming down her face.

Jesus. "I'm so sorry. This is all my fault. What did she say?"

Her lip quivered. "She said that if I don't come home tonight, to never come home again unless we get married."

What the fuck? "Married? Is she serious?"

"Yup. And if I spend the night with you as an unwed woman, I'm dead to them."

"That's insane. They can't mean that." He tightened his grip on the wheel.

"Oh, they do. I get that it sounds dramatic and literally unbelievable, but my parents take my perceived purity very seriously. It's ridiculous. You haven't even seen the half of it in my traditional family. My abuelo did the same thing to my Tía Luísa. She spent the night with her boyfriend and was never allowed back into the home."

"Really? That's awful. Do you ever see her?"

"Never. I have fond memories of her as a child. She took me to Disneyland once. The only time I ever went."

"I'm sorry your grandfather did that to her. And to you. She lives in Barrio Logan, right?"

Carolina's eyes widened; a momentary look of happiness crossed her face. "Yes, she does. Do you know her?"

"I do, actually. She owns the café next to Julieta's restaurant. Your aunt is beloved by the community. And she makes the best conchas."

"That makes me so happy. Maybe I can come visit her."

"I'd love to take you."

Carolina's brief distraction seemed to be replaced by the reality of the situation. She exhaled loudly. "I'm so sad they would do this to me."

Enrique's brow wrinkled. "Don't you own the house? Can they legally kick you out?"

"I do own it, but no. I consider it *their* house. I know it's hard for you to understand." She shook her head and bit her lip. "I'd never ask them to leave. I love them—family is complicated."

Wow, guess so. Enrique wouldn't hesitate to cut off his family if they did that to him. "I don't know what to say. I'm sorry."

"Honestly, I'm relieved."

"What? Why?"

She gulped, her voice in a somber whisper. "Because I don't want to go get married. Not anytime soon, if ever. I'm so young. I just want to be free." She placed her hand on his thigh, a smile emerging on her flustered face. "I like you, Enrique, I really do, but this isn't about you. This is about me. And I want to be independent. I want to be able to spend the night in Carmel, or go skinny-dipping in the ocean, or travel. As for the farm—I'll figure it out."

Enrique exhaled. "I feel like shit. This was not my plan. You have to believe me."

"I do." She grinned a little too wide. "So, where are we staying tonight?"

CHAPTER TWENTY

Awave of apprehension overtook her as she still clutched her phone and turned away to look out the window. Enrique's presence was calming. He had been a perfect gentleman. Still, she couldn't believe she was actually going to spend the night in a hotel room alone with a man. She closed her eyes and could hear her mother's words repeat in her head, cruel insults that she had previously reserved for girls in the community who slept around. *Whore, puta, sucia.*

Tears welled in her eyes. What was she doing?

Enrique squeezed her hand and looked over. "You okay?"

She gulped. "No. But I will be."

Enrique turned forward again to give her some quiet as they drove along the coast.

Carolina stared out at the water and its dark glory. The stars shone in the sky and reflected off the rippling ocean. The peaceful moon peered through the violent clouds. If only she could borrow some of that moon's tranquility.

Enrique pulled up to a quaint hotel on the rocky cliffs overlooking the beach. The A-frame was painted a bright boysenberry color, and the shingles on the roof had moss growing on them. It didn't seem to her like the type of place that Enrique would normally stay in, but it suited her just fine.

"Sorry, this was all I could get at the last minute. There's a nice lodge a few miles away, but they're booked."

"Why are you apologizing? This place is lovely." She smiled at the neon sign in the window that glowed under the huge bulb Christmas lights hanging from the roof. "I'm not like that, Enrique. I don't need the nicest hotel or the most expensive restaurant. I can pay if you like."

He shrugged. "No, of course not. Sorry. I guess I'm used to girls equating how much I spend on them with how much I like them because I have money."

She smirked. "I'm not rich, by any means, but I can take care of myself. I take care of my entire family, too."

Enrique put his thumb under her chin. "You're incredible."

She bit her nails. "Do you mind if I stay in the SUV while you check in?"

His brow furrowed. "Why?"

"I need a moment alone. Just check in. I'll wait here."

He kissed her again and went inside.

Carolina fired off a text to Blanca.

Carolina: Hey. Has Papá flipped?

Blanca: Uh, yeah. He keeps pacing around the room saying he no longer has ten daughters.

Carolina: He's so dramatic.

Blanca: Yeah, it's awful. Tiburón is here trying to calm him down. It's not working though.

Tiburón was there? So late? Wow, he must be really serious about courting Blanca.

Carolina: Sorry you have to deal with this. Love you, Blanca.

Blanca: Love you, too.

Carolina called her father's phone, knowing he wouldn't pick up. Once the voice mail answered, she left a message.

Papá, I know you're upset, but I did nothing wrong. I was caught in a storm, and it was too dangerous to come home. I'm an adult now, but I'm still the same daughter you've always loved. I'll see you when I return. Love you.

She hesitated and, after a moment, turned her phone off. She did not want to spend the rest of the night fighting with Papá. It would be better for both of them to calm down and talk in the morning.

Enrique returned a few minutes later with a key and two toiletry kits.

He helped her out of the SUV and led her to their room. When he opened the door, Carolina gulped.

There was one king bed in the middle of the room. She would definitely be sharing a bed with Enrique tonight.

Enrique glanced at the bed. "I'm sorry—they didn't have two queens. I can sleep on the floor if you feel more comfortable."

She shook her head. "No. This is just fine." She took a cautious step into the room and turned her attention to anything but the big bed that beckoned her. She fondled the pretty framed photos of seashells and admired the calming coastal decor. If Carolina ever moved out of her family's home, she would have a place decorated just like this.

She stood in a corner under a lamp, shifting from side to side. She didn't know what to do or what to say. How, at twenty-three, was she so sheltered that she had never been alone, truly alone, with a man?

She counted her blessings that she'd met such a patient one as Enrique.

Enrique stared at her with hunger in his eyes, but he didn't make a move, didn't push her for more.

Instead, he simply said, "I'm going to take a quick shower, if that's okay."

"Sure." She grabbed the remote from the nightstand and perched herself at the end of the bed, trying to find something to distract herself from the fact that Enrique was about to be naked with only a thin wall separating them. She heard the water come on and imagined his hard body—the water running down his chest, his muscular thighs. She tried to force the image out of her head, but it was impossible to turn off.

He emerged from the bathroom wearing the clothes he'd had on earlier. A surprise twinge of sadness passed over Carolina. She had hoped he would come out with just a towel on or at least nothing but black boxer briefs.

What was this man doing to her? She normally didn't fantasize about men, but she couldn't stop imagining Enrique kissing her, his strong body pressed on top of her soft one, his lips kissing down her chest. And she wanted to explore every inch of him.

She wiped a bead of sweat from her forehead. Flushed from the wicked way her mind was headed, she realized how sticky she felt after walking around all day and sitting in the car.

"I'm going to take a shower, too." She dashed into the bathroom, where his sandalwood scent still lingered. She took off her clothes and stepped into the steamy shower, the very place where Enrique had been naked just a few minutes prior. As she rubbed the vanilla-fragranced bath gel all over her body, she studied her curves.

She had always believed that her body was built for hard work, though her parents believed its purpose was to someday have kids.

But another thought passed through her head.

It was also built for pleasure. Despite what she had been taught by the Church, she truly believed that making herself and her partner feel good wasn't a sin.

She rubbed her nipples, and they hardened. The thought of Enrique kissing or even sucking on them sent heat between her legs. What would that feel like? Would she grip his hair, twist it between her fingers as he brought her to the brink of pleasure? Would his hardness throb against her stomach? Her hand dropped between her thighs, in between her warm folds. She imagined his tongue licking her.

Was she ready for this? For him?

Carolina turned off the water, considered grabbing a robe, but instead put her clothes back on and walked into the bedroom.

Enrique's eyes raked over her, but he didn't move from his cross-legged sitting position at the end of the bed. "I, uh . . . Look, I don't know what you want or feel comfortable with. You're gorgeous, and I'd love nothing more than to show you just how much I want you, but as I've said, I don't want you to feel pressured. I'll keep my distance, or we could just cuddle, or I really could sleep on the floor if you like."

Ah. Warmth filled her chest. He was just the sweetest. But she didn't want to hold back. She didn't have a reason to hold back. She didn't necessarily expect to lose her virginity tonight, but what was the harm in indulging in a little fun?

"No, I don't want you to sleep on the floor. I want to sleep wrapped in your arms—my head pressed against your chest." She sat next to him at the edge of the bed.

He gulped and his eyes widened. "Carolina, I . . ." His voice was husky and deep. "Are you sure? We really don't—"

She pressed her finger to his lips. They had done enough talking. "Kiss me, mi amor."

His cautious smile turned into a sheepish grin. He kissed her lips, softly at first, and then with each kiss the intensity grew. His tongue probed her mouth as he cupped her face. These kisses were more dangerous than the previous times their mouths had met. They weren't in front of a hospital, or on her farm, or in public. They were alone. In a hotel room. There was no need for them to stop.

Her belly ached. Was this really happening? How far were they going to go? Did she actually want to have sex tonight? Did he have protection?

She pushed all her thoughts out of her head. She wanted to be in the moment. Enjoy what was happening now. The stubble on his face grazing on her neck, the pressure of his hand on the swell of her back, the heat of his breath and hers commingling in the air. Yes, the beauty of this innocent budding love. She had dreamed for years of what this scenario would look like, and it was finally happening, and she wanted to savor every moment.

His teeth lightly gripped her lip and she moaned. He whispered into her ear, "Do you know how sexy you are?"

She most certainly didn't but refused to derail the moment by launching into a diatribe about how she was shocked that he found her so attractive. Instead, she let out a nervous laugh. "Glad you think so. I think you're so hot."

She put her hands under his shirt and traced his muscles. His chest was so firm—she wanted to see it bare. She wanted to lift his shirt off but decided to wait. Maybe he wanted to undress her first? She didn't know the rules on these things. Were there any? God, she was a mess.

He wrapped his arms around her back, his lower hand rubbing

her bottom, and his kisses became harder and rougher. She slid her hands all over his body and rubbed his cock through his jeans. She could feel his hardness press against her and sensed how badly he wanted her.

And she wanted him, too. What would it be like to feel this man inside of her? Would it hurt? Feel good? Both? Would she really bleed everywhere? Would that freak him out?

Carolina! Stop!!!

She needed an intervention from her thoughts. The only thing that seemed to work was focusing on him.

So that was what she planned to do.

She leaned back on the bed, which caused Enrique to flash a dazzling grin. He slid beside her and pressed his body on top of hers. One of his hands interlaced with hers and he pinned the other above her head. That was so hot. Carolina was in control of so much of her life—well, clearly not her living situation, but her farm and her finances were hers to manage. It was so nice for this man to take the lead. The more he kissed her, the hotter she got. She writhed under his body, her core aching for him. So, this was what it was like—this raw, insatiable desire. She wanted more. She wanted him in every way possible.

She tugged on his belt buckle, but he pushed her hand away. Uh-oh. Had she done something wrong?

He kissed her again. Hmm. Maybe he just wanted them to take their time. That was cool.

She kissed him more aggressively. As her lips made their way down his body, she pulled up his shirt and planted a kiss right above his waistline.

He reached down to grab her hand in his and looked into her eyes. "Babe, as much as I want you, I think we should stop."

CHAPTER TWENTY-ONE

Carolina's bottom lip trembled, and she pulled her hand away from Enrique's. "Oh, okay. Did I do something wrong?"

"No, babe. Not at all. I just think we're going too fast." Enrique couldn't believe the words that were coming out of his mouth. Too fast? What was he even saying? He'd spent his entire life going fast. Why was he rejecting a beautiful woman in his bed?

But the answer was abundantly clear. It wasn't just that she was a virgin—though that was a factor—but because he didn't want the responsibility of taking her virginity when they weren't officially boyfriend and girlfriend. Nor was it the most romantic evening— they were in a cheap motel by his standards after she'd had a blowout fight with her parents that left her in emotional turmoil.

No, his hesitation was still for an entirely different reason.

He liked her.

What if there was a future for him . . . with her? But she lived so far away, and who knew if she'd suddenly change her mind and run back to her family? Though was that even a possibility given their recent argument? She didn't seem to be that confident that her family would get over this.

Having sex could hurt her.

What if she was unintentionally using sex as a final act of revenge toward her family? What if he was just a tool?

Damn, he was such a sap.

"I thought that's what you wanted? I mean, if I wasn't a virgin, we'd have sex tonight, right?" she asked. "Not that I'm saying I'm ready for that right now. But we don't have to limit ourselves to just kissing..."

"Carolina, you just had a huge fight with your parents, who told you to never come home unless we got married because we were in a storm. You must be feeling super emotional right now. I don't want you to sleep with me as a way to prove that you're independent."

She gulped and turned away from him.

Enrique winced. He didn't want to cause her further anguish or make her feel rejected. He stroked her hair and forced himself not to run his hands over her body again. But damn, did he want to. He wanted to suck on her nipples until she screamed his name, slip his fingers between her luscious thighs, lick her pussy until she could do nothing but come and come for him.

He was starting to even *like* the fact that she was a virgin. Just the thought that he could be the first man to ever bring her pleasure enraptured him. And shocked the hell out of him.

What if he was the only man to be with her ever?

He'd never felt like this before. It must be some sort of primal thing beyond his control. At the same time, he couldn't help but think the fact that her innocence turned him on so much made him a bit of a douche. The only guys he knew who were obsessed with virgins usually were controlling pricks. He generally wanted a woman who already knew what she wanted in bed. Was he holding her virginity against her?

God, feelings were so *complicated*.

This was why he'd struggled in relationships—all this thinking and turmoil and teasing was so goddamn hard.

"Hey." He kissed her cheek and turned her toward him.

"Hey," she said softly.

"Let's just get a good night's sleep, and we can see how we feel tomorrow. We can drive back home, or if you decide you really don't want to go home, or can't, we can spend another night here or back in Montecito." He paused. "Or you may decide after you wake up that you want to talk to your dad. I don't want to be the reason you stop speaking to your family. I don't want to be something you regret."

She exhaled, squeezed his bicep, and gave him a soft and gentle kiss. "You're right. I'm so sorry. You must think I'm a complete and total mess."

He shook his head. "No, I don't at all. I just think you have a lot going on right now. Everything is happening so fast with us."

She placed her hand on his chest. "But I like it. Enrique . . . I can't explain it. Ever since I met you, I've been feeling all these things that I'd only heard about from Blanca."

"I haven't felt like this in a long time." And he didn't want to feel like this with a woman that he had no future with.

Could he make this work? Long distance would be too hard. He couldn't leave his business, and neither could she. What was he supposed to do?

She cupped his face and kissed him softly before lying down beside him, her back against his chest. "Good night."

He pressed a kiss into her hair. "Good night, babe." He wrapped his arms around her, his hard cock pressing into her plump ass. This was blissful torment, emotionally and physically.

She drifted to sleep in his arms while his mind raced. He had to figure out his feelings fast, before he headed back to San Diego and regretted fucking up a possible future with Carolina.

The next morning, Enrique woke first. He snuck out of bed and opened the window. The salty ocean breeze mixed with Carolina's sweet vanilla scent.

He checked his phone. A few missed calls last night from Tiburón and an early-morning text from him as well.

Tiburón: Dude, what are you thinking? Did you kidnap Carolina?

Enrique: Funny, but no. She's with me though. We're in Carmel.

Tiburón: Her dad's going to kill you. Like seriously. Good luck, man. I'll pray for you.

Enrique was pretty sure Tiburón was joking, but he couldn't be certain.

Carolina was curled into a tiny ball, her black hair fanned out on the white sheets. She was breathtakingly gorgeous—and Enrique was a complete fucking idiot for not at least trying to sleep with her.

Before long, she blinked one eye open, and then buried her head in the pillows.

He sat at the edge of the bed. "Morning, sunshine. How did you sleep?"

She stretched and smiled as she looked at him. "Great, actually." She crawled out of bed, went to the bathroom, and then came back to sit on the bed.

Enrique handed her a water bottle from the mini refrigerator. "So, what do you want to do today?"

She took a swig of water, then grabbed her phone. Her eyes scanned the screen, and then her face fell. "We can stay around here if you want? I'm not welcome at home. Sorry to be such a burden."

Ugh, his stomach coiled. This must be so hard for her. "Hey, I don't mind at all. Are you sure you don't want to go home?"

"Yeah, I'm sure."

She checked her phone—again. And shook her head.

Enrique had to ask. "What did he say?"

"Nothing. But my mom told me not to come home."

Enrique was surprised that she was shocked by their reactions. And as much as he wanted to be there for her, this was very intense for such a new relationship. "What do you expect? He's pissed."

She nodded. "Oh, I know. But radio silence is the worst. I'd almost feel better if he was yelling at me."

He frowned at that.

She bit her lip. "Can I ask you something?"

"Anything." He sat next to her.

"What's going on between us? Are you really going to go back to San Diego and that's it?" She fidgeted with the strap of her dress as she looked at the sheets.

Enrique exhaled. Though he was wrestling with these same thoughts, he didn't know the answer. And he hated to be put on the spot. "I don't know. I mean, maybe we don't have to put a time limit on this. I like you. A lot."

She met his eyes and smiled. "I like you, too. And to be honest, I want to see where this goes."

Enrique gulped. Did he want that, too? He stared into her eyes and took her hand. He was certain he wasn't ready to end this. But was that enough?

He took a calm, centering breath. And in that moment, it became clear.

He wanted that, too. "I do, too."

She grinned. "Really?"

Was he doing this? Did he want to try a long-distance relationship with Carolina? Enrique hadn't had an actual girlfriend in years. Friends with benefits, fuck buddies? Sure. But not girlfriends. He was open to seeing where this might go with Carolina, though. Committing to her didn't scare him; if anything, it excited him. And maybe the security of being in a relationship would make her more comfortable. They could both give this a real chance of working out. They could see each other on the weekends. Perhaps once a month he could justify a weeklong trip out to this part of California as a part of his efforts to improve farmworkers' rights, visiting his own farms.

"Really. Will you be my girlfriend?"

"Hmm," she teased. "What does that entail?"

He softly pinched her arm. "Well, we'll see where this goes. I won't date anyone else, and neither will you."

"That seems fair." Her gaze lowered. "But you have the raw end of the deal. I've never dated *anyone*, so it's not like I'm giving up anything. I'm sure you've been with hundreds of women."

Enrique winced. He didn't want to lie, but he also didn't want to make her feel insecure. "Look, my past is my past. Right now, you're the only woman on my mind." He twirled a lock of her hair. "So, is that a yes?"

She wrapped her arms around him. "Yes!"

Enrique pushed her down on the bed and climbed on top of her, and they made out like teenagers.

Her breath sped up in between her moans.

Nope. Not like this.

He pulled away, leaving her breathless, her cheeks pink.

"If we are spending some time up here, let's go to this other hotel. It's one of my favorite places. There are more things to do there."

"I'd like that."

He made a reservation at the Carmel Valley Ranch, a place where he had made some good childhood memories with his brothers. His mother would drop them off at the all-day camp while she would go to the spa. Ramón, Enrique, and Jaime played tennis, took golf lessons, rode horses, and even learned about honeybees.

They quickly tidied up the room, which was easy because they hadn't brought anything, checked out, and drove into town to buy some extra day clothes and get a light breakfast.

In the early afternoon, they pulled into the resort, which was a few miles inland. Though it didn't overlook the coast, this lodge was incredible. It was rural and rustic, almost like a grand farm.

He gave his car to the valet and checked in with the front desk. The bellman took them in a golf cart to their room.

Enrique exhaled. This was more like it.

They had a huge suite, overlooking hiking trails. And a private hot tub on the deck. Deer grazed on the hillside behind them, and couples teed off on the golf course down below.

Carolina ran through the room and sat in front of the fireplace. "Wow, you weren't kidding about this place being great. It's like a castle."

He brushed a lock of hair back off her face. "And you, my dear, are my queen." He kissed her. This place felt right. If they were going to actually sleep together tonight, he wanted to spoil her first. But he had no expectations about how far she wanted to go—he would let her set the pace. "Let's get massages."

Carolina's face crinkled. "I've never had one. I don't know how I feel about some stranger touching me. Will I be alone? Do I have to be naked?"

He shook his head. "You can leave your panties on if you are more comfortable. And we could get a couple's massage if you like. Or you can have a solo one. You work so hard—I think you'd really like it."

She threw her hands up. "Okay."

He booked them massages together in a couple's suite.

After their session, they showered in their respective spa rooms and met up in the lounge.

"Wow, that was really great. The woman worked this knot out of my back that's been there for months. How often do you get massages?"

Enrique didn't know if he should admit that he got them weekly and even had a massage room with an ocean view at his place. "All the time. I'm glad you liked it."

They walked back to their room and changed into their new clothes. After a romantic dinner overlooking the lavender fields and dining on local seafood and farm-to-table delicacies, they finally retired to their room.

Carolina walked over to the private deck and turned on the Jacuzzi, the bubbles starting to bounce in the water.

Enrique followed her and brushed his hand through the water. "That looks nice, but I don't have a swimsuit."

"Neither do I," she said with a smile. She held his gaze as her sundress fell to her toes. She was standing there in nothing but the new bra and panties and heels he'd purchased at the store. The yellow lace barely covered her nipples, and the thong accentuated her perfect ass.

Enrique wanted to fuck her against the hot tub until she screamed his name. But again, he reminded himself that he needed to go slow.

"You sure? I can run down to the gift shop and buy us swimsuits."

She shook her head. "No, Enrique. I just don't want to hold back anymore. I want you." She unhooked her bra and took off her panties, revealing dark curls between her legs. The sight of this beautiful naked woman caused his cock to spring to attention.

She carefully slipped out of her shoes, stepped into the tub, and sat down.

He'd assumed she would be shy, but apparently that girl was gone.

Well then! Enrique stripped down, his cock at full attention. Her mouth opened at the sight of his naked body. He grinned and then slipped into the bubbles and sat next to her.

Enrique was about to kiss her when she straddled his thighs.

"Are you sure you want to do this?" he asked.

She kissed him. "I'm sure."

"Carolina . . . you're so beautiful."

He kissed her neck, and she tossed back her hair. His cock was pressed up against her soft belly. He so desperately wanted to be inside of her.

Her hands rubbed all over his body, and she hesitantly touched his throbbing cock underwater. Her delicate fingers felt incredible with the current from the jets.

Her nipples were glistening from the water, and he sucked on one. She moaned as he touched her pussy, sliding a finger inside of her while thumbing her clit. God, she was tight.

"Enrique. That feels so good."

He smirked. "You haven't seen anything yet." He lifted her to sit on the edge of the tub, spreading her legs as he knelt on the seat inside.

She shook her head and closed her legs. "Oh, I don't know if I'll like that."

He laughed. "Yeah, you will."

She bit her lower lip. "Do you like doing it?"

"Babe, I've been dying to eat your pussy since I met you."

Her jaw dropped and her cheeks seemed redder, but maybe that was from the heat of the spa. "Enrique! That mouth!"

He grinned. "My dirty mouth speaks the truth. Now spread your legs and relax."

She cautiously opened her legs.

Time to feast.

Enrique grasped her waist and planted kisses in between her thighs. Then he slowly licked her, savoring her sweet taste. He licked and licked again, picking up the pace. She was quiet at first, then her hand dropped and rubbed the back of his head.

"Ay, Enrique. Wow."

He licked her sweet clit as she came alive under his mouth. Her body trembled, and he'd never seen anything sexier in his life than watching her above him.

Her breath came more rapidly, and her chest began to heave. She was so fucking hot, and she tasted like sweet sex. The fact that she had never been with anyone but him, that no one had ever made her moan, drove Enrique wild. This was his woman and *only* his woman.

What if he was the only man to ever touch her? Ever?

He pushed that thought out of his head.

"That's my girl."

Enrique pressed his finger into her beautiful pussy. It was so damn tight. He couldn't wait to feel her clench around his cock. But for now, he just wanted to make her come.

He sucked on her clit as he worked her pussy. He could sense that she was close, but he was in no rush. He could eat her all night.

Her thighs trembled and Enrique pressed his tongue flat against her.

"Ay, Dios mío!"

She came all over his face, and he lapped up her juices. After catching her breath, a gorgeous smile graced her face as he pulled back, loving the beautiful sight in front of him.

"You're right. I loved it."

CHAPTER TWENTY-TWO

*W*hoa.

Carolina was breathless and more satisfied than she'd ever imagined.

That had been incredible. Why on earth had she waited twenty-three years to give in to pleasure? Was it because she hadn't met the right man? Or some deeply internalized Catholic guilt that made her think she was going to hell?

Instead, she had experienced a little slice of heaven. And she wanted more. Now that she had a taste of sin, her mind raced. What would it be like to be in an actual relationship with Enrique? To see him daily, kiss him every morning, make love to him every night? And though they were both so different, they did have a lot of things in common. They both loved their family and were interested in farming. And clearly their sexual chemistry was off the charts.

Enrique retrieved them both towels and led Carolina back inside. She quickly changed into some lounge clothes she had purchased earlier in the day.

The night had become cooler. He turned on the fireplace and they curled up on the sofa. Carolina couldn't remember ever being so happy.

A slow pitter-patter of rain began on the roof. The sound grew louder, and it reminded Carolina of the ticking of a clock.

Or maybe that was her heart beating.

Carolina checked her phone, but there were still no calls or messages from Papá. She had to tell him the truth about Enrique—that he hadn't been her boyfriend, though now he actually was her boyfriend. And more importantly, that her goals had changed. She was ready to stand on her own.

One decision became clear to her—she wanted to get her own place, away from his watchful eye. Well, at this point, technically, she was kicked out of her home, so she had no choice, but even if he hadn't forbidden her from coming home, she was certain that she wanted some privacy, not just because of Enrique, but because she really wanted to live alone.

But standing up to her father could cost her everything. Her reputation, her honor, her family, her farm.

Ay, Dios mío. The farm.

Her farm meant everything to her. She had fought so hard to buy it, worked ceaselessly in and after school to raise the funds. And she had done good, meaningful work. She was proud of how all the farmworkers were treated there.

But was it enough? Just to have one ethical farm when so many people around the state were being treated horribly?

What if she could expand her reach? Invest in a new farm? Change the lives of others? A real impact on the lives of farmworkers.

She closed her eyes and said a quick prayer for guidance. She needed to think about her career aspirations long and hard when she wasn't so overwhelmed with her personal issues.

She opened her eyes back up and caught Enrique's gaze. As much as she just wanted to relax and watch a movie with him, she needed to confront her father.

Her belly ached. "I'm going to call my dad."

"Good luck. I'll be in the other room if you need me." Enrique kissed her on the cheek, then grabbed her hand and gave it a squeeze before he walked into the bedroom and shut the door.

Carolina dialed. The phone rang and rang; Carolina's nerves jumped each time. Papá didn't answer, so she left yet another message, this one with a profuse apology, in Spanish for extra points. "Papá. Call me. We need to talk."

Carolina was shocked when a few minutes later, he called back. Maybe the groveling had done the trick.

"Papá. I'm sorry I didn't make it home last night, but I did try. It was not intentional. It was a flash storm."

"Not intentional? You went on a road trip with a man alone. No chaperone. You disgraced us in front of Tiburón. There are rumors that you ran off with this man because you are pregnant!"

She stifled a laugh. How ridiculous. She was still a virgin. Well, technically. But maybe she wouldn't be for that much longer. Would that truly be so bad?

Not to mention, she'd only met him a little over a week ago. Even if they'd slept together on that first night, it would be too early to tell where things were headed between them.

"That's crazy. People can talk all they want. I'm a good woman. I have not disgraced you or the family. But I need some freedom. I want to live my life on my terms."

Her father let out a loud huff and a wheeze. Carolina's heart dropped—was this stress exacerbating his medical condition? "Your terms, mija? You meet this man, this pendejo, and suddenly you ruin your life? Our lives?"

"He's not an idiot. He's kind and handsome and loving." She stopped herself before she revealed to her father how much she was infatuated with Enrique.

"Loving! He has no respect or honor. And neither do you! You spent the night with him! And you are still with him now. ¿Verdad?"

Her voice lowered. This was her moment of reckoning. She lowered her voice to a whisper. "Sí, Papá. I am. But I didn't do anything wrong."

"You have ruined me! You have ruined my name. And the reputations of your sisters. Do you think any decent man will date them now?" His voice broke. Were those tears?

As angry as she was, she had compassion for her old man. She knew that this was heartbreaking for him; it shattered the traditional life he'd known for so long. "No one will care, Papá. It's the twenty-first century. We live in America and I'm an adult. I own the farm. I should be able to take a day off and spend time with someone I'm dating."

"Those are not the rules, and you know it. I don't care what other girls do. You are *my* daughter. And you have brought shame on me and our family. You cannot come home."

Rage seethed inside of her. "So, what? You're kicking me out of our home—that *I* bought? Off the farm that *I* own? Right before Christmas?" The emotional turmoil of this happening just before the holidays was almost too much for her.

"You spent the night alone with a man in a hotel. About to be two nights. You aren't married. It's unacceptable. You know this."

"But I love him, Papá!" she gasped.

He gasped right along with her.

Oh my God! What had she said? The words had flown out of her mouth before she'd even realized what she was saying. How could she love a guy that she had only known for a few days? She didn't, couldn't love him. She was sure of it.

But how would she know if she did anyway?

What was love? Her parents claimed to love her but didn't hesitate to throw her out on the streets for spending a night with Enrique. Was *that* love?

Carolina was practically obsessed with Enrique. She couldn't stop thinking about how sexy he was, how kind he had been toward her, how he made her insides tingle. She had been resisting giving in to this fantasy of a future with him, but she couldn't stop herself anymore. Was *that* love?

No. It wasn't. It was lust. Infatuation. But definitely, most certainly not love. Love is a choice. Love grows. Love involves commitment.

What a delusional fool she was.

"Does he love you, too?" His voice was quiet.

"I don't know."

"Well, if he loves you, then he can marry you and save your reputation and our family's name. If not, I don't ever want to see you again. I will not have such a horrible role model around the rest of my pure daughters."

Carolina cringed at the word *pure*. How misogynistic. But before she could call her father out and get a final word in, the phone went dead.

Carolina tossed it across the room and began to cry. The sobs came rapidly. She tried to stop them. She knew her father was dead serious about his threat. He could hold a grudge. Her life as she knew it was over. Everything she had worked so hard for was gone.

Sure, she could kick her family out of the home and farm, since she was the legal owner, but she would never, ever do such a thing. No matter how awful her dad had just been to her, she could never throw her family out. She just didn't have it in her to displace her sisters from their school or her parents from their home.

He'd never allow her back around her sisters—not unless Enrique married her. And what hope was there of that? They'd only just met. Not that she even wanted to get married. She definitely wasn't ready now, and she wasn't sure she would be ever.

She could buy a home nearby and still work on the farm, but how could she go to work every day and not be allowed in her home? Would she walk by her family and look the other way? No. That would be torture. What if Baby ran up to her for a hug—would her little sister be scolded for talking to Carolina?

No matter how she looked at it, all these options were terrible.

Enrique knocked on the door. "Can I come out?"

OMG. Had he heard her say she loved him?

She slowly opened the door, scanning his face for some signal as to what he heard. He didn't seem shocked, so maybe he hadn't heard her confession, but she decided to ask to be sure. "Did you hear our fight?"

He shook his head. "No. I was watching TV. I wanted to give you privacy. What did he say?"

Even the thought of telling Enrique what her father said was horrifying. She tried to speak, but only a sob came out.

He placed his arm around her. "Don't cry. It'll be okay."

She shook her head. "No. It won't. My father reminded me never to show my face again unless we got married."

Enrique grimaced. "He'll calm down. I'll go over and talk to him."

"He won't calm down. The town will gossip about him, about me. His reputation in Santa Maria is *everything* to him. He would rather disown me and be seen as a hero for casting out his slutty daughter than accept me back with the scrutiny."

Enrique turned her face to him and held up his hand. "Stop. You are not a slut. Don't ever say that again. I hate that word—women aren't sluts for enjoying sex. Sex is natural; you did nothing wrong. I need you to believe that."

God—he was too good to be true. Carolina was waiting for the other shoe to drop. "I mean, rationally, I realize that. But it's hard to get over a lifetime of indoctrination."

Enrique shook his head. "Maybe I'm naive, but I can't comprehend how traditional your father is. Pardon me for saying, but is this tradition or abuse?"

Carolina gulped. Her father's behavior was definitely unacceptable. "I don't know. It's just how it is." Maybe she did need to go to therapy. Well, if she didn't have Blanca around to commiserate with, who would she talk to? Definitely not Enrique. He would never understand her family. And she didn't want to tell him her concerns about him.

"Well, not my place, but his behavior is not okay. You really think he won't budge about you going home? That's brutal." He grabbed her a box of tissues and rubbed her back.

"I'm positive. I've known this about him since I was a little girl. Perhaps one day he'll forgive me, but when? And look at my Tía Luísa—her father never forgave her. And my father, her own brother, won't let us see her."

"I'll take you to see her."

"I'd like that."

Enrique ran his hand through his dark hair. "I hate to say this, Carolina, but you don't need him if he's like that. I know he's your father, but you bought the farm on your own. You raised the money. You could take it from him, and even if you don't want to—which I understand—you could buy another farm. You have options."

"Any option that involves not being able to see my family is awful." Carolina felt trapped, like her world was caving in on her. She knew what her father demanded was completely fucked-up, but she wanted her farm. She wanted her family. And she also wanted Enrique. But those things were mutually exclusive. They weren't possible unless she and Enrique got married.

They sat in silence around the hearth and Carolina stared at the fire. It was almost poetic—the smoldering embers looked so enticing and warm, just like how good the idea of being with Enrique had seemed, but the closer she got to the flame, the more certain she was that she was about to get burned.

Chapter Twenty-Three

Jesus. Did Carolina really love him?

He hadn't been trying to eavesdrop, but she had literally screamed those words so loudly to her father that Enrique couldn't help but hear them.

How could that be possible? They hadn't known each other for that long.

They were infatuated with each other, sure. In lust with each other. But was that love?

That Van Halen song that Ramón used to play on his guitar during his metal phase blasted in Enrique's head. "Why can't this be love?"

Was there a timeline on love, anyway? Ramón had fallen fast and hard for Julieta. His father had known he was in love with Julieta's mother in less than a week, but that had been a disaster. Then his dad had dated his mother for a full two years before they'd gotten married, and that hadn't worked out, either.

In his own life, Enrique had fallen in love a few times. Each time, he'd known he was in love months before he'd had the courage to tell his partners.

There was his high school girlfriend, Taya. But they had one of those first-love situations. Taya meant the world to Enrique—she was kind and sweet and loved to go surfing with him. They were each other's firsts. It had been a blissful teen love affair, but they had decided to break up before college. Enrique had held out hope that one day they would reunite, but she had eventually fallen in love with her college sweetheart, and they had recently gotten married.

In college, Enrique had dated Ruby. She was fun and quirky and nothing like Taya—or Enrique, for that matter. She had grown up in Mariposa, California, and loved to be outside and hike. They had a great relationship, but she didn't want to be tied down and ultimately ended things. Enrique was crushed but figured it was for the better because they were graduating. She now had a successful YouTube travel channel and lived in a van.

And lastly, there was the beautiful Alisa. They had dated for a couple of years after college. His attraction to her was purely physical, and ultimately, he ended the relationship after he finally realized that he didn't feel they truly connected on his core values. She was a bit too materialistic for his taste. And though he definitely had a taste for the finer things, when he tried to realign his life goals, she wasn't receptive to him wanting to focus more on giving back to the community.

Since then, Enrique had just casually dated. And he had been fine with that.

Until he met Carolina.

But Carolina hadn't told Enrique she loved him; she'd said it to her father. Maybe she was just trying to justify spending the night with Enrique to her dad—that made perfect sense. Enrique was almost entirely responsible for trapping them up here. Granted, he'd checked the forecast before they left that morning, but he shouldn't have risked taking her somewhere a few hours away from her home.

Enrique had a deep emotional connection, intellectual curiosity, physical chemistry, and respect for Carolina. When they talked about their families or even the farm, she seemed to really share his core values on what was important in life. Not money. She was wicked smart, and he was still blown away by her business acumen and creativity, especially in starting that farm-to-table delivery service during the pandemic. He found her body wildly intoxicating— her curves, her curly hair, her soulful eyes. When she kissed him, it just felt . . . different. More intimate. And he admired her. She was such a great woman. If she saw good in him, it would make him a better man. And he would love to support her in all her endeavors.

Was that enough to build something lasting? Maybe.

But he was certain he wasn't in love. Not yet, anyway.

They had agreed to date for now, but they still hadn't smoothed out the details. They didn't live in the same place. Hell, Carolina currently didn't live *anywhere* if she wasn't allowed to return home.

How would this ever work?

After relaxing by the fire for a bit, Carolina had said she was tired. She had seemed to shut down after her conversation with her father. Enrique didn't want to further pressure her or add to the intensity of the night, so they settled in for a quiet evening. Enrique wrapped his arms around her and stroked her hair as she stared at the fire. They finally retired to bed, where she fell asleep in his arms.

Enrique woke early the next morning. Carolina was still asleep, so he snuck into the bathroom, took a quick shower. Then he went on the deck, did a few sun salutations to ground himself, and called Tiburón, who picked up on the first ring.

"Homie, you done fucked up. Her dad is livid. He won't even speak her name in the house. Blanca is so upset."

"I know. Carolina is upset, too. She thinks he's seriously not going to let her back in the house."

"He's not."

Ugh. This was really bad. "At least you're making headway with Blanca."

"Yeah, I'm courting her. Respectfully. It's not that hard, man. All you had to do was have a civil dinner with her family and ask to date her. And not spend the night with her. Why couldn't you do that? If she were my daughter, I'd knock you out."

Great to know that Tiburón was on his side.

"Because I wasn't even trying to date her in the first place. And those archaic rules are stupid and misogynistic. Even so, I showed up when she lied and said I was her boyfriend, and gladly met her parents. But you were there. Carolina's a firecracker. I hadn't even asked her out, and she didn't want to go through with that charade, either. But she's the one who left home and blew off her family and their rules. Granted, I did invite her to Carmel and probably should've planned a date closer to her home. It was a totally messed-up situation. And she's great. I'm crazy about her. And if she really wanted me to, maybe I would've eventually played her dad's games despite my feelings about them, but she didn't want to be held to his standards anymore. Not just in dating, but in *all* aspects of her life. She doesn't want to feel like she has to marry me because we go out on a couple of dates."

"Whatever, bro." Tiburón sighed. "You didn't just go on a few dates with her. You spent the night with her."

"Come on—now you're defending him?"

"No, I'm just saying that you didn't take her to Starbucks or a movie, man—you spent the night with a woman from a super traditional Mexican Catholic family. I just want you to understand exactly what happened. She's not one of the girls you meet on Tinder."

Enrique sighed. "I know that. But we were in a storm. It wasn't safe to drive back. I offered."

"I get it. I do. But *you* don't. To her dad, it's all about honor. He feels like you disrespected him."

Enrique could not understand it no matter how hard he tried. He wasn't trying to disrespect anyone. Not Carolina, not her father—no one. He just wanted to take a day trip with a girl he liked. Wasn't it that simple? "I don't know what I can do."

"Marry her." Tiburón laughed.

Enrique gulped. "Not that."

"Well, all of this made it easier for me. They love me compared to you. They don't even care that I did time."

Great. This was the first instance in Enrique's life when a woman's family despised him. "Well, I'm happy for you."

"You do realize that we came up to Santa Barbara for *you*, and you ghosted us this whole trip. Everyone else is still back in your house. It's the holidays. Where are you, anyway?"

"Carmel-by-the-Sea. But we're coming back today. We will spend Christmas Eve together, I promise." Enrique paused. "I don't know if she's going to try to go back home. She may come with me."

What would Christmas Eve be like with Carolina and his family? It would be his first holiday season with Julieta's family, so Enrique didn't even know what to expect. Carolina didn't cook, so he would be the one assisting Julieta and Linda in the kitchen, which was fine by him. Maybe Carolina could hang out with Rosa. And then Enrique and Carolina could take a romantic walk on the beach and snuggle by the firepit.

"Can't say that I blame her. I'll catch you later, dude."

"Bye, Tiburón."

Enrique ended the call. He walked back into the bedroom and sat by Carolina, who was now awake. She curled up by his side. "Morning."

"Morning, sunshine. So, I'm going to check out in a bit and then we'll start driving back to Santa Maria." He kissed her forehead.

Her face paled.

"Or you could spend Christmas Eve with us."

"Definitely the latter." She gulped. "I can't even believe that I'm not going to spend Nochebuena with my family."

He had never really traditionally celebrated Nochebuena, with the exception of his nanny teaching him to make paper poinsettia flowers. He was so disconnected from his culture that sometimes he felt like he wasn't really Mexican. How could he ask about it without sounding like an idiot?

"How do you celebrate?"

Her face lit up. "Well, my mom, her sisters, and my sisters would make tamales. I usually got out of it because I'd perform with the Ballet Folklórico. There would be mariachis at the performance. When we'd get home, we would drink atole and each open one present." She gulped and her voice became laced with sadness. "It was really wonderful."

She paused over the word *was*. "Do you want to go home?"

She shook her head. "No. I don't want to ruin my sisters' holiday by making it a big fight with Mamá and Papá and me."

"Well, I'll be honest. I never celebrated it. My parents were usually on vacation, so we stayed with our nannies. They thought presents were good substitutes for love. But Julieta and her mom have planned to have it at our home. Not sure exactly what they are going to do, but Julieta is an incredible cook, and they go all out for holidays, so it will be fun."

She nodded and looked down.

Enrique lifted her chin with his hand. "Spend it with me?"

She grinned. "I'd love to."

They packed up the few things they had brought or purchased on this unplanned trip, grabbed coffee and Danish from the hotel café, and then checked out.

Highway One was still closed from the storm the other night, so they took the 101, which didn't have as nice of a view. Instead of miles upon miles of the glorious rocky coast and driving through one of Enrique's favorite places in the world, Big Sur, they were relegated to views of asphalt and wall-to-wall traffic and tacky billboards. Not to mention smog instead of the crisp ocean air.

The drive was, well, awkward. Carolina stayed mostly silent, surely processing and planning for her future.

A future that Enrique hoped to be part of.

But what would that look like? Would she move to San Diego? Buy a farm down there? Work on his? Get her own place?

Though Enrique was crazy about her, he felt strongly that Carolina needed to stand on her own and not jump from her father's house to his.

And how would she cope with being cut off from her family? Enrique needed Ramón and Jaime—no matter how often they fought. He couldn't fathom a life without them.

A wince of sadness spread through him. Though he didn't agree with his father's actions, it must be hard for his dad to be cut off from his sons. Maybe he would reach out when he returned.

Enrique didn't regret coming to Santa Maria, but he had to admit that in entering Carolina's world, he had blown up her life.

But he believed that these tumultuous events, no matter how much they hurt, were meant to be. And that he and Carolina were destined to be in each other's lives.

Maybe it was crazy enough to work.

Chapter Twenty-Four

Enrique parked his SUV in front of the blue-shingled beach house in Montecito. He exited the Tesla and opened the door for Carolina.

Nerves swirled inside of her. Instead of celebrating with her own family, she was here at her new boyfriend's oceanfront second home for Nochebuena, a holiday he didn't celebrate. Enrique was Mexican, but their backgrounds were vastly different. The guy was about as SoCal surfer as you could get. He didn't even speak Spanish, which wasn't his fault. So many Mexicans didn't speak Spanish because their parents and grandparents had tried to assimilate. Then their children and grandchildren had to struggle to learn their native tongue and be accepted among fellow Mexicans.

Still, the fact remained that they had wildly different lifestyles. He woke up early every morning to surf; she rose with the sun to sow seeds. Why was she delusional enough to think that this could possibly work out?

But, as she assured herself over and over again, her newfound freedom and independence were only sparked by him, not because of him. Yes, she had been comfortably complacent in her rigid ways, but for a long time she had secretly wanted more. Every time her father had nagged her about when she would meet someone, she had just politely told him that she wasn't ready yet, instead of saying what was really on her mind. She had even set this whole course in motion by lying to her dad about Enrique being her boyfriend. Had she never felt that pressure, she wouldn't have done that.

But then again, she wouldn't be here with Enrique now. And she was really enjoying spending time with him.

Until now, there had never been a valid reason to disrupt her life.

She caught a glimpse of herself in the car mirror. Her hair was frizzy, and her skin looked blotchy. Would Enrique be embarrassed by her? This was the first dinner with his family. And since her family had disowned her over this situation, his family's approval was important.

He studied the expression on her face and put his arm around her. "Don't be nervous. Everyone is super chill."

Ha. Chill. Her family was the exact opposite of chill. But she didn't want to rewrite them in her memories as villains. Her home had a lot of love and warmth. She loved singing songs by the fire and making up silly dances with her sisters. And her parents weren't awful, despite their recent actions. Her father loved to make funny accents when he read stories to her younger sisters, and her mother was never too busy to soothe a boo-boo or give a hug.

The cold hard truth was that she loved her parents.

She could never replace them.

Carolina wore a brand-new red dress that she had just purchased for herself. It was modest and long and suitable for a holiday dinner, but still formfitting. For the first time, she wanted to be seen as sexy. Enrique had again offered to buy her clothes, but she didn't need his money. She didn't need him, either—she just wanted him.

She had briefly been introduced to his family at Las Posadas but had been so flustered about her father's health that they didn't have time to get to know one another. And she had met Tiburón at her house but had spent most of her time outside with Enrique.

Tiburón opened the door. A momentary flash of shame flew over her. Had he heard the horrible things her parents said about her? He was properly courting her sister—what must he think of her spending the night with Enrique?

He smiled and gave her a big hug. "Hola, Carolina."

His warmth put her at ease. She didn't sense a hint of judgment from him about her fight with her family.

She hugged him back. "Hola, Tiburón."

He grinned. "I figure we will be celebrating many holidays together."

She pursed her lips and tried to interrupt his words. Was he thinking he would be with Blanca, so she would see him because she was her sister? But that didn't mean anything, because she could be forbidden to see Blanca. Would Blanca stop communicating with her? Would they buy burner phones to maintain their relationship like the Hernandez sisters did when their father kicked Juana out when he found out she was pregnant? God, all this drama in her traditional community sounded like a telenovela.

Or did Tiburón mean that Carolina would be with Enrique, so she would see him because they were soon to be related by marriage?

The only thing that was clear was that she was overthinking.

"That would be nice. How's Blanca?" She shuddered. She was asking a man who she barely knew how her own sister was. Tiburón had spent more time with her family in the past few days than she had.

"She's wonderful. I dig her." He took a step back, gestured down the hall, and motioned for her to come in.

Carolina's eyes zoomed in on the view, which was by itself enough for this place to be breathtaking. The interior was painted in light blue and white tones with natural wood accents. And it was decorated in a pretty coastal style—there was a rope-encased mirror, seashell accents, and wicker baskets galore. It wasn't as big as she had imagined, but it was still glorious. The deck looked out over the ocean, and there was a firepit and Adirondack chairs beckoning her.

The scent of cinnamon and cloves lightly spiced the air. Though this house smelled similar to hers, everything else was different. There were no young children running around, no dogs barking, no noises from the farm.

This was a house—hers was a home.

But it wasn't hers anymore.

Maybe it was time Carolina bought a home of her own—a cozy coastal casa.

An older woman with her hair in a tight bun embraced her. "Carolina, nice to meet you. I'm Linda, Julieta's mamá. And this is my niece, Rosa." She pointed to a gorgeous young girl who had to be her sister Blanca's age. Rosa waved, then turned her attention back to Jaime, who was playing a video game on a white fabric sofa. This definitely wasn't a home lived in year-round—Carolina couldn't imagine keeping that couch clean.

"Mucho gusto. Thank you for inviting me to join you to celebrate."

"Of course, mija. Don't mention it. We're honored for the company."

Once Linda was out of earshot, Carolina whispered to Enrique, "Is Jaime dating Rosa?"

Enrique laughed. "No. Definitely not. My younger brother has always been a player."

Carolina nodded but paused on the word *player*. Wasn't Enrique a player also? What made her think that despite his actions and words this wasn't just a game for him? She knew he could get practically any girl he wanted. What was he doing with her?

She looked up at him and his smile calmed her anxiety. It was just so hard to trust that his intentions were good. Carolina was, however, grateful that Blanca was interested in Tiburón and not Jaime. Even though Blanca was a bit boy-crazy, her sister was a good woman who wanted to be in a serious relationship. From what Enrique had told her about Tiburón, he seemed to fit the boyfriend bill.

Julieta walked over to them. "Hey, Carolina. Nice to see you again. So glad you can join us. I made tamales and buñuelos." She pointed to a table with a white Christmas-themed runner with appliquéd poinsettias adorning it. Carolina could see serving ware filled with rice and beans. "Would you like something to drink? Ponche?"

"I'd love some, thank you."

Enrique rubbed her back.

Julieta returned with a cup of the warm liquid. The aroma surrounding it made Carolina nostalgic for home.

Carolina took a sip. Wow. This ponche was unlike any she'd ever had, and she considered herself a ponche snob.

"This is so good! It has a tart taste I'm not familiar with. What's in it?"

Julieta grinned. "Oh, I use tejocotes. They are simultaneously sweet and sour. Super hard to find, but I discovered an orchard in Julian that supplies them for me. I brought them up for the holiday."

Carolina liked this woman already. Tejocotes were a small stone fruit that tasted a bit sour, kind of like a guava-laced bitter apple. She loved the colors of them—they could be variegated shades of orange, yellow, or red. She had only had them once when she found them at a specialty grocery store, and she had been curious about them ever since.

Why had she never considered growing them?

"Where is Julian?"

"It's about an hour or so east of San Diego. In the mountains. I love it up there. I go every fall for apple picking in their orchards. There is even snow there in the winter."

That sounded like so much fun. There was so much of this beautiful state to explore. She was excited to leave the confines of Santa Maria. Carolina smiled and imagined going down there with Enrique and picking the lush fruit from the trees. And Carolina had never seen snow. Maybe they could visit. It would be so fun to take Baby! She could make a snow angel.

She took another sip of ponche, drinking down the pain knowing that she might never be able to take Sofía anywhere again.

"Wow. That's so cool. I don't know anyone who grows tejocotes locally." Her mind started racing. Her farm grew the standard crops for the region—lettuce, strawberries, tomatoes, garlic. She used innovative drought systems and didn't rely on toxic pesticides.

But she had never really broken the mold. Tejocotes were super expensive in the United States due to their rarity and the border importation restrictions. With the cartels threatening food inspectors, Carolina wondered if there would be a market in the United States for growing them along with other specialty Mexican crops. There had to be! If other Mexicans tasted this ponche, the demand would be high!

But it wasn't just about the tejocotes. Carolina realized that there was an entire world of opportunities for her in farming outside her current farm.

"Dinner!" Linda called everyone to the table.

Ramón shut his laptop from a desk that was overlooking the ocean. He kissed Julieta and then greeted Carolina. Tiburón carried drinks in from the kitchen, assisted by Jaime, who waved at Carolina.

Jaime smirked. "So, Carolina, you're the reason that we're celebrating the holidays up here. My brother was obsessed with meeting you."

Enrique punched Jaime on the bicep. "Obsessed is a bit strong."

Jaime laughed. "It's all good. I like Santa Barbara. Glad you could join us."

"Thanks for having me."

Rosa helped her tía bring the tamales.

Enrique pulled out a chair for Carolina. After she sat down, she gripped his hand on the table and he put his other on her thigh.

Carolina nervously glanced around. Were they going to bless this food?

When Enrique picked up his fork, she knew she had to act fast.

"May I say grace?"

Enrique dropped his fork and nodded toward Carolina.

Linda smiled. "Please do."

"Bless us, O Lord, and these Thy gifts, which we are about to receive from Thy bounty, through Christ our Lord. Amen."

Everyone said amen, even Enrique, but he fidgeted a bit in his seat. Had she made him uncomfortable? She hoped not. It was just a blessing.

But then again, it was okay if he was. She was uncomfortable. They were so different, and if there was any chance of this—whatever this fledgling relationship was—working, they needed to learn about each other's similarities and differences.

Carolina filled her plate with pork tamales, beans, and rice. Her fork pierced into the masa, and she brought the first bite to her mouth. *Wow!* These were the best tamales she had ever had!

She'd better not tell Mamá.

But the second that thought graced her head, her heart fell.

Would she ever taste her mamá's tamales again?

Chapter Twenty-Five

Enrique's first Nochebuena had been great. There'd been excellent food, he'd been surrounded by family, and he had even had a date to kiss under the mistletoe.

After dinner, Enrique exchanged presents with the rest of his family. He had always received gifts on Christmas morning but had since learned that many Mexicans celebrated on Nochebuena instead. Julieta had gifted him some rare epazote seeds for his garden, Tiburón had crocheted him a scarf, and his brothers had pitched in and purchased him a new hand-crafted surfboard that was made specifically for the San Diego waves, with an ornate Aztec trim.

He leaned over to Carolina. "Maybe I can teach you how to surf?"

She shook her head. "That's a hard no. I hate sharks."

Tiburón scoffed. "Watch it, Carolina. I feel a special affinity toward my namesake animal."

She laughed. "No, but seriously. My primos forced me to watch *Jaws* when I was younger, and I never recovered."

Enrique stroked her hair. "There hasn't been a shark attack in La

Jolla since 1959. Up in Del Mar—ten minutes north, there was one the other week. Where I surf, it's really safe."

"Still a no from me."

Enrique laughed. "That's cool—no pressure. But I think you'd like it."

When Enrique had realized that Carolina might not be going home for Christmas Eve, he had snuck away to the gift shop in Carmel to get her a present. There hadn't been too many options, but he purchased a pretty butterfly necklace with matching earrings.

Once they were alone in the room, he took out the small wrapped box.

Her eyes lit up. "Enrique! You didn't have to get me anything."

He grinned. "I know. But I wanted to. Open it."

She carefully unwrapped the box. "Oh, mariposas! I love them. Gracias."

"You know, the butterfly represents rebirth. Carolina, you can do anything. I know you are struggling with what is going on with your family, but I want you to know that you are amazing, and I believe in you."

Tears welled up in her eyes, and she kissed him. He placed his hands under her ass and lifted her up, wrapping her legs around him. She ran her fingers through his hair and kissed him madly. Enrique was wild for her.

He laid her down on the bed, pressing his hard body into her soft one.

"Enrique, don't stop. I want you. All of you."

He didn't want to stop—but he forced himself to. Not like this, with his family in the next room. If she really did want to have sex with him, he wanted to make it special for her.

"Babe, let's wait. We are in no rush. Let's get a good night's sleep, and we can maybe go somewhere tomorrow."

She gulped and nodded. He kissed her good night, and she fell asleep in his arms.

The next morning, Enrique rolled over to cuddle Carolina, but she was not in his bed.

Where was she?

He quickly dressed, brushed his teeth, and exited his bedroom. Carolina was standing on the deck with a coffee mug in her hand. Wind blew her hair in her face and also caused her long dress to ripple like the waves below them.

He poured his own cup of joe and joined her. "Morning. Merry Christmas."

"Feliz Navidad. Hope I didn't wake you?"

He shook his head. "No, you didn't." He took a sip of his coffee—it was good, but he missed the local shop in his neighborhood. He had to tell Carolina that he had to go home, but he wanted to ease into it. He would miss her if he left now. And more importantly, he wanted her to come with him.

"How are you feeling about things with your family? Have you decided if you want to go home?"

"I haven't made any long-term decision, but I think that it's best if my parents and I both have some space, a bit of time to calm down. Maybe I'll try to talk to them again after New Year's to avoid disrupting my sisters' holidays. I can just stay in a hotel or an Airbnb until I figure it out."

Enrique nodded. "That sounds like a good plan. I intended to leave tomorrow to go back home with the rest of my family." He paused. "You're welcome to come with me if you want to, but if you want to stay up here, I understand." He didn't want to pressure her into coming, and he also wasn't ready to plan their future at this moment.

Would they visit each other on the weekends? Since she was fighting with her family, would she consider moving? He didn't want her to make life decisions because of him—but he did want to make concrete plans to see her. He had asked her to be his girlfriend, after all. "Have you ever been to Disneyland during Christmastime?"

She pursed her lips and shook her head. "No, actually. And I've only ever been there once, years ago with my Tía Luísa when I was a little girl."

"We could go there today. I can take you wherever you want after our time in Disney." Hopefully back to San Diego with him, but he wouldn't press.

She blinked rapidly. "Actually, I'd love that. You really want to go today?"

He grinned. He had never taken a girlfriend to Disneyland. "Yeah, let's go."

"Okay!"

He kissed his beautiful woman.

Enrique made sure his family was cool with him bailing to Disneyland on Christmas, but they assured him they were fine and would just enjoy the last day in the home and then head back to San Diego. Julieta made them some breakfast burritos, and Enrique and Carolina hopped in his SUV for yet another road trip.

They took turns choosing the music—she was open to listening to his punk-pop music selections, and Enrique tolerated her endless stream of Selena.

After a leisurely drive down the coast, where they stopped at a few beaches and took some pictures, they arrived in the afternoon and checked in to their hotel. After freshening up, they entered the park. Enrique bought her some Mexican floral Christmas Minnie Mouse ears, and they strode around the park.

Christmas at Disneyland was always breathtakingly beautiful, especially at night. The huge tree was strung with multicolored lights, and there were red bows hung on the poles.

They enjoyed some rides and walked hand in hand, finally making their way to Disney California Adventure.

"Look! They have Ballet Folklórico dancers here!"

Rows of dancers wearing ornately colored gowns walked in a procession and then began to dance to traditional Mexican music. Carolina studied their movements intensely.

"Wow! They are really good!"

They looked great to Enrique, but he didn't have a clue how to judge their ability. Their full skirts flew in the air and waved around their bodies. The men's steps were sharp and joyful. Enrique laughed when the men would simultaneously drop their hats in front of the women's mouths to pretend that they were kissing them.

He gave Carolina a real kiss.

Enrique ordered them two Mexican hot chocolates and a plate of churros, and they sat on nearby chairs. The parade came by, with the Three Caballeros dancing on an elaborately colored stage flourished with Talavera tiles.

Carolina stared at the multicolored lights lining the street. "Wow, it's magical during Christmas—it's so amazing that they honor our culture. Have they always done this?"

"I think they have for a while—I know they do a big thing for Three Kings Day." Enrique had once come to the park in January having no knowledge it was Three Kings Day, another Mexican holiday he didn't celebrate, and there had been a big parade.

"I wish Baby could see this." Her words were laced with sadness.

"Well, you can bring her someday."

She nodded. "I hope so. Papá may never let me see her again."

"He'll come around." *But he may not.*

Carolina tapped something on her phone and then stared at it.

"I don't know. Blanca hasn't even texted back."

"Well, you just texted her. Give it time."

"That's like the fourth text I've sent today."

Enrique was trying to help her stay positive, but it was pretty obvious her parents were not budging. But even Blanca? "There has to be an explanation. It's Christmas. Maybe they are busy."

Carolina shook her head. "We don't celebrate on Christmas—we give gifts on Christmas Eve. They are ignoring me."

Enrique's stomach clenched. Their courtship might've ended Carolina's relationship with her family. Forever.

A photographer approached them. "Can I take your photo?"

"Sure." Carolina stood, a forced smile on her face.

Enrique hoped he could take her mind off her family. He finished his churro and then stood up.

Enrique and Carolina posed, and after the first flash, Enrique wrapped an arm around her waist, dipped her back, and captured her mouth in a Disney-worthy kiss. Someone wolf whistled, but when they straightened up and he saw the smile on Carolina's face, heard the laughter from her lips, he felt . . . *love*. This was magical. This was perfect.

She was perfect.

He twirled her around one more time and she stared intently at the dancers.

"I wonder how they find their dancers?" she asked.

Enrique shrugged. "No idea. Have you ever wanted to dance professionally?"

She nodded. "Yeah, as a little girl. But I was always focusing on school and the farm."

He held her close to him. "Carolina, you're young. It's never too late. You could find out and possibly dance with them."

She shook her head. Her brow furrowed and she placed a finger on her cheek.

"That would be crazy. I didn't go to college to be a professional dancer."

"No, you went to college to grow as a person. To learn how to think for yourself. To expand. You would've never accomplished what you did with your farm or at those speaking events without college." He wanted to make her understand that she didn't have to spend the rest of her life doing what she was supposed to do. "And now you're questioning everything because you see things differently. Your family's traditions, what you want in life, what makes you happy."

"You're right." Her face tilted toward him. "I honestly don't think I could be a dancer, but maybe I could do something different with the farm. Or start another one."

"You could be anything. You know, Ramón wanted to be a musician; Jaime wanted to play professional soccer. Both were great, but my father wouldn't hear of it. They were both expected to go into the family business. Like I was. And who knows? Maybe they would've failed . . . but what's wrong with going after your dreams?" He paused. "I never found a true passion like they had, though I've always liked to cook. And grow things. For me, the most important thing was to live my life with no regrets and try to be a good person. And be happy. My parents were so miserable. And for years Ramón was stuck on this endless cog. He was a workaholic just like my father. But I didn't want that. I just wanted happiness. And peace. And love."

She placed her hand on his face and kissed him, his stubble grazing her cheek. "You're truly exceptional, do you know that? I've literally never imagined a man as kind as you. This has been the best night of my life."

He smirked. "Well, it's not over yet."

CHAPTER TWENTY-SIX

Enrique booked a room for them at the Grand Californian. Carolina didn't even want to know how much it cost but was certain it was a near fortune—this place truly was grand like its name.

It reminded her of the Ahwahnee lodge in Yosemite, a place she had visited only once when her parents had taken the girls camping. She hadn't stayed there, just been inside the lobby, but she remembered it vividly. Just like there, this hotel had a rustic vibe with a huge ceiling, a massive Christmas tree, and Craftsman-style architecture. There were wreaths everywhere and it even smelled like fresh pinewood. The scent made her giddy—or maybe that was Enrique's pheromones.

Carolina had gone from never being alone with a man to staying in her third hotel room. She felt like she was on her honeymoon.

But they were not married.

All her emotions swirled inside of her. Love, lust, desire—years of pent-up and repressed feelings. She had once convinced herself that she didn't desire sex and would never meet the right guy. That she was somehow above it. And then she met Enrique.

There went that theory.

And sure, he'd been making a lot of the decisions for them as a couple when it came to where they went and what they did, but it wasn't like she had anywhere else to be or go—and she wanted this moment, this physical intimacy, for herself.

She was ready. She wanted to lose her virginity tonight.

"I'm going to take a quick bath."

"Take as long as you want."

Carolina went to the bathroom and turned on the water. She slowly undressed and looked at her naked body in the mirror. Though personally she didn't think there was anything wrong with premarital sex, despite her upbringing and religion, she had always imagined that she would lose her virginity on her wedding night, and if she never got married, she would never have sex.

Yet here she was, certain she was about to have sex, if he wanted to, with a man who was not and probably never would be her husband.

She exhaled out her doubt and slipped into the tub. The warm water cascaded over her breasts. She wanted this. She wanted him. He made her feel empowered, beautiful, and unique. And she realized she was all of those things. She wasn't giving this man a priceless gift, as she had been told her entire life, but instead, she was giving herself one.

She didn't want to be seduced—she was in power. She was in control. She wanted to initiate intimacy with him. And dammit, she was going to.

Twenty minutes later, she emerged from the room wearing nothing but a robe.

A smile spread across Enrique's lips. His eyes raked over her body, worshipping her curves. He made her feel like a goddess.

She walked over to him, and she removed her robe confidently, even though inside her nerves were on fire.

She stood in front of him, naked. Empowered. Anxious. Excited. "I want you to be my first." And only, but she didn't say that.

He grinned. "Well, that makes two of us." He scooped her into his arms and carried her to the bed.

She laughed. His hands caressed her body. He cupped her face and gave her a slow kiss as he gently placed her on the bed.

He took off his shirt as she fumbled with his belt. His jeans dropped to the floor, and she pulled down his boxers. His body was so beautiful—dark, hard, chiseled.

But then a chill came over her.

This was actually happening. This was *real*.

"Enrique, I'm nervous."

"It's okay. That's normal. You're sure you want to do this?"

"Yes. I am." She was going to have sex with the man she loved, even though she hadn't told him how she felt yet.

But she was sure about it. She loved him.

"I'll go slow. We can stop at any time."

His words relaxed her. Enrique kissed her neck and slowly made his way down to her chest. He licked her nipple, and she moaned. "You know, you are absolutely perfect. And completely and totally mine."

His wavy dark hair hung around his head like a crown.

Like Jesus.

Wow, she was messed up. She was naked in bed with this man she adored, and she was thinking about Jesus. Could she be feeling any more guilty?

No. No. Stop it. There was no room for guilt in the bed. There was nothing to feel guilty about. Having sex with a man she wanted did not make her less worthy as a woman. She closed her eyes, shoved her shame out the door, and centered herself back in the present.

His hands dropped down to her thighs. He kissed her belly, and then blew kisses in between her legs. She experienced nothing but pleasure as he made her body sing.

He licked her like he had the other night, and she gasped. She clutched his hair. He touched her bud and stroked her. It felt amazing, and she wanted him to lick her forever, but she didn't know if she was being selfish. She hadn't done anything to pleasure him.

She sat up and pulled him next to her. "You don't have to do that again. We can just have sex. Or I can try to do it to you, though I don't know how to."

"Babe, sex isn't just about penetration. I want to please you. I love this. You taste so damn sweet. I want you to enjoy yourself and do anything that feels good. I want you to come in my mouth again."

"Enrique!" she gasped, her cheeks turning red as she was laughing. She had never talked freely about sex. And she loved how open he was being with her.

He smiled. "You're mine now. And I think you're sexy as hell. I'm going to tell you every chance I get—how much I want you, how badly I wanted to touch you from the second I saw you. How you have the most incredible plump ass. How much I want to eat your pussy."

She exhaled. "I've never seen myself as sexy or attractive. But you . . . you're a god." She rubbed her hand down his abs and stroked his cock. "I've fantasized about this since I met you."

He grinned and kissed her neck. "I can pretty much guarantee not as much as I have. Now relax, babe."

He kissed her back down to her belly, and in between her thighs. Sweet heat. He licked her pussy and her breath quickened. Her moans came rapidly. He rubbed her nipples with his free hand as she clutched the sheets, writhing against his tongue. She looked down at Enrique, who was settled between her legs, lapping at her as if she were his oasis in the middle of the fields.

She took a deep breath and did exactly as he said.

Relax.

As she loosened up, pressure built between her legs and waves of pleasure washed over her. Her chest heaved. "Enrique. That feels really good."

He grinned. "I'm going to make you feel even better."

He rubbed her clit. She felt as if she was going to explode.

"That's it, baby. Come for me."

Carolina closed her eyes and let go. The intensity pulsed through her as her body shook and ecstasy took over. "Ah, Enrique!"

He kissed back up to her breasts.

The moment she caught her breath, she pushed Enrique onto his back and straddled him.

He put his hand up. "Are you sure? We can wait. You don't have to sleep with me tonight. Or ever. I'm fine, Carolina. Really. We are in no rush."

"No. I want to. I want to feel you inside me."

Enrique grinned. "Don't have to ask me twice. But babe . . . it might be painful."

"It's fine. I'm ready."

"Okay."

He kissed her on her forehead and then slid out from under her and stood up to get a condom.

What a gorgeous man. His body was chiseled and strong. She couldn't stop staring at his huge penis as he rolled the condom over it.

She winced. Fear and anticipation swirled inside of her. The moment was finally here.

He climbed back on the bed and gently pushed her on her back. He rubbed her pussy, and he slid one finger inside her. She clenched.

"Relax, babe. Look at me." He leaned over on top of her, pressing slowly into her body. "You ready?"

"Yes."

He paused but then smiled and gazed into her eyes. "I'm crazy about you."

He kissed her neck as he slowly entered her.

There was a moment of piercing pain. "Ay."

"You okay?" He held his body still and didn't move.

She nodded. "Yes."

"God . . . you're so tight!"

She inhaled a sharp breath, and he pushed, inch by inch, as he gently kissed her. The pressure was almost unbearable, but she breathed through the tightness.

He was finally inside.

"I got you. Just look at me."

She relaxed her body and touched his chest. After a few deep breaths, she wrapped her arms around his back and pulled him closer. "Make love to me."

He laced his fingers with hers and rocked slowly in and out. Pleasure replaced the pain as they moved together, finding their own lovely rhythm.

She loved this. Not just the sex, but the intimacy. Having him on top of her. This special dance they engaged in that was just between them.

He looked into her eyes. "You're incredible."

And now they belonged to each other.

His pace quickened and she let herself go. Her joy came in waves, like it had earlier, but this time it was different.

She was lost in this moment, lost in Enrique.

How could anything feel so amazing?

Her heart beat so loudly, she was certain he could hear it. Blood coursed through her body; she was on fire as he rubbed her clit. Pleasure prickled through her veins. Over and over again.

"Come on, baby. Don't stop!" he said.

She didn't want to stop. She wanted to feel this great every day for the rest of her life. He was like a drug, and she was addicted.

He gazed deep into her eyes. Her body throbbed as she cried out.

Her thighs quivered as he pressed closer. Finally, she broke into a million pieces. "Enrique!"

He released inside of her. "Babe . . . you are so beautiful."

He collapsed on top of her and then kissed her as her body recovered.

For several moments they lay there, lost in each other, two hearts beating as one. Eventually, she excused herself to the bathroom. When she returned, he quickly disposed of the condom, then came back to bed, pulling her close to him once more and *yes*. This was where she was meant to be. This was where she belonged.

"How do you feel?" he asked, his voice kind. "Was it everything you hoped it would be?"

"It was and more."

"Carolina . . ." He had a twinkle in his brown eyes.

"What?"

"Would you like to spend the New Year with me? In San Diego?"

"I'd love to!" She wrapped her arms around Enrique. She kissed this handsome man, and as happy as she was, the thought of not seeing him regularly after the holidays were over made her heart ache.

CHAPTER TWENTY-SEVEN

The next morning, Enrique woke up with Carolina by his side.

The sex had been incredible. He'd had no idea it would mean so much to him, being her first. The more he thought about it, the more it meant. Not so much that she hadn't been with any other man, but that she had chosen *him*.

But the vacation would soon be over. They had fallen hard and fast into some sort of fantasy romance that didn't have any place in reality. Romantic nights in hotel rooms, carefree days . . . He knew that she would soon have to make a huge adjustment to living without her family's emotional support.

They spent the next day at Disney again, holding hands and sharing cotton candy. When they collapsed into their hotel room bed that evening, their bodies physically spent, peace washed over him. This was such a beautiful life.

It was a shame it had to end.

Carolina had been calling her parents and Blanca, but none of them were returning her calls.

He stroked her hair in the bed. "Do you want to spend another day here?"

She shook her head. "Can we go to your place? I've never been to San Diego."

"Oh, you'll love it." He kissed her. He wanted her to have a fun time in San Diego. He would show her around and then see what she wanted to do after the holiday break. Either way, she could stay with him until she decided if she wanted to pursue buying another farm. She didn't seem to need his help financially, but he wasn't sure if that was going to change depending on what happened with her family. He'd be happy to support her, but he didn't want to overwhelm her.

The next morning, they left for San Diego.

"I can't wait to show you around."

"Oh yes?" she asked, sitting up, her eyes alive. "What will you show me?"

"Well, the beaches are a must. They're so clean, and there isn't any smog in the sky."

"That sounds divine. I love the beach; well, gazing at it. Not actually going into the water. I still refuse to go surfing with you."

He grinned. "We will see about that. But San Diego is the best. I love the rich culture of our border town. The food is incredible, especially Julieta's. We're going to have a great time."

They arrived in La Jolla. He'd never felt nervous about taking a woman to his place before, but he did with Carolina.

He drove along his beachfront street and pulled into his driveway and opened the garage. He held the door for her and led her upstairs.

He led her through the open-concept living area to the large balcony overlooking the beach.

Her eyes scanned the coast. "It really is beautiful. I can't believe you live here."

Enrique always felt a bit uncomfortable when he invited people to his place—it was over-the-top. She slid her hand over the leather furniture and lifted up a vase, her eyes squinting at the name.

"Yeah, I'm very lucky. Ramón, Jaime, and I bought it a few years ago. Our beach bachelor pad. But Ramón now lives in Coronado with Julieta. Tiburón has been crashing here a lot."

"Wow. I imagine that would be fun. I would've loved to get a place with Blanca and Adela." Her voice dropped. "I wonder how they are."

"Blanca still won't respond?"

She shook her head. "No, not yet. Though I'm not blaming her for that. Papá probably forbade her from talking to me. She's living there, so she has to obey his rules."

"You're welcome to stay here as long as you like. But you shouldn't run away from your life. Don't worry about me, about us. We can make this work. But you own that farm. How is it even running without you?"

She cast a downward glance. "Well, we always shut it down for the holidays until Three Kings Day, so the timing at least on that end is good. But after the holidays, I'll need to go back to check in on everything. I can't just abandon it."

"So you have a week or so until you have to leave?"

"Yeah. But I don't think anything will change with my family. I will never kick them out of the home, and they will never let me back inside. I think I'll have to run the farm myself and live somewhere else. Doing it solo would be hard because I've always had my family's support. Papá should retire anyway. And I guess I could replace Blanca, though I don't want to. I'm sure Papá will forbid her to work with me. She should focus on doing something she wants in her life, instead of being my administrative assistant. Maybe this whole mess was meant to happen for her freedom. Now she can date, and pursue a career that she wants, though honestly, she really just wants to get married and start a family."

How could she even consider letting her family stay in the home she bought if they weren't talking to her? "Kick them out if they won't talk to you. Or make your parents leave and let your siblings stay, of course. Don't let your father bully you out of the life you have worked for."

"Well, I won't. It's my farm—people depend on me. I don't care about the house, though—he can have it. And if he wants to disown me, that's his problem. But even if I go back to the house, he will treat me differently. I want to grow. Evolve. I need my own place."

"That's good. I just think that it's messed up that he can kick you out of your home."

"I just want to be happy. And it's not about the house. The issue is that I stood up to him. He's never wrong. What he says goes. I was raised to always defer to Papá, and then my future husband."

He pulled her toward him. "I hope you know that I don't want that." He paused. "If we were to get married someday, I would want an equal. A partner in life. Not a servant."

She bit her lower lip. "Married . . . ?"

"Yes, married. I want to get married one day and have a family. I love kids. You don't ever see yourself getting married?" He pulled her closer to him. She felt so good in his arms, in his place.

She looked away. "Not really. And I'm not even sure about kids. I practically raised my sisters when my parents were in the fields. I just want to focus on myself."

Ah. She had made a similar comment before, but he had wanted clarity on her feelings.

Enrique tried to brush off her words, but they bothered him. He *did* want to settle down. He *did* want to have kids. He understood that she had no desire to be in the type of marriage her parents were in, but she could never see herself getting married? Ever?

"I get it. You're young, though; maybe you will change your mind."

"And maybe I won't." She turned on him, pain flashing in her eyes.

Enrique wanted to swallow his words. "Damn, I'm sorry. I didn't mean to invalidate your feelings. All I meant is that you will change a lot in the next five to seven years, especially if you are independent from your family. Forget I said it."

"Already forgotten," she said quietly.

Maybe she would change her mind one day.

But maybe she wouldn't. Enrique never bought into the fact that all women should want kids.

But he knew that he did.

It was way too early in the relationship to be thinking about that. Even so, he couldn't let go of a nagging feeling that they weren't right for each other.

He kissed her and showed her around the rest of his home. It was already pretty late, so they ordered takeout and then went to sleep.

The next morning, they woke early, and he led her to his local bakery, Wayfarer, for some bread and pastries.

She ordered a blood orange croissant, and he had an egg sandwich.

"This place is great. I wonder where they get their fruit." Carolina looked out on the deck toward the ocean.

He laughed. "I don't know. You scouting new business? We could start working on my farm and lure them in as clients."

She bit her lip and gave a noncommittal laugh. "We will see."

Another awkward reaction. Had he said something wrong? She

had left her home, and, after a wild, romantic road trip, they'd come to San Diego together. They were boyfriend and girlfriend, and she had lost her virginity to him. Was he wrong to entertain the possibility that she would consider moving to San Diego to be with him? How else could this work? Sure, they could have a long-distance relationship, but this was infinitely better. They didn't even have to live together; she could rent her own place as soon as she decided if she was staying.

And besides, now that they'd had sex, things between them felt different. He was almost thirty and wanted to move on to the next phase of his life. He had spent years fucking around and not taking things seriously. He wanted a partner. He wanted someone to share his life with, the good times and the bad. And he wanted to start a family of his own.

Even though she had clearly said she wasn't sure if she wanted one. Ever.

That was a deal breaker for Enrique. He would never ask a woman to change her mind about wanting a family, but he knew that children were something he wanted in his future.

He would wait to bring that up later when they were more established in their relationship—he didn't want to waste her time— or his.

No matter what happened between them, she had to make decisions about her own future. She was at a very personal crossroads.

All Enrique could do was support her.

Then it hit him.

"Hey—do you want to visit your aunt while you are here?" he asked right as a seagull flew by and landed on the nearby railing. "That's why this part of town is called Bird Rock."

Carolina laughed. "That's so cool. As for my aunt, I'd love to see her."

He leaned forward, enjoying the smile that lit her face. "I love talking things out with you about the future—but sometimes family can help you see things clearly, too. And she obviously knows your parents better than I do."

Carolina grabbed his arm and held it tightly. "You're the best."

She reached for her phone and called. "Tía Luísa? It's Carolina—your niece. I'm in town. Can I come see you?"

CHAPTER TWENTY-EIGHT

Enrique drove her down to Barrio Logan.

"This place is really special to me." He pulled the car adjacent to Chicano Park. "Let me show you the murals."

He opened the door for her and led her around the glorious art. Carolina loved seeing all the historical Mexican heroes bigger than life and getting the recognition they deserved. But one stopped her cold.

It was a massive multipart mural on a large column. There was a quote from Emiliano Zapata painted up top.

La tierra es de quién la trabaja con sus propias manos.

The land belongs to those who work it with their own hands.

Carolina's breath hitched.

The work was astounding. It depicted a farmworker on the left side pulling a cog with a man in a black suit with a metal claw for a hand also grabbing it. There were farmworkers striking underneath, one of whom was dead. The bottom two sections showed migrants working in a field and then two boxes of produce.

It had a plaque describing the piece.

Death of a Farmworker.

In memory of all the farmworkers who have struggled for a better life—the artists.

Carolina was speechless.

She looked up at Enrique, who was watching her look at the mural.

He reached down and squeezed her hand. "Powerful."

"Sure is."

He turned to her, and now took her other hand. "We can make a difference. As a team. My company has the funds to invest in making farmworkers' lives better. Effect real change. We're unstoppable together."

She kissed him passionately in the park.

He was right. They could be great together.

And she could live here.

She could move to San Diego with Enrique.

She wanted to so very badly—but what if she was simply moving out of the control of one man to fall into the sway of another? Enrique wasn't forcing her to do anything, but he also always had an answer for everything—and that felt dangerous. She was adrift, and he could sway her far too easily.

And then there's the fact he wants children.

Then they walked over to the public garden. Emotions washed over her. For a community so entrenched in farming not to have outdoor space to grow their own herbs was unfathomable to her. Her head filled with the possibilities of other ways she could give back to her community.

He finally pulled up to a small house a block away from the bridge. "Do you want me to come in?" he asked as he idled at the curb.

She shook her head. "No, thank you. I haven't seen her since I was a child, so I'd love to catch up. But maybe next time. It's very kind of you to offer, though."

"No worries. I'll stop by Las Pescas. Text me when you want me to come pick you up. Or you can come by, and I'll show you the restaurant."

"That sounds great." She gave him a long kiss. "See you in a bit."

She got out of the car, and he waved and drove away.

The house was a quaint Craftsman sandwiched between a tire shop and an apartment building.

Carolina knocked at the door, and her aunt's dogs came running to the screen door, barking wildly. "Tía Luísa!"

Her aunt opened the door, clutching the leash of a one-eyed pit bull. The years had been kind to Tía Luísa. There were only a few lines on her face, and she was in great shape. Her hair was dyed a bright red, and she wore a long kaftan robe.

Her aunt hugged her, and the scent of roses overtook Carolina.

"Sobrina, you look so pretty!"

Carolina smiled at the pit bull. "Thank you. He's so cute. What's his name?"

"This is Gordo. He's very calm."

Carolina knelt down to pet Gordo. "Oh, you're a good boy." Carolina wanted a dog of her own. A place of her own. A life of her own.

"So—to what do I owe this wonderful surprise? I'm surprised your father let you visit me."

A lump grew in her throat. Carolina should've reached out to her aunt years ago. Her father should've never forbidden her from communicating with her. "You'll never believe this . . . but I'm here with Enrique Montez. You know him."

Her aunt's jaw dropped. "Qué? Are you dating a Montez? Though I must say, Enrique is my favorite."

Carolina laughed. "Mine, too!"

She grabbed Carolina's ring finger, staring at its nakedness. "You are here alone? Without a chaperone? Your father allowed that?"

Carolina shook her head. "Yes, I'm dating him, and no, Papá most certainly did not. That's why I'm here."

Tía Luísa nodded. "I understand completely about my brother. But forget about him—you have to tell me how you met Enrique! Come on in."

Carolina walked into her aunt's kitchen, which was full of knick-knacks and crystals. Open shelves were covered with plants, and there were candles with herbs sprinkled in them on the counter. A couple of cats lounged in the window cuddled up next to a fluffy white dog. Out back, there was a tiny Chihuahua sunbathing with some black mutt.

Tía Luísa stirred a clay pot on the stove, and the sweet and spicy scent of café de olla filled the room.

"Do you want some coffee?"

"Sí."

Tía Luísa grabbed some mugs. "Carolina, tell me everything."

Carolina exhaled. "Well, it's a long story, but the ending is similar to yours—Papá kicked me out."

Tía Luísa shook her head. "Cari. No. Lo siento."

"I'm sorry, too. Enrique drove up to Santa Maria to meet with me. He wanted to partner with my farm. I never saw the email he sent requesting a meeting—Blanca impersonated me and invited him up. She wanted to meet the infamous Montez brothers and knew I'd think it was a terrible idea."

Tía Luísa grinned. She ladled the coffee into the cups and handed one to Carolina.

"I always liked Blanca—though I haven't seen her since she was a little girl. She loved her dolls. But if I were her, I would've done the same thing."

Carolina laughed. "Well, that decision changed the course of my life. I met Enrique, and even though I was determined not to like him—I just couldn't help myself. He volunteered to be Joseph to my Mary in Las Posadas, and when Papá got sick and thought Enrique was my boyfriend—"

"He's sick?" Luísa asked as another cat ran across a back room.

"Yes, he had a pulmonary embolism, but he is doing better. Or was. He's not speaking to me right now."

"I'm sorry. I had no idea."

"Don't apologize—it's his fault you don't speak."

"True."

Carolina continued. "Anyway, Enrique was there for me, but when he visited for dinner, Papá made him do this elaborate song and dance and I flipped. I went dancing with him alone—and you can guess what happened next."

"I can only imagine. Your father always overreacts. He's just like my father."

"Yeah, they share a temper." Carolina sipped her coffee. It was smooth and lovely. "Anyway, Enrique and I went to Carmel-by-the-Sea together, but we got stuck there in a storm and we had to stay the night together. And . . ."

"And?" her tía asked gently.

"And he's wonderful, Tía. He was super supportive and patient. He makes me smile, and I feel more relaxed being around him. And he wants to start supporting farmworkers and making real changes in his farms. He was absolutely wonderful to me."

"Wow. Sounds like a great guy."

"He is. And . . ." She couldn't believe she was actually going to share this intimate detail out loud, but she hadn't been able to talk to Blanca and she was dying to tell someone. Plus she knew Tía Luísa didn't talk to her parents, so there was zero chance it would get back to them. "I slept with him! I still can't believe it. But I really wanted to, and it felt so right. He didn't pressure me at all, and I don't regret it." And she didn't. No matter what ended up happening with her and Enrique, she would never question her decision.

"I'm so happy for you." Tía Luísa clasped her hands together. "You know, I was once just like you. I know our family sees me as the tipsy spinster dog mom, but I didn't want to live by your grandfather's rules. I had suitors, but I wanted my own life. To come and go as I pleased."

Independence. That sounded dreamy. But also hard. "Do you have any regrets about leaving home?"

"No, not about leaving home. Sure, I get lonely sometimes. But no. I'm happy. Your grandfather never forgave me when I left and wouldn't even let me come visit. I missed him terribly, and you, your sisters that I met, and your father, but I wanted to live my life."

"I understand. But it's not that easy." She glanced toward the window where, moments ago, Enrique had been. Was she living her life if she was with him? Or living his?

"Tell me, Carolina."

"Tell you what?"

Luísa waggled her finger. "We may have been apart for many years, but sometimes an aunt knows when her niece has man troubles."

Carolina sighed. "I just worry if maybe this is all moving too fast. Enrique has suggested that I move to San Diego, and he's even spoken of marriage and babies, and I don't know if I'm ready."

"Carolina," her aunt sighed. "Be careful about going from one controlling situation to another. I'm glad you are exploring what you want in your life, but you need some time alone. You are strong, smart, and independent. I support you wanting to get out from under your parents' restrictive ways, but don't run from one problem to another. Find yourself first."

Her words hit Carolina. Did she actually want to start a relationship? Was she using Enrique to escape her family's control?

And was he controlling her? It hadn't occurred to her at first, but . . . he wanted her to move down to San Diego. He even already mentioned marriage and having kids.

What was she doing?

She didn't know—all she knew was that she needed some time alone to process what her aunt had said. "Tía Luísa—is there any way I can spend the night here with you tonight?"

Tía Luísa's lips spread into a wide smile. "I would love that! We can watch telenovelas and order in a pizza and chat."

Carolina picked up her phone to call Enrique to tell him about the change of plans, but it went to voice mail. Instead of leaving a message, she sent him a text.

Carolina: Hey. I've decided to spend the night with my aunt. I haven't seen her for years and really want to catch up with her.

A few seconds later, Enrique replied.

Enrique: Cool, sorry I missed your call. Glad you're having a great time. I'll call you tomorrow. Do you want to go to yoga with me? There is a class at eleven.

Carolina paused. She didn't, actually. Years of heavily preached Catholicism had her unsure of the spiritual nature of it all. But she had vowed to try new things.

Carolina: Maybe. I'll text you tomorrow.

Enrique: Miss you, love.

Carolina wanted to say *I love you* to him. She felt it. But she wasn't sure of the implications of the words.

So she replied with a smiley face.

CHAPTER TWENTY-NINE

Enrique hadn't heard from Carolina all night. That was fine, but he missed her. In such a short time, he had become so used to having her around. Funny, how love could make you feel that way.

Was it love?

He couldn't stop thinking about her. But it was too soon for love. Wasn't it?

He went surfing late at night. Tiburón decided to spend more time up near Blanca, and Jaime was visiting some friends in Malibu, so Enrique spent a rare night alone in his house.

The next morning, Enrique drove back to Barrio Logan to pick Carolina up and take her to yoga. She had texted in the morning saying she wanted to try it, which made Enrique happy.

He greeted her with a kiss. "Did you have fun with your aunt?"

Her face lit up. "A great time," she said as she settled in the seat across from him. "I never wanted to leave."

Ouch.

Well, that hurt a little.

"I mean, of course to see you I did." Carolina reached her hand out to rest on his leg. "It was just nice to reconnect."

"You might be able to reconnect more," Enrique suggested. "What if you stayed with her here in Barrio Logan?"

"I guess I could possibly," Carolina said, gazing out the window at the many murals under the freeway.

Enrique sensed the tension in the air, but surely his anxiety was messing with him again. He changed the subject.

"Hey, have you ever done yoga?"

She shook her head. "Is it fun? I'm a dancer, so I like movement, but it always seemed slow and boring to me."

"It's great. My studio, Riffs, is down the street from my house. We practice on an outdoor deck surrounded by bamboo. Sometimes they have live music. In today's class, they use a sound bath to help get you into a meditative state."

She scratched the base of her neck. "You lost me at sound bath."

"Come on. It's fun. We're taking the Yin Yoga class."

"I'm sure it will be great."

They stopped at a boutique, and Carolina bought some yoga clothes, which hugged her smoking body.

Enrique went back to his place to change into his own clothes, and then they headed toward the studio. Enrique was proud to show her off around his town. When they got to class, he helped her with her borrowed mat, bolster, blocks, and blanket. She followed him out to the redwood deck.

"Wow, this is really nice. Thanks for bringing me here." She gazed at the hummingbirds flying overhead.

"I come here every day. It really helps me focus. Being here, on the mat, is my version of church."

She gave him a quizzical look. "I think yoga seems great and all.

Like the stretching part and relaxation. But I can't even fathom comparing it to going to church."

His heart sank. Was she judging him? He'd be the first to admit he wasn't the type of man her father would probably want her to date. For one, he wasn't a devout Catholic. And Enrique hated toxic masculinity and machismo. He saw women as equals and cared as much, if not more, about his mental health as he did his physical health.

Maybe he was just a novelty for her, and she would soon realize she *did* want a man more like her papá. Sometimes those things were ingrained in you since childhood, no matter how hard you tried to fight them.

Or maybe, now that she'd had a taste of the joys of sex, she would want to explore them, maybe find another partner. He couldn't fault her for that, either. But the thought of another man touching her, fucking her, made his skin prickle. He hadn't expected to have such an emotional connection to her so quickly, but he allowed his feelings in and sat with them.

But the biggest difference that was apparent to him was that she didn't want to get married and have kids, and he did. It was early in their relationship, but this was definitely something he wanted in his life. He would never pressure a woman into starting a family if she didn't want to. He wanted to have a family with someone who wanted that as much as he did.

They sat side by side, waiting for the teacher to begin.

The instructor sat in lotus pose and started some chanted Kirtan meditation.

Enrique followed the yogi, repeating her words. He exhaled and tried to center himself.

He looked over at Carolina. She was not chanting, and that was okay. Hopefully, she was enjoying herself.

After a few deep breaths, he was in the zone. He loved the slow yin style of practice. Relaxing into each pose, stretching his muscles. He was completely at peace and in the moment.

At the end of class, the teacher made the gesture of no fear. She ran the sound bath. The calming noise vibrated in Enrique's soul.

"Namaste. I honor the light in you and me." She thanked the class. Then they were dismissed.

Around them, people began rolling up their mats, slowly moving out of the class. Enrique turned to Carolina.

"Did you enjoy yourself?"

She shrugged. "It was okay. Not really my thing. But thanks for bringing me."

"That's okay. We can try again tomorrow. I usually go every day when I'm in town," Enrique said, smiling. "We can probably get a discount on your membership with my pass."

"Enrique, slow down." Carolina was smiling, but her voice shook. She sprayed her mat with a disinfectant and wiped it down with a towel. Then she rolled it up and stood, her shoulders shaking.

"Sorry. It's totally okay if you don't like it. I can go alone."

They left the class and walked down the street toward his house. He led her to a bench overlooking the ocean. The salty scent of the air enlivened him. He saw surfers in the distance but didn't dare ask Carolina to try another new hobby today.

He exhaled. "So, have you thought about what you're going to do? Did you get any clarity with your aunt?"

"A bit. But I haven't made any decisions yet."

"You could move to San Diego. You have your aunt here? And me?"

"Move to San Diego?" she repeated.

"Yes."

"In with you?" she asked.

"Yes," he said again, and damn, he'd been expecting a happier look on her face than this. "Of course, it's fine if you don't want to. I just thought given the situation with your family and everything..."

"That's sweet, Enrique." She placed a hand on his thigh. "But I think we're rushing in a little too soon. I have dreams of my own. I can't just become a housemistress—even if it would be fun to do this all the time."

Regret consumed him. He shouldn't have asked her that. Not yet. It was way too soon. "Totally understand. Forget I asked."

"No worries." She kissed him on the forehead. "I hope you don't mind, but I—I'm going to take a walk alone in the park. I'll call you later."

"Carolina, wait, I—"

"Please, Enrique," she said. "I just need some space."

His inner peace turned again to turmoil. Enrique tried to not let her words bother him, but it felt like a punch to the gut.

He had gone too fast, but he couldn't help himself—he was crazy about her. It was fine with him that she didn't like yoga . . . but he sensed that she was pulling away from him for other reasons.

CHAPTER THIRTY

Carolina walked away from the yoga studio down to Calumet Park.

She stopped in the middle of the grass to get a breath of fresh air. Then sat on a bench and overlooked the rocky cliffs. How amazing to have a park above the ocean. San Diego was incredible. She was glad she had come here.

Even so, she had to gather her thoughts.

Ever since leaving home, she hadn't spent a moment alone. Aside from the night with her tía, Enrique had always been with her, and though he was great—truly the best—she felt overwhelmed by her thoughts. He was talking to her about the future, and she wasn't even sure what she was doing tomorrow. He wasn't controlling like her father, but it still seemed . . . suffocating?

And the yoga class had not been her scene. She'd felt supremely uncomfortable. She knew that yoga wasn't inherently religious, but it felt contrary to her beliefs. Sure, she was a complete sinner by now, but she still was Catholic, and her spirituality involved saints and

Sunday school, not incense and mantras. She knew some people just saw yoga as a workout, but she didn't feel comfortable chanting and praying in that way.

Enrique seemed at home there. It was beautiful to see that he was connected to something he believed in. But it made her feel farther apart from him.

Who was she now? How could she reconcile her past and present? And what would she do next?

She couldn't live with Enrique. Staying with her aunt had been helpful and it had made her realize that she wasn't comfortable moving in with Enrique, but that hadn't brought her any closer to a solution. She had her farm, and she had a whole life back home she'd miss too terribly. And she would need to find a new place to live if she went back. She was lost.

What she desperately wanted was to talk to Blanca.

She called one more time, listening to that lonely ringing tone over, over, and over again.

"Carolina?"

She nearly dropped the phone in surprise. "Blanca!"

"I don't have long to talk. If Papá finds out I'm speaking to you, he'll take my phone."

"So, nothing has changed?" Carolina's heart sank.

"Nothing. Baby asked about you, and he yelled at her. It was awful."

Nausea swirled in her stomach. Poor Sofía. "That's horrible. I miss her. I miss everyone."

"I miss you, too. Are you okay? Are you with Enrique?"

A bird landed on a rock in the ocean.

"I am staying with him, Blanca, but I'm not going to move in with him. And I spent last night at Tía Luísa's."

"Really? I'm so jealous. How is she?"

"She's great. She has a wonderful life. Her dogs are so cool. You should come and visit."

Blanca laughed. "Papá would never allow me, that is, not unless I marry Tiburón, then he could take me, or we could move down there. Oh my God. Tiburón is so amazing. I think it's really going to work out!"

Carolina's throat closed. She should be happy for her sister, but anguish overtook her. "That's great."

"Come home. I miss you."

"You know I can't." Her throat itched. What if Blanca married Tiburón? Would she be allowed at their wedding? What other events would she miss out on? Births? Funerals? Would Carolina ever see her family again?

"What's going on with Enrique? Are you in love?"

"I think so. But what is love?"

"Ay, Cari. Love is love. It's easy. I love Tiburón."

"What do you love about him?"

A goldendoodle dashed in front of her, retrieving a ball his owner threw.

"I love how he makes me feel. How he spoils me. How he talks about the future with me in it. I love how good he is with our sisters. How respectful he was to Papá. He has made me feel like a queen. He's sexy, too. I know he will do anything for me. He calls me his princesa."

"I'm so happy for you, Blanca, I really am."

It was so black-and-white to Blanca. Meet, talk, court, propose, get married, have babies. Happily ever after. But Carolina didn't want that life. Oh my God. What if Carolina was already pregnant? They had used a condom but those didn't always work.

She brushed that thought aside. Clearly, she was getting paranoid. Now that Carolina had actually had sex, she no longer regarded it as the holy act that she'd always believed it would be. Then again, she'd had premarital sex, so maybe it would've felt different if Enrique had been her husband?

She loved sex. It made her feel amazing, and she enjoyed sharing that special intimate moment with Enrique. She wanted to have it again. And again and again. But she didn't want to feel like she had to make their relationship work solely because she had lost her virginity to him.

And she didn't just like Enrique because he was a great lover. She enjoyed his calm personality. How kind he was toward others. How he really wanted to change people's lives.

He was wonderful.

Whether she was with Enrique or not, she needed a plan for her life. If her father wouldn't forgive her, what were her options? She could work awkwardly on the farm and live off-site, but running into him, enduring his cold silence every time she saw him . . . it would be too much. It would break her heart.

And if she didn't go back, what would happen to the farm and all the workers who depended on her?

Could she buy another farm? Did she have enough money to do that? And where would she do it? If she set one up near home, she would be essentially competing with a business she'd already established. And if she set one up here . . . well, she knew no one. Had no contacts. No workers or managers she trusted. No one except her aunt.

But was love enough?

Was *he* enough?

"What about you? Are you moving in with Enrique?"

"No. Definitely not. Though he asked." Her aunt's words rang in her head. *Don't go from one man's house to another man's house.* But unfortunately for Carolina, her father's words *also* rang in her head.

¿Por qué comprar el cerdo entero si sólo te interesa la salchicha?

Not much better than the English version of "Why buy the cow when you can get the milk for free?"

Carolina didn't want to be purchased like a pig, a cow, or a house.

She just wanted to find herself. She needed to stand alone and figure out her feelings toward Enrique and make sure she wasn't just caught up in the turmoil of her life.

"Are you coming back here? I mean, you can't. Like, not to the farm. But to town?"

"Blanca, I own the farm, and the house. But no, I don't want to come back to Santa Maria. Not yet."

"Well, I love you. I'll try to call you when I can sneak away. I hope to see you soon." She paused. "You know, if you ended things with Enrique—came back here without him—I'm sure Papá would forgive you. Life could go back to how it was. Simple."

Her gut wrenched. She didn't want to end things with Enrique just to get back in her father's good graces, to tuck her tail between her legs and go back home, to be forgiven for a crime that she hadn't committed.

But she wasn't sure staying with Enrique was the right idea, either. No matter how much she wanted to.

"I'm not going to do that, Blanca, at least not for Papá. But promise me something—don't rush into anything with Tiburón. Make sure you really want this."

"Whatever, Carolina. I know what I want. Stop warning me. I'm not you."

"Noted," Carolina snapped back.

"Maybe you just need to stop worrying about how independent you are and take a chance and love someone. Loving means taking a risk. It means not knowing how things might work out. Sometimes it means moving somewhere else or doing something new. But change isn't always bad. Worse things have happened, you know."

"Got it." Did her sister really see her like that? So desperate to always be in control? So resistant to change?

"I'm sorry, Cari." Blanca sighed. "I just—I really wish you'd stop needling me about Tiburón. I know what I want. Respect that."

"Okay." Carolina's hair blew in her face, momentarily blinding her. "Bye, Blanca."

She hung up the phone, but Blanca's words were ringing in Carolina's ears. Was that the problem? Was she too afraid to take a chance on love?

She continued walking along the street, and after exploring the town, she checked into a small hotel. She needed to be alone. Not with Enrique. Not with her aunt.

Just her and her thoughts.

The walk in the park hadn't been quite enough—she needed more.

She glanced at her phone.

Enrique: Hello?

Enrique: Are you alright?

Enrique: What's wrong??

Enrique: Please answer the phone. Are you upset with me?

She hadn't been in the mood to respond, which she knew was just plain awful of her. But she needed space.

She sat on her bed overlooking the ocean.

A few hours later, she finally texted Enrique back.

Carolina: Sorry. I just need some space. Don't worry about me. I got a hotel room nearby.

Enrique: Wow. Okay. Wasn't expecting that. I was worried about you, Carolina. Are you okay? What did I do?

Why did everyone always think that what she wanted had anything to do with them? Could she ever be selfish and just focus on herself? Not her mom, not her dad, not her sisters, not her employees, and not her new boyfriend?

Carolina: Nothing. You're great. I'll come by tomorrow.

Her phone rang. It was Enrique. She couldn't ignore him anymore. She picked it up.

"Hey."

"Hey? Please be honest with me. What's going on?"

The tears started coming, cascading down her face.

"Are you okay? Talk to me, dammit."

No, she wasn't okay.

"I just . . . I just think we are too different. Like you want kids one day and I'm not sure I do."

"I get that. But this is new. We don't have to decide our lives. I just want to date you."

"I know." Her shoulders hunched. She felt nauseous. "There is just so much going on for me right now . . . I didn't want to do this over the phone."

He groaned. "Are you breaking up with me, Carolina?" His voice broke. "After all we've been through together?"

Ay, she was awful. "It isn't about you. It's about me. I've been like a caged bird my entire life, dying to break free. You came along and gave me a taste of that freedom. And through being with you, I realized that I need to figure out who I am. Without you, and without my father."

"So . . . you used me? Was this some sort of test I didn't pass?"

"No! There was no test."

"Then why are you doing this to me?"

Silence echoed down the line. Carolina's chest shook as she tried to steady her breath, her racing heart. "I'm so sorry. I'm just a mess. I can't even think about someone else until I find myself."

"I'm crazy about you. I'm falling in love with you."

"I think I love you, too! But Enrique, I need to figure out who I am on my own."

"Got it." The phone went dead. She dropped it on the bedside table.

She was awful. Truly awful.

Everyone hated her now. She knew she needed to be selfish, but she couldn't seem to stop hurting everyone in her quest to figure out who she was.

Carolina crawled under the covers in the room and sobbed as the sea lions' barking drowned out her tears.

CHAPTER THIRTY-ONE

L ater that night, Enrique poured himself a glass of whiskey and sat on his beachfront balcony, gazing at the dark ocean.

Another night alone. Ramón was with Julieta, Jaime was still out of town, and Tiburón was still up in Santa Maria.

And Carolina had dumped him.

Where had he gone so wrong?

He was completely aware that this whole relationship with Carolina had gone fast. Way too fast. He had only wanted to meet her. Then he had stupidly volunteered to play Joseph in Las Posadas. Once she told her father he was her boyfriend, everything seemed to spiral hopelessly out of control.

Christ, he had taken her virginity. Yet she'd walked away and was spending the night alone in a hotel.

How had everything become so hopelessly fucked-up?

She'd seemed so callous and heartless on the phone. And her words cut him deep. Sleeping with Carolina had meant something to him. Because she had chosen him, he'd felt special and worthy.

He needed to talk to someone.

He called Tiburón, who answered on the first ring.

Loud metal music played in the background along with a low hum of voices.

"Hey, can I call you later? I'm with Blanca."

Of course. He was with Carolina's sister. "Where did you take her? A Death Angel concert?"

Tiburón laughed. "We got jokes? Nah, just some bar up in Santa Barbara."

"Sounds fun. I'll catch you later."

"You okay?"

"I'm fine. Give me a call when you get a chance."

"Bye."

Was Tiburón really going to move up there to be with Blanca? Tiburón knew she couldn't move down to San Diego unless they were married. Enrique just wanted to get off this crazy train and go back to hanging out with people who made sense and who weren't affected by someone else's rules when it came to their relationships.

Had he been so desperate to find a deep meaning and someone special that he had projected those feelings onto Carolina?

He really didn't want to be alone tonight.

He called a few friends, but they didn't answer. He went inside and looked around his empty house on the beach. He called his mother, who also didn't even answer.

There was only one place left to go.

He got into his car and drove to his father's house.

Enrique and his brothers lived less than a mile away from their father, but Enrique hadn't seen him in half a year. Papá had reached out a few times, but Enrique didn't know what to say. His father had behaved horribly when he was attempting to take over the block in Barrio Logan, especially when it came to light that he'd stolen Julieta's mom's recipe years ago, basing his entire fast-food empire on the woman's fish tacos. His actions were reprehensible, to say the least.

He pulled up in the long circular driveway and stared at the perfectly manicured lawn. He was so used to seeing maintenance workers toiling around the home that the house seemed empty without them. For years, he had aspired for his father's approval. But he no longer wanted that. He just wanted advice. But was this even a good idea? Who was his father to give out relationship guidance?

Well, he was already here. He rang the doorbell.

Papá answered the door. His mouth had more lines than it had the last time Enrique had seen him.

For a second, Papá studied Enrique. Confusion clouded his dad's eyes as if perhaps he had seen a ghost. Then he rushed forward, embraced his son in a long hug. "Mijo! What are you doing here? I thought you went to Montecito."

"We did. But I'm back." He paused. It was easy for him to be open with his feelings to anyone but his father. It wasn't just the childhood neglect. As an adult, Papá had always focused on Ramón's role in the business and had brushed off both Enrique and Jaime. Enrique often felt that there was no need to try hard because no matter what he did, he was compared to Ramón and found lacking.

He had come here for counsel. But now, in the arms of the man who had not been there for him through his childhood, he changed his mind. He pushed through his old pain and tried to forgive him. "I've missed you, Papá."

Arturo hugged him again—and then burst into tears. "I'm so sorry, Enrique. For what I did in Barrio. For how much I was absent when you were a child. For every soccer game I missed. Forgive me."

Enrique pulled away. "Thanks, but it's not that easy. And I'm not the only one you need to apologize to. The childhood trauma is bad enough. But you caused irreparable damage to our company and wanted to destroy Barrio Logan. It's not as easy as saying sorry."

"I know nothing I can say will fix anything. I'm just glad you're here. Come on in."

Enrique walked into his home that no longer felt like a home. He sat on the leather sofa in the living room.

"A drink?" his father offered. "Another pillow? That couch is too uncomfortable. I said so in the shop, but the sales associate said it was the best one."

"It's fine. I'll have a bourbon."

His father poured him a glass and then handed it to him. He then poured himself one and sat in a reclining chair. "I have wanted to reach out to you all, but I know Ramón will never forgive me."

"Yeah, I'm not sure if he will."

Papá shook his head. "I know, I know. I've been racking my head on how to fix it."

"Sometimes you can't fix things. Ramón did a pretty good job of mitigating the damage. A formal apology is the first step. To Linda and to the residents of Barrio Logan."

"I will never apologize to her," his father sneered, anger threaded through his tone. His fist slammed into the coffee table.

"You can't keep bottling up this anger. You need to talk to someone, a professional, and work through it."

His father nodded. "You're right. I know. I should go to therapy. I messed everything up with this deal. I was so stubborn about Barrio Logan."

Enrique stood up and walked over to a huge Christmas tree that was in the center of the room. Enrique crouched down and looked at the presents. There were ones for each of his brothers. But most interesting was one for Julieta.

"Dad, *why* were you so stubborn about Barrio? Ramón told you for months that what we were doing was wrong. Why didn't you listen to him?"

"Because. I carried resentment in my heart."

"For Linda? That was forty years ago."

"Yes. And the pain only grew." He took a sip of his drink. "I never got over her betraying me with another man. I wanted to hurt her like she hurt me."

Enrique was astounded. He had no idea that his father had been so wounded by Julieta's mother.

Would Enrique feel the same way about Carolina years from now? Would he want to hurt Carolina as she had hurt him this week?

No. He wasn't like that. Carolina was overwhelmed. It was clear to his heart. Their timing was off.

Enrique sat back on the soft brown leather sofa under the window and gazed into the fire in the massive marble fireplace. Christmas stockings hung from the mantel. It was the picture-perfect Christmas scene—the only thing missing was a family to share it with. "You should go talk to Linda. At least see what she has to say. It may heal you."

His father shook his head. "No. It is in the past. I had kept it in the past until I saw her again. And then, it all rushed back."

"I'm sorry."

"No, mijo. I'm sorry. I don't even care about the deal anymore. I miss my family."

"We miss you, too."

"I may never earn everyone's forgiveness. But will you forgive me?"

"I'll try."

Enrique could even forgive his father for his years of neglect, but he couldn't forget. He tried to heal from his childhood, but here he was, a grown-ass man, and he felt more alone than ever. He shouldn't need a girlfriend to fulfill his life, but he had really fallen for Carolina. It wasn't just her beauty, or that he had been her first lover—it was that he truly felt inspired by her. He loved the way she was so caring about her family. And she made him laugh and challenged him.

And just because they had broken up—that didn't mean that he had to say goodbye to all the good things she'd made him want to do.

It was time for Enrique to be a man. To build his own family. And that responsibility extended to the workplace.

He didn't need Ramón's permission. He was determined to implement changes in the farms that partnered with his company, starting with the Montez Group farm in Encinitas.

And to thank that wonderful woman for inspiring him, he needed to do something for her. He wouldn't contact her again. He wouldn't beg her to reconsider.

He needed to set Carolina free so she could grow and decide if she truly wanted him.

Even if he never saw her again, she had changed his life.

CHAPTER THIRTY-TWO

Carolina woke early. Her stomach was upset, and she had no appetite. She'd spent the night tossing and turning. How could she have done this to Enrique? He was so great. He must completely hate her.

And she didn't blame him.

Maybe someday he would forgive her. Maybe someday she would forgive herself.

But sometimes people fall in love at the wrong time. Right now, she needed to focus on herself. Take some time alone. Figure out what she wanted.

For once in her life, she had to give herself permission to be selfish.

She called her aunt and told her she needed a place to stay for a few days until she decided what she was going to do. Tía Luísa invited her over without hesitation.

Carolina took an Uber to Tía Luísa's house. Though she hadn't had any contact with Enrique, he had sent her a text that he had packed up her things and dropped them by Tía Luísa's house, but she didn't see him.

The Uber drove down the freeway. A little girl with her parents walked through Chicano Park. Carolina idly wondered if Baby loved the doll she had bought for her. It had already been wrapped and under the tree when she'd left. What had her parents done with the presents for Carolina?

Tears came as she imagined everyone pretending that she had never existed.

After all she had done for her family, after how much she had loved them and sacrificed for them, she was being erased.

Tía Luísa opened the door clutching an orange cat. "Come in quickly or one of these rascals will escape."

Carolina rushed in and Tía Luísa slammed the door behind her.

Carolina petted the cat. "What's his name?"

"Nacho."

Sobs came suddenly and Carolina couldn't stop them. Nacho nuzzled her and her tears dampened his fur.

"Mija. It's okay. Come sit."

Tía Luísa sat on the sofa and placed Nacho on her lap. Carolina sat next to her.

"Now you tell me exactly what happened with Enrique. Did he break up with you?"

Carolina shook her head. "Oh no. The opposite. He has been nothing but a gentleman. But it's like you said. I was going from my father's home to his. And though I could still date him no matter where I live, I just need to figure out who I am."

"I understand. I'm proud of you." She squeezed Carolina's hand. "There is no rush. Take some time alone. Figure out what you want." She wagged a finger at her. "But don't make my mistake."

"What was that?"

"Years ago, I was in love with a man. He was good to me also. But I didn't want to be tied down. I was so insistent on being free, a reaction to my own papá. Your papá is nothing compared to your abuelo. But I loved this boyfriend. And he was patient and kind and waited for me a long time. Until one day, he met someone else. I was finally ready to tell him how I felt, and it was too late."

Carolina's eyes bugged. "Is that why you never married?"

"Yes. I dated through the years and never found anyone else I loved as much. You can meet the right person at the wrong time. Luckily, time keeps moving."

Carolina had no right to ask Enrique to wait for her. Not that he probably ever wanted to see her again.

But was finding herself worth the risk of losing Enrique?

She didn't know anything.

Carolina finally calmed down. Petting Nacho helped. She really needed a pet.

"Do you want to check out my café?"

Carolina nodded. "I'd love to."

They walked a few blocks back to the main street. The homes they passed were small but full of character. But Carolina couldn't help but notice how many brand-new lofts and buildings were in this neighborhood.

Carolina passed Las Pescas. Rosa was standing by the hostess sign. She waved, and Carolina gave a guilty wave back.

She just hoped Enrique wasn't around. She couldn't face him.

They stopped outside Café Mariposa, a vivid purple building with brightly painted butterflies adorning it.

Carolina loved her aunt's café. It was so adorable. There were freshly baked conchas in the case and a list of Mexican-style coffees. Her aunt had accomplished so much without the support of her family. Carolina especially loved the mural inside the café of a cholita holding a rosary. She sat at a small table in the shop.

Tía Luísa greeted the girl who worked there and then served Carolina a Mexican mocha and a concha.

The whipped cream from the mocha cooled down the spicy heat. And the concha was crunchy and cloudlike.

Too bad Carolina didn't get her aunt's cooking gene.

Tía Luísa sat across from her, then she gave Carolina a little box.

"Ah, you didn't have to get me anything."

"I know I didn't. Open it up."

She opened the tiny little box.

It was a key.

"It's the key to my place. I thought you could use somewhere to stay for a while until you know what's happening with the farm back home," Luísa said with a smile.

"Oh, thanks, Tía. I appreciate it." She swallowed down the lump in her throat. "But, whether here or closer to home, I'm going to get my own place."

She didn't know a lot about her future, but she knew that much. "After Three Kings Day, I'm going to go home. Figure out what to do with my farm. And deal with Papá."

"Well, if you change your mind, the offer stands."

Carolina embraced her auntie. "Mil gracias." They finished their coffee and pan dulces. Her aunt offered to show her around Barrio Logan, but since Julieta was such an integral part of the community, Carolina wanted to keep a low profile.

They spent the next week doing touristy stuff in San Diego. They went to the zoo; Carolina loved the hippos and the way they played ball in their pool. They saw a production of *The Taming of the Shrew* at the Old Globe in Balboa Park. And they even celebrated Three Kings Day with her aunt's friends.

One day, they spent the day collecting seashells in Coronado. And through it all, Carolina began to smile a little more. Thinking about her family started to hurt a little less.

Tía Luísa was just so easy to be around. Maybe true family wasn't always about those who raised you.

Maybe true family was simply based on love.

On her final night before she returned home, Carolina cuddled on the sofa with one of Tía Luísa's dogs. Carolina loved the black mutt. His name was Siete and he had severe separation anxiety, but he always wanted to be near her.

This freedom was what she wanted. What she needed.

And she was going to get it.

Chapter Thirty-Three

Enrique drove up the coast. Just a couple of months ago, he was taking the same trip, but for a very different purpose. Back then, he was full of hope that he would be able to meet Carolina, partner with her farm, and alleviate the guilt of his company contracting with unethical farms.

Well, that had blown up in his face.

Even so, he was grateful for the experience. In the time since he'd last seen Carolina, he had stopped by each farm with which the Montez Group was contracted. After evaluating their operations, he gave them feedback and detailed reports of what they needed to improve on. Top of the list was the conditions of farmworkers. When some of the farms balked, Enrique threatened to pull their contracts. He even offered funding for health care pop-up clinics on each site. All the farms but one was in the process of complying, and he had terminated the relationship with the one farm owner who refused. Ramón even told Enrique he was proud of him. More importantly, Enrique was proud of himself.

Tiburón pointed at the exit to Santa Maria. "Sure you don't want to stop by and see Carolina?"

Enrique shook his head. "Positive. If she wants to reach out, she will." Tiburón had told Enrique that Carolina was still running the farm but no longer living in the house. Enrique asked him not to give him any more details about her life. The truth was, though Enrique understood why Carolina left him and cut off contact, it still hurt, and the less he knew about her life, the better.

He was grateful to have Tiburón on this trip with him.

"Blanca says Carolina is still in love with you."

Enrique seriously doubted that, but what did he know?

"At least things are still working out in your relationship."

Tiburón laughed. "It's tough, man. Her dad is brutal. And long distance is a bitch. But she's young. I don't want her to rush into anything with me and then resent me later."

Tiburón was still seeing Blanca a few times a month when he could drive up there. He was serious about her, and her father loved him.

"How did you get so wise?"

"I read a lot of philosophy."

Tiburón was such a great dude.

A little over two hours later, Enrique exited from the freeway. The gravel road to the farm tore up his tires, but he didn't care.

He pulled into the driveway. Two men walked over to their door. Enrique jumped out and embraced one.

Tío Jorge held his nephew tight. "I'm so glad you came to see me."

Enrique finally pulled away and studied his uncle. His face was hardened by the sun and his full head of hair was now gray. "I just apologize for not doing it sooner. My brothers couldn't make it but plan to come up together later in the month."

"I can't wait."

Tiburón and his tío Tomás walked toward the house.

As it turned out, both of their uncles were friends and had even worked on a farm together for years. Unfortunately, Tiburón's uncle had some pretty severe health problems. Enrique offered to fundraise for his health care and so did Julieta, even though he wasn't her uncle—he was Tiburón's father's brother. But Tiburón insisted on doing it on his own and had raised enough funds and scheduled him appointments at Stanford Hospital. They ran a bunch of tests, put him on new medications, and he was doing great.

Tío Jorge grabbed four bottles of Pacifico Clara beer and handed them to his friend, Enrique, and Tiburón.

They sat on the wraparound porch in front of Tío Jorge's house. He raised his bottle. "¡Salud! To family."

"Salud," they said in unison. They clinked all the necks of the bottles, and the four men drank the night away under the sunset.

Chapter Thirty-Four

Shortly after leaving San Diego, Carolina had returned to Santa Maria and had found a small place in town to live while she figured out her next steps. She had spent the last few months working on herself. She'd found a therapist and had been going to weekly sessions, dealing with her relationship with her father. After he still refused to talk to her, Carolina had made the difficult decision to cut emotional ties with him—for now. She held hope he would one day come around. The good news was his health was stable. She had ultimately decided it was in everyone's best interests to deed the farm to her father but had first refinanced it and received a hefty sum.

And she was at peace with that decision.

She was still talking to Blanca and Adela on the sly and hoped to reunite with her other sisters soon. Blanca was still dating Tiburón, though it was a long-distance relationship. Blanca hoped that he was going to propose, but Carolina urged her sister to take the relationship slow.

"And Downward Dog," the instructor on the Zoom video said.

Carolina placed her hands on the floor. Instantly, her aunt's dog Siete licked her face.

"Ugh!" She collapsed on the floor in a heap. Yoga was definitely still not for her.

She closed the Zoom chat when one new email notification popped up and she opened it and—*yes.*

An email from the real estate agent.

The strawberry farm in Carlsbad was officially hers.

She clicked through to look at the photos of the property one more time. There was a tiny cottage among the fields of strawberries. Sun-hatted tourists were dotted along the rows, picking lush red berries to take home. And beyond that, acres and acres of space, where Carolina planned to plant tejocotes in the future.

She already loved all her new employees, and they were excited for the changes she planned to make to the farm. They would be using organic pesticides, and she would provide health care for all the workers. And they were all getting substantial raises.

Things would be perfect.

Well, almost perfect.

Her heart twinged as she closed her laptop. There was still the matter of Enrique to sort out.

She had never given him a chance. She had used him as an excuse to blow up her life.

But after the gift of time, she was certain that even though their timing was terrible, the emotions she felt for him were unforgettable. He was a wonderful man.

Carolina loved him. She was sure of it.

She owed him an apology. And she finally knew exactly how she'd do it.

But first, she had someone to welcome home.

The door opened and a floral whiff of roses announced Tía Luísa's arrival. She strode inside to the cacophony of dogs barking, her hair as wild as ever.

"Oh, I had such a glorious trip. Thanks for watching my pups. Let me tell you all about it."

Carolina kissed her aunt. Once Carolina entered escrow, she asked Tía Luísa if she could stay with her. Her aunt took the free pet-sitting opportunity as the perfect time to enjoy a long-needed vacation. "I'm all ears."

Her aunt told her about all the places she visited. How she saw the flamenco dancers in Spain and shared a torrid love affair with a former priest in Rome.

Carolina loved her aunt's stories; they made her want to travel.

But not alone.

The next morning, Carolina took her new car, a Toyota 4Runner, to her farm, after a short pit stop getting the keys from her real estate agent. She spent the day greeting the workers and telling them how excited she was for the future.

But that wasn't the real reason she was visiting today.

When she had hatched this plan a few weeks ago, she had reached out to Ramón to help her.

As she stood alone in a field of strawberries, she heard the SUV pull up. It stopped right with her heart.

Enrique and Ramón got out.

Enrique's mouth dropped open at the sight of her. He looked hotter than hell. He was wearing board shorts and a T-shirt. He was still the sexiest man she had ever seen.

But more importantly, he was the kindest. He was sweet, and honest, and open.

And whatever he told her today, she would accept, just like he had maturely accepted when she broke up with him.

Ramón smiled. "I delivered him safe and sound. I'll leave you two alone." He reached down and grabbed a strawberry from a bush. "These are delicious. Julieta will love them."

"Tell her I'm planting tejocote trees!"

"I will."

Ramón walked away.

Finally, Carolina was alone with Enrique in this field of juicy strawberries.

She gave a nervous wave. "Hola, Enrique."

Enrique ran his hands through his hair. The shock that had been on his face had turned into a scowl. "What am I doing here, Carolina?"

"I wanted to see you." She took a step closer.

He clenched his fist.

"I'm sorry. I was super immature and selfish." She had practiced this speech so many times in her head. "But I felt so stunted. I couldn't be responsible for your love when I was trying to figure out my life. I hope one day you can forgive me."

He took a step back. Not a good sign. "I don't know if I can. You hurt me."

Her lip trembled. "I know. And that's something I'm going to have to live with." She exhaled. "And I want to help you with your farm. All of the ones you work with. At the very least, I hope you accept my guidance, which is why you originally came to meet me." She paused. "If you still want my help, that is."

"I appreciate it, but I've taken care of it on my own."

She gulped. She had no right to ask him how. "Oh, wow. Congratulations."

He gave a slight nod. "What about your father?"

"I've deeded Flores Family Farm to my father. We're still not speaking. But I'm looking to start a new partnership, and I . . . I hope it can be with you."

His jaw dropped. A flicker of joy graced his face.

"You're serious? You want to work with me? Doing what? You just said you sold your farm."

She nodded. "Yes. I did. But I bought this one. I moved here, Enrique. There is a small cottage on this property."

He looked away from her toward the ocean. "Carolina . . . I don't know what to say."

She took a step forward. "That's fine. I do. The thing is . . . I love you, Enrique. I've never met anyone like you. You are kind, compassionate, gorgeous, and most importantly, respectful. I needed time to work on myself to be someone who is your equal in every way. And I know I screwed up." She choked back a sob. "But I was hoping you would give me a chance. I'm not asking to be your girlfriend—real or fake. I just want to get to know you. Maybe go on a date. And if you still hate me, I'll leave you alone."

He licked his bottom lip. "I can't hate you."

She stepped toward him and brushed her hand on his face and stared into his eyes. "Forgive me."

Enrique stood still for a moment, but a smile slowly spread across his lips.

"I can try." He leaned in and kissed Carolina.

A few months ago, she had never even been kissed. And now she was in love with a man, and with herself.

And she had found a true partner. A good man. Carolina had never thought that she would be happy in a relationship. She wanted to be there for him and support him as well.

She had been hailed in the media as a strong, independent woman before. But it wasn't until today that she truly felt like she was living her authentic life.

EPILOGUE

The following December, Enrique and Carolina went up to Santa
María. This time, as a couple.

But again, they weren't alone. Enrique couldn't do anything without his family.

Ramón, Julieta, Rosa, Jaime, Tiburón, and Linda had all gone to
spend the holidays up at the Montecito home. But they weren't in
town for Enrique to make a business connection.

They were here to celebrate Las Posadas.

Blanca was set to be Mary this year, and it was Tiburón's turn to
tame the donkey—he would be Joseph.

Carolina had been a nervous wreck since hearing about Las Posadas. She wasn't going to come, but Enrique insisted. Tiburón was
Julieta's cousin and soon to be part of Enrique's family—they had
every right to attend.

She smoothed her dress in the mirror in his bedroom at the beach
home.

"How do I look?"

"Gorgeous."

She gulped. "What if my father kicks me out and I ruin Blanca's night?"

"If that happens, we will leave. But I'm sure he wants to see you."

"I don't know."

Enrique and Carolina had settled into a stable loving relationship over the past eight months. They still lived apart, which suited them both fine. They spent their weekly date nights exploring new restaurants or heading to the beach.

Enrique had even agreed to take a few Ballet Folklórico lessons so she would have a partner. It was fun, and he was a good sport.

And she had grown to like yoga, especially the restorative type, which focused more on relaxation and less on dogma.

But surfing was still off-limits. There was no way she would get in the ocean.

The family drove in two separate vehicles, just in case Enrique and Carolina had to make a quick getaway.

Enrique pulled down the driveway into the farm where Carolina had spent so much of her life. The house looked the same, though the trim was worn. She pushed the thought out of her head to text Manny to find someone to fix it.

This house was not her problem anymore.

"A year ago, when I came here, I was so nervous to meet you."

Carolina laughed. "Well, I wasn't. I didn't even know you were coming."

"That sister of yours." He gave a fond smile. "Tiburón has his hands full."

"True. I can't wait to see her."

He parked his Tesla and opened Carolina's door. Then he walked her to the house, carrying flowers for her mom.

"You got this, sunshine."

"Thanks." She gave a light knock.

Her father opened the door. His hand flew to his mouth the second he saw his daughter.

Before he could speak, Carolina hugged him.

"I'm so sorry, Papá. I love you so much. Please forgive me."

Señor Flores hugged her back. "No, mija. It is me you need to forgive. I'm so stubborn. I've missed you so much. I love you."

Enrique choked up. After their embrace ended and they separated, Enrique reached out his hand. "I'm sorry for everything, Señor Flores. I need you to know that I love and respect your daughter."

Señor Flores folded his arms across his chest. "And you think a simple apology will be enough for me to forgive you?"

Enrique gulped. "I had hoped so . . . yes. Sí, Señor."

Carolina's father's face broke into a broad smile. "Then you would be right. Come here." He opened his arms for an embrace. Enrique grinned and fell into them. "You're a good man, Enrique. Tiburón has told me a lot about you. I am hoping he will soon ask for Blanca's hand." He paused, studying Enrique. "And I'd welcome you in as well. I'd love to have two sons."

Enrique choked on his saliva.

Carolina shook her head. "Papá! Stop!"

Her father threw up his hands. "What? He loves you? We can have a double wedding."

"Ay, Dios mío. Blanca isn't even engaged."

"Yet. I have a good feeling. Maybe I reimpose the old rule with a new twist! She can't get married until you do!"

"You're unbelievable."

Papá laughed again. "I tease. Come inside. Carolina—go greet your mother and help her in the kitchen."

Carolina laughed. Some things would never change.

"I'll be there in a moment."

Her father walked back into the house.

Carolina shrugged and turned to Enrique. "Sorry about that."

"It's okay—it went better than I thought it would." He squeezed her hand and his voice lowered to a whisper. "I love you. I would marry you, but I know that's not what you want."

"Well, I'm not ready yet. But one day, maybe. And I've been thinking . . ." Her eyes lit up. "I may want kids eventually. But not anytime soon."

"If that's what you want, I would love that, too." He pulled her close. "But as long as I have you, I am happy."

"Good." She grinned. "Because I was hoping you'd move in with me."

His heart leapt. "Are you serious?"

"Ye—"

He didn't let her finish. "Kiss me, mi amor."

Enrique cupped Carolina's face and kissed her. She passionately kissed him back, not caring if her sisters were all probably watching from the curtains.

"Get a room!" Tiburón called as he opened the door. Carolina and Enrique broke apart.

Blanca hugged her sister. "You can have mine!"

"Blanca!" her mother chastised. Adela and Eva burst into giggles. Baby ran out and leapt into Carolina's arms.

Everyone embraced Enrique and Carolina.

Tiburón took Enrique aside. "You can thank me for getting her father to come around."

Ha. "Gracias, primo."

Tiburón grinned. "Primo, shit, man. You're going to be my brother one day."

ACKNOWLEDGMENTS

Kiss Me, Mi Amor was a labor of love. I had long wanted to write a book featuring a big, traditional Mexican-American family and was overjoyed to be able to publish this.

I would like to thank my incredible agent, Jill Marsal. Thank you so much for all your support on this book and in my writing career. You are the best!

To my fabumazing editor, Sarah Blumenstock—thank you for letting me go there with this book and depict a super old-school family. I adore you and am so excited about this book.

To Liz Sellers—your edits for this book have been so wonderful and I love working with you!

To my film agent, Carolina Beltran—thank you for lending your name to Cari. I'm so excited for our future endeavors.

To my producers, Gina Rodriguez, Kristen Campo, and Molly Breeskin—the news keeps getting better! Can't wait to see where this goes.

To Dailyn Rodriguez—I'm so in awe of you. Can't wait to make magic together.

My old-school first-look peeps: Kelli Collins—my first, my last, my everything. Lauren McKellar—this book would be a disaster without you. Gwen Hayes—I adore you. Tamara Lush—thanks for being my sounding board in this insane career we chose. My DD peeps—I love you all. Christine Hutton—so glad I met you this year! Thank you for all your support during the writing of this book. I honestly don't think I would've finished it without you. To my amazing betas Karla Silva and Jade Hernández—thank you both for helping me make Carolina shine. To all the authors in my classes—you are all so wonderful and talented.

My publicity and marketing team: Jessica Brock, Kristin Dwyer, Anika Bates, and Chelsea Pascoe—you are all so talented and I'm so, so, so excited about working on this project together.

To my amazing cover designer: Carina Guevara—thanks for the stunning cover!

To my copyeditor and proofreaders—thanks for saving this timeline (I'm so sorry!) and your great fixes.

To my family—without your support I would not be able to live my dream. To my late father, Joseph Chulick Jr.—I miss you so, so, so much. To my mother, Diana—you inspire all my books and my love of reading. To my brother and sister-in-law, Joe and Susie Chulick—thanks for putting up with me through the ups and downs of this crazy career. To my in-laws, Ron and Pam Albertson—thank you for all your encouragement.

To my two beautiful sons, Connor and Caleb Albertson—I love you both to pieces. I'm so happy that we have been reading books together. Can't wait to write the baseball book for you both.

To my husband, Roger—thank you for supporting me in this crazy lifestyle and watching the boys when I go to events. One day, all our sacrifices will finally pay off. I love you and thank you for not giving up on me.

And to all my fans—I have met so many of you this year. Hearing what it means to you to see characters like ourselves in books is the reason I write.

To my booksellers—you are all so great! Special shout-outs to Warwick's and Bay Books, and to Mando, Yuli, and Harrison at Barnes & Noble.

Kiss Me, Mi Amor

Love & Tacos

Alana Quintana Albertson

READERS GUIDE

DISCUSSION QUESTIONS

1. *Kiss Me, Mi Amor* shows the contrast between traditional Mexican families and more progressive ones. Which family did you relate to most?

2. Have you ever tried to date someone with a more traditional background than you have? What challenges did you face? What did you learn?

3. Farmworkers' rights is a central theme in the novel. What responsibility do the restaurants that contract with farms have for workers' treatment?

4. Tiburón is happy to traditionally court Blanca, but Enrique struggles with the restrictions set by Señor Flores. Do you see any benefits in his rules?

5. Carolina has achieved career success at such a young age but feels she has little control over her life. Do you agree with her ultimate decision to give the farm to her family and start over? Why do you think she made that choice?

6. How does Enrique's relationship with his father compare to Carolina's relationship with her father? How do they contrast?

7. The Flores family and the Montez family celebrate year-end holidays very differently. What holiday traditions do you share with your family?

8. To many, yoga is considered exercise, but Carolina struggles with the spiritual aspect of it due to her religious upbringing. Do you consider yoga exercise or something with a deeper meaning?

9. Shakespeare's *The Taming of the Shrew* was used as a framework for this book. It is a problematic play, especially for its portrayal of women. How does the novel engage with its inspiration? Do Carolina's strength and rebellion make her a "shrew" in her traditional family? How would you define this term? How would you characterize Carolina?

10. This book is set in Central and Southern California. How does the setting enhance the book?

Photo by Meg McMillan

ALANA QUINTANA ALBERTSON has written over thirty romance novels, rescued five hundred death-row shelter dogs, and danced one thousand rumbas. She lives in sunny San Diego with her husband, two sons, and too many pets. Most days, she can be found writing her next heart book in a beachfront café while sipping an oat-milk Mexican mocha or gardening with her children in their backyard orchard and snacking on a juicy blood orange.

VISIT ALANA QUINTANA ALBERTSON ONLINE

AuthorAlanaAlbertson.com

 AuthorAlanaAlbertson

 AuthorAlanaAlbertson

 AlanaAlbertson

 AuthorAlanaAlbertson

Ready to find
your next great read?

Let us help.

Visit prh.com/nextread